The Chocolate Assassin

Peter Durantine

ISBN: 1451579527

ISBN-13: 9781451579529

To my wife, Angela, for all her love and support.

Prologue

Heidelberg, Germany
March, 1945

By the hour, the rumble of American guns drew closer to the medieval city. A frantic SS general puffed on a cigarette, anxiously pacing his dark-wooden lair. His young adjutant entered and told him the call he had been awaiting had finally come through.

Von Rhonen – tall, stocky, broad-shouldered – gave the man a sharp, impatient glare. He marched over to the desk, ripping the black-handled receiver from its cradle, and barked into the mouthpiece at the man on the other end of the line.

"*Der Reichsfuhrer* is not taking my calls, Gerhard. *Warum?*"

SS General Walther Gerhard smiled to himself as he sat in his Munich office, more than three hours south of Heidelberg by train. To his delight, the ever-confident, unorthodox Joachim von Rhonen sounded shattered. He had only himself to blame for this.

Gerhard warned him, but he refused to listen. Now he would suffer the consequences of devising and launching such a misbegotten mission.

"You have failed and your agent is missing. Himmler has no more use for you; he's too busy with home-front defenses, as you should be."

"I don't believe you!" Rhonen shouted.

"He's not taking your calls, is he?"

Gerhard spoke calmly. Wailing air raid sirens and the distant drone of aircraft engines wafted into his office window from across the bomb-devastated city. "Believe it, von Rhonen. You've no more time. The enemy is closing in."

He waited for Rhonen's reply.

"Hello? Von Rhonen?"

Silence filled the earpiece. A moment later the adjutant came on the line. He sounded shaken. "The general … is dead."

Gerhard hung up abruptly and stared at the black phone. His fingers carefully felt for the capsule in the cuff of his black tunic. *No*, he thought to himself, *there was too much to live for.*

Explosions from Allied bombs neared. An aide rushed in and urged him to the air raid shelter immediately. Gerhard hurriedly followed him down to the cellar. They stood, smoked, and listened as bombs thudded overhead for twenty minutes.

Gerhard thought about von Rohnen. *The damn fool and his mission,* he scoffed. What a waste. Had the man not heard the rumor circulating in SS officer circles? The *Reichsfuhrer* had his own secret mission – one not even known to the *Fuhrer*. Himmler was attempting to make a deal with the Americans for the surrender of Germany.

The very idea was almost too fantastic for a Nazi officer such as Gerhard to believe, but he was much less an ideologue than he was an opportunist. It was clear to the less fanatical like him that the Third Reich was ending. Where was von Rhonen's agent? What would he do?

The wail of the all-clear signal drew Gerhard out of his thoughts. He emerged from the cellar to hear the screaming ambulance and fire sirens, and to smell the acrid smoke from fires burning across the city. The air bombardment hardly damaged SS/Gestapo headquarters.

Back in his office, Gerhard prepared to depart. He was expecting the Americans to arrive in the city within days. Before leaving, he ordered the burning of files and records, then he went to the radio room to give one more order – an order he knew would be his final as an SS officer.

"*Leutnant*," he said to the waiting lieutenant. "Release the Werewolves."

The officer stiffened, clicked his heels with a nod, and directed two radio operators to send the message across a nearly beaten Germany, torn asunder by war's ravages; its cities in flames, its military desperate, its fearful people holding on to ever thin strands of hope.

Gerhard listened as the calls went out. When the operators finished, the general gave a defiant speech about sacrifice in defense of the Fatherland, proclaiming undying allegiance to Adolf Hitler and National Socialism.

"*Siege Heil!*"

He left the building, climbed into his black Mercedes coupe and drove alone, toward the front lines – and the Americans who he knew were waiting for him.

Chapter I

Lewes, Delaware

Fifty-five years later

Three days passed. Oskar Franks had neither heard from nor seen his friend and neighbor, although the lights in the lonely bungalow up the road burned through the nights.

Franks stood at the dining room window while Rosemary, his wife, a petite, dark-eyed woman who always suspected the worst, fretted about their neighbor as she went about clearing the breakfast table dishes.

"It's so unusual for Eric not to have called," she said. "Just go and see if he's all right."

Shafts of sunlight pierced heavy clouds gathering over the mouth of the Delaware Bay and the Atlantic Ocean beyond. It was unseasonably cool this August morning. Oskar stepped onto the porch of their old Victorian.

Wind gusts whipped his hair and face. A ship's horn blasted from down the shoreline, where huge boats ferried cars and trucks across the water to Cape May, New Jersey.

Oskar watched a ferry steaming against choppy white-caps and sensed something was terribly wrong. Rosemary, wrapped in a tweedy sweater, joined him. She folded her arms and shivered against the cold wind.

She touched her husband's arm and urged, "Why don't you go and see?"

His unease growing, he nodded and gave Rosemary a faint smile, descended the porch stairs and trudged up the road to Eric Hoest's house. He climbed the steps to his friend's porch, strong gusts ruffling his thinning gray hair, and rapped on the door.

He waited, but no answer. He peered through one of the small door-side window panes. The place was oddly still. He turned the doorknob; the latch released, the door swung open, its hinges groaned at the burden.

As he stepped inside he cleared his throat.

"Eric."

He stood and listened; nothing but the blowing wind and an unsettling silence. He went to the study; Hoest liked to spend time there. A putrid odor and a bloated corpse greeted him. Hoest lay on the floor, blood soaked his shirt and stained the rug. Angry green flies buzzed the room.

Trembling uncontrollably, Oskar stumbled backward, trying to escape. He almost ran into the front door as he hurried outside onto the porch, where a panic seized him and he vomited. His legs turned wobbly and he groped the handrail, struggling down the steps.

He reached the road and forced himself to run. Rosemary had been watching for him and now hurried toward him. Her eyes grew large with fear as she approached and could see Oskar's ashen face and vomit-splattered trouser leg and shoe.

"My God! What's happened?"

Oskar gasped, "Eric ... is ... dead."

"What?"

"Murdered!"

Rosemary threw her arm around her husband as he wept and brought him home. She set him in his old overstuffed chair and called the police. She put a kettle of water on for tea as they quietly waited for the authorities to arrive.

"Mr. Grey?"

The exasperated tone echoed from the well of the amphitheater classroom in Gore Hall, where, seated in the upper-most row, a deeply absorbed Samuel Grey busily jotted notes, totally unaware he was being called or even that the lecture had ended. He glanced absently at a gaggle of students chattering and gathering their belongings and returned to his writing.

"MISS-TUR GREY?" Professor Jennings loudly and emphatically repeated.

The noisy throng quieted. Several students turned their heads to look in the direction their professor stared. Grey's cocoa-colored eyes now darted to the lectern and an imperious Jennings, head of the graduate history program, standing with a contemptuous glare.

Over the murmur of departing students, Jennings filled his voice with sarcasm. "Now that I've captured your attention, see me in my office."

Grey nodded and hurriedly collected his books. At forty, he was the oldest student by at least a decade in the school's doctoral program. From mind to appearance, he was studious and methodical. He wore his hair neat, close cropped. Although ten pounds heavier from his college athletic days, he maintained a trim build.

He chased after the professor, but the lean, long-legged Jennings, wearing his customary light seer-sucker, had already left the lecture hall and crossed the pedestrian bridge over College Avenue, headed to Munroe Hall on the University of Delaware's sprawling, tree-lined campus.

Haughty Charles Jennings liked to remind students of his scholarly descendents who had taught at what he called "our finer institutions." Students tried to work around his resentments at having to settle for less than Ivy League, where his grandfather and great-grandfather taught. He belittled students who failed to meet his high measure.

As a man who was half African-American and half Hispanic, Grey was less concerned about the professor's eccentricities. He worried whether Jennings accepted minorities. He was surprised by his concern – he long disciplined himself not to be judgmental about such things – though he found himself wondering at times.

Jennings never directly came out about it, but still he spoke in a manner that made a dark-skinned human being like himself suspect a white Anglo-Saxon authority figure.

The professor was removing his jacket when Grey caught up with him in his office.

"Tell me," Jennings demanded, sinking his lanky frame into a chair, "what was so God-awful important in your notebook today that you could not spare time to listen to my lecture on Germany's naval mutinies of 1918?"

Grey set his heavy book bag on the floor. "Look, I'm sorry – "

"No," Jennings interrupted. "No apologies! Tell me what you were writing about."

"An outline for next month's essay, it's on Russia's aging sub fleet."

"What about it?" Jennings demanded.

Grey paused. Jennings made him nervous, but why he was not entirely sure, although he suspected it was the influence this fop had on *his* future as a professor. Jennings would, after all, sit on the dissertation committee.

"Russia's struggling with a weak economy," he began. "The government lacks funds for upgrades, and, therefore, because of constant technological advances in the West, particularly in the United States, the fleet is fast becoming antiquated."

Jennings nodded. "I see," he said, approvingly. "Why not make *that* your doctoral thesis instead of bothering us with the tired subject of German naval policy in World War I?"

The comment irritated Grey as he realized the professor's purpose in calling him to the office. "What's wrong with what I've proposed?"

Jennings stared at his student. "That ground has been so well covered that I doubt you could find any new insights into the argument that Germany may have won had it maintained unrestricted submarine warfare; but if you insist, I'll want something fresh – very fresh."

Grey departed, questioning whether his chosen subject was worth Jennings' pressure. He pushed this out of his mind as he strolled past the lawns of the idyllic red-brick campus to Morris Library, where he planned an afternoon of research.

His cell phone vibrated on his hip, warning him otherwise. He flipped it open, looked at the screen, and answered reluctantly.

"Jack?"

"Hate to take you away from your studies," Davis said.

No you don't, thought Grey. "What's going on?"

"Homicide in Lewes."

Grey had misgivings about a cell phone and now, less than one week after his lieutenant assigned him one, regretted it. Not all modern conveniences were convenient, he decided. Some are damned nuisances.

"Isn't there anyone at the barracks down there?"

"They can't free a man." Davis lied. He wanted Grey.

"I'm leaving for Europe in a few days; there isn't another trooper who can handle it?"

Davis spoke firmly. "Not really."

By his superior's tone Grey knew other troopers were available. But when Davis smelled an interesting case, he liked to turn to Grey, one the state police's leading investigators, and Grey obliged because Davis worked around his school schedule so he could study.

"Don't worry," the lieutenant said. "I'll make sure you get your time off."

Grey sighed. "What's the location?"

When he hung up he shut the cell phone off and dropped it into a zippered pocket in his book bag, where, he decided, it would remain … permanently.

Lewes Police Chief John Christopher, a stout man with a mane of sandy hair that swept the brow of his bronze yachtsman's face, stood on the porch of the white-framed bungalow, its cedar shingles long gone gray.

He waited impatiently, his hands shoved inside his windbreaker's pockets.

It annoyed him to wait three hours for the state police to send an investigator; it annoyed him that the coroner could not remove the body until an investigator arrived; it annoyed him that he had no means or authority to conduct a murder investigation himself.

A little Victorian town on the bay, Lewes was a quaint, but vital ferry boat stop, nestled along the southern corner of the Delaware's mouth. The town was not large enough to afford a homicide team, relying, as many towns did, on the state police.

Christopher watched as Grey stepped from an unmarked sedan that pulled up, driven by a blue-uniformed trooper. He was annoyed all over again.

Grey lifted his sturdy arms to stretch while he took stock of the scene. As he let his arms drop he smiled at Christopher.

"Chris," he said. "It's been a couple of years."

"That it has."

Grey climbed the porch steps and said something to the chief he immediately regretted. "Parker suicide, wasn't it?"

"Yup," Christopher sniffed. "You pissed on me then and you haven't been on this case more than two minutes and you're pissing on me again."

Grey frowned uneasily. The hostility still lingered, he thought, the embarrassing memory of a new police chief acting like a fool in his zeal to prove a murder without ever scrutinizing the evidence that quickly showed otherwise.

Had he, as Grey had, examined the girl's bedroom and the autopsy report, and searched the room to find an asthma inhaler under her bed, Christopher would have asked another set of questions. Had he examined her medical records and found no history of breathing ailments, he would have spoken to the coroner, who would have told him about the unusually high levels of an inhalant in her system, large dosages of which can constrict the lungs and cause suffocation.

And had the chief spent more time talking to Lilly Parker's friends and family, he would have learned, as Grey did, about a girl's life plagued by emotional problems. Grey's conclusion, that she poisoned herself, but tried to make it look like she had been murdered, leaving a pillow on her face and her ground-floor window open, was angrily dismissed.

They were in the Sussex County morgue, where Grey was explaining his theory and the coroner, a soft-spoken, narrow-nose man, was supporting it. Christopher looked incredulous.

"Sam, that's too damn complicated to believe," the chief said.

"Maybe, but it best explains what happened."

"I'm afraid it is, Chris," the coroner said.

The police chief glared at Grey. "I just don't understand why you don't like trying to help your own kind."

The remarked surprised Grey. "What do you mean, 'my own kind?'"

"She's black, isn't she?"

"What're you saying? Because she's black I don't care."

"Well, she's your people."

"She's not 'my people,' I don't know the girl." Grey tried to hold his temper. "I don't do my job or live my life based on skin color. Now, look, the coroner has determined cause of death as suicide. Do you want to sign off on it or waste more time looking for a nonexistent murderer?"

Christopher had no alternative. He was left sounding foolish explaining to the press why his initial investigation called the girl's death a murder.

Grey would not mention the Parker case again. He apologized for his delayed arrival, but Christopher only shrugged and grumbled. "Let's go inside."

"What've we got?" Grey asked, following him into the house.

"Three-day-old body, no witnesses and no one heard anything, so, I dunno; but that's why you're here."

Grey cheerfully tried to lighten the mood. "When are you getting that detective squad?"

"We don't need one when we have the state police."

"Ah, but the taxpayers may appreciate a local force handling their affairs."

"Unfortunately," the police chief snapped, "they're happy just the way things are."

Grey would not mention municipal financing and local police initiatives, either.

Inside, police officers wearing white masks pulled tight around their mouths and noses photographed the corpse and dusted for fingerprints. A foul odor permeated the room.

Grey placed a handkerchief over his nose and looked around. "Anyone touch anything?"

"No. We've been waiting your grand entry."

Grey ignored the remark. His eyes roamed over the body and the blood-stained rug. Two brass cylinders on the floor by an armchair caught his attention. Using a pen he delicately poked at one to find an opening at the end. He inserted his pen in the cylinder and stood to examine it.

"Shell casing," Christopher said.

"Yeah; there's another on the floor."

Grey found four numbers – one, nine, four, four – and three letters – D W M – on the casing. He collected the other and found it had identical markings. He slipped a hand into his jacket pocket and removed a plastic bag, dropping the casings inside and sealing it.

With the handkerchief over his nose and mouth, Grey gently leaned over the body to examine the chest. He noted two bullet wounds. He looked at the dead man's gray hairs and wrinkled face and estimated his age at roughly mid-seventies.

He looked the body over once more and nodded. "Okay, they can take him."

The police chief barked. An ambulance crew wheeled a stretcher with a black body bag spread over it. As they attended to the corpse, Grey looked around the room. On the floor near where he found the casings, a piece of newspaper lay crumpled. He slipped on latex gloves he took from his pocket and retrieved the paper.

He unfolded an article with an accompanying photograph. Grey read the caption beneath the photo. He called to Christopher who had left the room.

"Chris, victim's name is Eric Hoest? Right?"

Christopher returned and Grey showed him the newspaper clipping.

"What about it?" Christopher said, unimpressed.

"It was on the floor." Grey looked quizzically at the police chief and said, "Are we having a problem here?"

"No, no problem."

"Look, if it's any consolation, I was off duty when I got the call."

Christopher shrugged. Grey went back to the article and read the headline: "FORMER U-BOAT CAPTAIN FINDS HOME IN AMERICA."

Grey scanned the story. "I know this. It ran in the newspaper about a week or two ago. Did you know this guy?"

The police chief shook his head. "Knew of him; people said he was quiet, respectable."

Turning, Grey walked to where he had collected the shell casings and stood looking at where the body had been.

"He was shot at close range."

"That's what we figure," Christopher said.

"And that may mean he knew the murderer."

Grey folded the clipping and placed it in another plastic bag. He would examine it later for fingerprints. He examined the study once more, removing his gloves and putting them back in his pocket as he did.

A black-and-white framed photograph on one wall depicted a young Hoest, squinting into the sun with a broad smile. He stood on deck of a U-boat moored somewhere, its coning tower in the background. The dashing seaman in his white cap and worn leather coat.

Grey turned his attention to two walls in the study, lined with large floor-to-ceiling book cases, their shelves laden with history books, most of them about conflicts in Europe and North America in the 19th and 20th centuries.

Strange, Grey thought. He had never investigated a murder in which he shared an interest with the victim. He concluded history and war were integral to the old U-boat commander.

Grey turned to Christopher, who had been watching him. "Anything missing?"

"Not that we can determine."

"Robbery's not a motive then?"

"Doesn't seem to be, but we're still looking around."

Grey walked to the desk and looked at the blotter. On the note pad by the telephone was written, "*der kleine wolf*" and the initials HJ. He smiled and said to himself, "Little wolf."

Christopher heard him. "What did you say?"

"Little wolf. It's written here in German. Mean anything to you?"

"No, but it may to the Franks."

"The Franks?"

"The deceased's neighbors; they found the body."

"Where are they?"

"Next house down; one of my officers is with them."

Grey nodded and looked at the telephone note pad on the desk.

"Chris, let's ask the phone company to get us a record of outgoing *and* incoming calls made over the last week, okay?"

Christopher nodded as he removed a small notebook from his jacket pocket to jot down the request.

Grey gave one last look around. "I don't want anyone trampling through here. Does he have any relatives – wife, children?"

Christopher shook his head. "Wife died a while back, never had children."

"Okay. Let's go see the Franks."

The two men walked along the wind-swept road past grassy dunes. Christopher informed Grey it was Oskar Franks who had found Hoest. At the Frank's house, Oskar and Rosemary rose from the sofa as the officers entered.

"Please, sit down," Grey said, introducing himself. He sat in an over-stuffed chair offered by the couple and leaned forward, speaking softly.

"Mr. Franks, you found the body?"

Oskar nodded.

"Why were you at the house?"

The Franks looked at each other. Oskar said, "We hadn't seen Eric for three days and we were wondering what happened to him."

"You and Mr. Hoest were good friends?" Grey asked, detecting a slight accent in Oskar's voice and waiting for the reply to hear it again.

"Yes, for quite a few years. Rosemary and I, we retired here back in – " he turned to his wife, who nodded and said, "'94." Oskar picked up the story, " – yes, in 1994. That's when we met Eric."

"What made you good friends?"

A curious look crossed Oskar's face. "I'm sorry I don't understand."

"How come you got along? What did you have in common?"

"Oh, I see, yes," Oskar began, before Grey interrupted him.

"Mr. Franks, excuse me, but I detect an accent."

"Yes. I am German, but I became an American many years ago."

"When was that?"

"My parents brought me here in the late 1930s."

"Thirties?"

"We fled Germany because of Hitler."

Grey thought for a moment. "You're Jewish?"

"Yes."

"Is that what you and Mr. Hoest had in common, your German backgrounds?"

"Yes, that was part of it, but Eric was just a wonderful man. Very thoughtful. We always found things to talk about."

"But he was a Nazi at one time, wasn't he?"

The Franks shook their heads and Oskar said, "No. I don't believe that. Eric was a sailor, yes, but not a Nazi. He loved the sea, not Hitler."

"Still, he fought for him," Grey said.

"No! He fought for his country, which was at war, but not for that monster."

"Did he know you were Jewish?"

"Of course, but it never mattered to him."

Rosemary interceded. "Eric was a tolerant man," she said, wrapping an arm around her husband. "His wife, Didi, she was Jamaican."

Grey nodded. "Did Mr. Hoest ever say anything about a little wolf?"

The Franks gave each other perplexed looks. Oskar shook his head. "No, nothing; what does it mean?"

"I don't know," Grey said. "Do the initials HJ mean anything to you?"

The couple shook their heads.

Grey said to Franks, "You two talk much about his U-boat experiences?"

"Somewhat, but he loved more to read about history. We often talked about that and his fishing. He liked to fish and sail his old trawler on the bay."

"What kind of history?"

"Oh, I guess American mostly."

"German?"

"Yes, German, usually in comparison with American."

"Did any of his war buddies ever visit?"

"War buddies? I don't know. Like I said, Eric didn't discuss the past much."

Grey thought about this remark and said, "That's odd, don't you think?"

Oskar shrugged. "I'm not sure."

A gust of wind buffeted the house, startling Rosemary. "Oh, my," she said. Grey glanced out the window to see dark-gray clouds billowing over the bay.

"Storm's coming in," Christopher said, matter-of-factly.

Grey rose from his chair and thanked the Franks, promising he would be in touch. As he and Christopher started to leave, he stopped to ask another question:

"Mr. Franks, I'm curious about something."

"Yes," Franks said, uttering the word slowly.

Grey could hear a slight tremble in the man's voice.

"Why did you wait three days to go check on your friend?"

Oskar looked at his wife, who pleaded with her husband, "Tell him, he should know."

Franks nodded reluctantly as Rosemary slipped her arm through his.

"We had an argument a few days ago over what now seems so unimportant and we were not talking. I'm afraid it got a little violent."

"How violent?" Grey said.

"It was silly, really, two old men pushing each other on a fishing boat."

"What were you arguing about?"

Franks recalled the warm, overcast afternoon. He sat in a cedar deck chair on the 36-foot Monk trawler, rationalizing to Hoest the Israeli's military tactics against the Palestinian Intifada in the late 1980s. Hoest listened as he checked the row of fishing lines he had in the water.

"They did what they had to for peace," Franks argued.

Hoest stopped, his body stiffened. Franks watched the old U-boat captain turn slowly, his face contorted in rage. "No! I won't believe that," he said. "Good God, man, don't you see they acted like Nazis? Like Nazis! They're still acting like Nazis."

Franks looked at Grey with watery eyes and sighed, sorrowfully. "It got worse."

"Why didn't you want to tell me about the argument?"

"I'm feeling guilty," Franks said.

"How so?"

Franks shook his head. "Corporal Grey, it's sad enough to lose a friend, but it is worse to lose a friend before you can make peace with him again."

Outside, the wind picked up considerably. Christopher glanced at Hoest's house.

"Well," he said, "what do you think?"

"I don't know," Grey said, as he waved over the unmarked sedan. "I'd like to get the slugs analyzed quickly."

Christopher promised to send him the coroner's report within 24 hours.

"And you'll have Hoest's phone records checked?"

"Yeah, but why?"

"The 'little wolf' notation by the phone has me wondering."

The sedan rolled to a stop beside Grey. As he started to step into the vehicle, Christopher stopped him. "By the way, what's with all this history talk?"

Grey shrugged. "I thought the victim's background was interesting, didn't you?"

The police chief gave him a sideward glance and shook his head. Grey laughed, slipped into the passenger seat and pulled the door shut. Christopher waited for an answer. Grey poked his head out the window and said, "I don't know yet, Chris. It's just a hunch."

The sedan sped off as a gust of wind kicked up sand on the road. Rain began to fall. The sudden cry of a Laughing Gull startled Christopher. He shot a look into the sky darkening above him to see the wide-winged bird glide downward behind the dunes, presumably toward refuge.

Shit, he thought. *It's going to storm.*

Chapter 2

Heidelberg, Germany

September 1944

Daily broadcasts by Propaganda Minister Goebels claiming victories on the eastern and western fronts left 19-year-old Martin Hahn in doubt. The destruction and degradation brought by five years of war belied those reports. The broadcasts had come to sound surreal.

Hahn no longer found coffee, butter or meat in shops that managed miraculously to avoid the relentless Allied bombing raids pulverizing Germany's cities, leaving blackened, smoldering ruins and desperate, hollow-eyed people, many still believing in victory despite the misery.

He'd had growing doubts about many things since Hamburg's firestorms. Another, more darker perspective was overshadowing what he had been taught in school and at the *Hitler Jugen* – Hitler Youth – camps, which promised a life of prosperity and thrills:

"*Jugen!* We march for *Der Fuhrer!* For our Fatherland!"

What camps they were! A boy's paradise; young males freed to act aggressively through military training and athletics. Hahn enjoyed it all – grenade throwing, map reading, pistol firing and bayonet practice. Hand-to-hand combat left him bloodied, but he was thrilled at the physical exertion allowing him to demonstrate his strength.

Hahn did what the youth leaders taught him was natural to his gender and his race. They drilled it into him and into millions like him; they were the superior race. They were training for a future in which Germany would perfect its Aryan heritage and rule the Earth.

Initially, playing war and the all-for-one comradeship exhilarated him.

Unfurling swastika flags and banners in torch light that flickered shadows over enormous pictures of Adolf Hitler, fresh-faced, blond-haired boys demonstrated their superiority by leaping through camp fires, challenging the flames to burn. They stood proudly in formation to sing and pray, *"Heavenly grace gave us the Fuehrer. We promise Hitler loyalty to the end."*

Total devotion to the Fatherland remained drummed into him, but he started to question what they taught him to believe about Hitler, race superiority, German hegemony, German will and German domination.

The questioning began earlier in the summer, at the solstice camp in the Black Forest, where he joined in nightly ceremonies around the *Thing-statte*, a stone-constructed temple-like structure. Their faces shimmered in torch-cast light as youth leaders frothily extolled German virtues in one breath and implored the boys to embrace battle in another – "*Jugen!* March!"

At that moment, hours after the news from Hamburg, Hahn began to understand a little about why his father opposed the party and the new Germany. Yet it wasn't enough for him to consider changing his view, still intoxicated as he was with Hitler's vision for Germany.

Such thoughts occupied Hahn on the train from Munich. On a worn, green cushion he sat, fingering a wallet-size black-and-white photo of his parents before field and forest slipped into an urban landscape. The conductor barged by his compartment: "Heidelberg! Next station! Heidelberg!"

The train slowed entering the yards. From his window, everything looked normal. Allied bombers had so far spared the old medieval city, he thought. The train shuddered to a stop as the engine hissed a dying breath.

Hahn's blue suit bore a red and black swastika armband. As a young man, he looked out of place among the many boys of his age in uniform. He put the photograph back inside his coat pocket, gripped his suitcase, and ambled off the train.

As he walked along the platform, a large poster caught his attention. A brave young boy superimposed on Hitler's face: *Jugend Deint Dem Fuhrer. Alle Zehnjahrigen in die HJ.* "Youth Serves the Fuhrer. All 10-year-olds into the Hitler Youth."

Outside the station, he climbed aboard a crowded tram that snaked slowly along the tree-lined cobblestone streets, then down the shop- and restaurant-lined *Haupstrasse,* stopping near a red-stone medieval church on a square. He stepped off to see a huge red-stone castle overlooking the city from atop a steep hill.

As he admired the massive fortification's partial ruins and its jagged turrets, a lilting voice observed sweetly: "*Der Schloss.*" A smiling young woman with brown hair and an interested eye walked past. He gave her a shy nod and awkwardly called after her.

"Um, *Fraulein*? Can you tell me where I can find *Rohrbachstrasse*?"

She stared at him, an impish grin on her face, and pointed to the street sign behind him.

Hahn thanked her, noting curiously her happy, carefree attitude in such a dark time. The young woman smiled warmly, but before he could ask her name she had gone on her way.

He wandered down *Rohrbachstrasse*, searching tall buildings lining the narrow street for number 42, where Waffen SS Lieutenant-General Joachim von Rhonen waited.

42 *Rohrbachstrasse* was dark-stoned and baroque, headquarters of Rhonen's espionage operations. On the second floor, behind a fine mahogany desk next to an unlit fireplace, sat the general, a scion of Upper Silesian aristocracy. Tall and thick, in his early fifties, Rhonen's face was oval, smooth-skinned; his dark hair receding; his eyes azure blue. Unlike others in his rank, he kept arrogance and pompousness in check.

Dressed in a double-breasted charcoal-gray suit – not his uniform – he smoked a cigarette as he listened to his adjutant speak crisply while reciting from a dossier on Hahn's life:

"His father was a German chocolate maker, his mother was an American. She was loyal to the party; he was a member in name only. They met as students at the University of Chicago; Martin had been their only child."

The general interrupted. "Had been? You refer to them in past tense. *Warum?*"

"They were killed in the fire-bombing raid on Hamburg last summer; according to the reports, burned alive."

"How did the young man escape?"

"At the time he was in Bavaria, *eine Hitler Jugend* summer training camp. He was to return home the week following the raid to celebrate his nineteenth birthday."

The general nodded as blue smoke from his cigarette lingered around his face. He said, "How well did he do in the Hitler Youth?"

"Excelled as a leader; dutiful; showed exceptional language skills, particularly English. Mother insisted her son speak the language as well as his American cousins."

Rhonen grunted and the adjutant continued: "An excellent student and athlete; he played soccer and tennis. Aspires to the party's ideal German male, serving *Fuehrer and Vaterland* – "

Impatient, Rhonen interrupted. "*Ja, ja,* what else is there?"

The adjutant paused, nervously glancing at the dossier. "Since his parent's death he has frequently expressed an eagerness to fight."

"Why hasn't he?" the general demanded.

"His academic skills convinced his youth leader to recommend him to General Gerhard for special espionage, for which he trained at Bad Toelz. He then infiltrated a group of Munich students planning an uprising. Hahn identified the leaders, who were tried and sentenced."

The adjutant concluded, "Although he's effective, General Gerhard believes he's better suited for the work you have in mind."

"I see," Rhonen said, wondering whether the young man would indeed be suitable for the mission he planned. "What time are we expecting him?"

"Shortly, *Herr General*."

Rhonen dismissed his adjutant with a wave and leaned back in his chair. This was likely the most important mission of the war, he thought. Could he entrust an eager youngster?

Devoted to the cause, Rhonen was among the first to join the party, against a backdrop of mob-controlled streets and the weak Weimar government. He marched with Hitler in the leader's failed beer-hall putsch in 1923; helped the party seize power in '33; joined the SS in '34; reached the rank of lieutenant-general in '43.

Now as Germany faced inevitable defeat, Rhonen devised a mission with a philosophical, rather than military, objective; to show the world National Socialism's inevitability.

Hahn, he thought, sounded devoted to the cause, but was he capable enough to endure the mission? Did he have the will? The will that brought Germany victories, the will that empowered National Socialism, the will of overcoming overwhelming odds.

As the general dwelled on these questions, Hahn rang the bell. The black-uniformed SS adjutant opened the door and beckoned the young man inside. He led Hahn across thick carpets in a well-furnished hall, up a sweeping staircase, and down a hall of elaborate-framed paintings by Eugène Delacroix and Egyptian statuary. At a heavy dark-wood door the adjutant instructed the young man to wait before disappearing into the Rhonen's cavernous lair.

Hahn marveled at the Delacroix's paintings; the vibrant colors in *The Fanatics of Algiers* depicting a mob of angered Arabs roiling in street violence. The rich textures in *The Entry of the Crusaders into Constantinople* were inspiring, provocative.

The paintings were among the art works looted by Hermann Goering when the Germans occupied Paris in 1940 then later given to Heinrich Himmler. When Rhonen transferred from his post in Serbia, Himmler presented him with 17 canvasses of North Africa that Delacroix painted, gifts for extraordinary service.

Hahn wandered around the hallway, admiring the paintings when the door opened and the adjutant ushered him inside.

The general sat at his desk and quickly sized up Hahn. The blond, blue-eyed young man was strapping, serious-minded. He would not let a smile break his sharp jaw line as the adjutant announced him. Hahn gave a stiff-armed salute and waited for one in return.

Rhonen ignored the regimental display, a Hitler Youth trait that annoyed him because he felt it lacked true spirit. The young had not fought, as their elders had, for National Socialism. It was given to them and he doubted their appreciation of it.

He offered a chair. *"Herr Hahn, setzen Sie sich bitte. Setzen Sie sich."*

Hahn nervously took his seat as the general tried to put him at ease. "Would you care for a cigarette?"

Hahn shook his head.

"Very well, then, you won't mind if I have one."

Rhonen lit the cigarette. He expressed condolences to Hahn on the loss of his parents to which the young man responded coolly. *"Herr General,* this is not necessary."

"Oh? *Warum?"*

"They died for the glory of the German Reich, for *Der Fuehrer."*

"I see." Rhonen marveled at how well the Hitler Youth trained their young charges to be dispassionate about everything but the state. He questioned the young man. "Hahn, *was denken Sie ueber diesen Krieg?"*

"What do I think of the war?" Hahn repeated, surprised by the question. Was the general testing his loyalty, he wondered, "We will be victorious, of course."

The general snapped. "You're wrong! The war is lost." Rhonen leaned back in his chair, dragged off his cigarette and exhaled. "The Reich is doomed, defeated."

Hahn angrily spat, "Traitorous talk!"

"It's true," Rhonen said, studying the young man. "The war *is* lost."

Uncertainty gripped Hahn. "The Fuhrer assures us victory. How dare you speak this way when German blood is spilling in the battle against Bolshevism and Jewry."

"The Fuhrer's High Command betrayed him." Rhonen's voice rose. "They've tried to kill him once; they'll succeed next time."

Hahn sat, reeling in thought. "If that's true, what's left for us?"

"The spirit of National Socialism," the general said defiantly as he leapt from his chair to stand over Hahn. "That, they can never defeat. It will last *beyond* a thousand years."

Rhonen demanded, "You believe that, yes?"

Hahn nodded, unsure. "Yes – yes, I want to believe that."

Rhonen roared angrily. "Are you questioning the cause? Did you not learn anything about loyalty from your parent's death? What right do you have to question?"

Hahn leapt from his chair and stood at attention: *"Herr General."*

"Sit down, Hahn."

Hahn sat stiffly, staring straight ahead, using his discipline to suppress questions roaming through his mind. The silence became menacing. Rhonen let it hang for what to Hahn seemed an eternity.

Rhonen's voice, now calm: "Hahn, look at me."

The young man looked into the smooth oval face. The general, speaking in soft, caring tones, lead him through a creed.

"You believe in the party?"

"Ja."

"You believe in the Fuhrer and the work he has accomplished?"

"Ja."

"You believe the struggle we've embarked on is eternal?"

"Ja."

"You remember what we've taught you about loyalty to family, to Germany?"

"Ja."

"You remember what that means, that loyalty? That it means forever?"

"Ja."

"You want vengeance for your parents so their deaths are not in vain? So that Germany has not fought in vain?"

"Ja."

"You trust me?"

"Jawohl, Herr General."

"The party and the Fuhrer ask that you accept a mission of utmost importance."

"But – "

Rhonen sighed. "You have a question?"

"Herr General, if, as you say, the war is lost, what does it matter?"

The general smiled. "Perhaps nothing now, but for future generations what you do will show the world the party's indomitable will. We may lose this war against the Bolsheviks and Jews, but we will return to triumph. It is our will."

Hahn thought for a moment. "What must I do, *Herr General?*"

Rhonen smiled as he removed a note pad from his desk. "Begin your training."

He tore off a slip of paper and handed it to Hahn. "This is the address to a pension near the university. You will live there. Tell no one why you are here, understood?"

Hahn nodded as he stood and took the paper. He stared at the address. Rhonen watched him. "You have *another* question, Hahn?"

"With respect to you, *Herr General*, just what is my mission?"

Rhonen smiled. "You'll soon learn." He pressed a button on his desk and a moment later his adjutant appeared.

Hahn prepared to leave and the general said, "You look hungry." The young man's only meal that day had been a few slices of bread and ersatz coffee. "You'll find sausage waiting for you at the pension."

Rhonen's fears were allayed. Hahn was more than qualified for the mission, but he was surprised General Gerhard, his Waffen SS superior in Yugoslavia, had recommended him.

Gerhard had shown no interest in Rhonen's special espionage unit when it was activated months ago, perhaps because Himmler authorized it. The SS leader and Rhonen had known each other since the early party days when they manned street barricades together.

Rhonen's undermining of Yugoslav Partisans caught Heinrich Himmler's attention and when the Reichsfuhrer visited SS headquarters in Sarajevo the winter before, he was impressed by the guerilla unit of Bosnian Muslims the general had organized.

"Fearless, relentless, disciplined by their religion, *Herr Reichsfuhrer*," Rhonen said.

In his field uniform and black shiny boots, Himmler stood in a dusty courtyard peering through wire-rimmed spectacles at the regiment of olive-skinned men in black uniforms, each wearing a fez with the SS skull-and-cross-bone insignia.

Fresh-cut pine permeated the air from newly constructed gallows that stood along a high stone wall where a dozen Partisans, hung by piano wire, dangled under the morning sun.

"Reports on these men are exemplary," Himmler said, shifting his gaze to the gallows. "I wish we had armies of them on the Eastern Front."

Sensing the Reichsfuhrer's limited time, Rhonen invited Himmler into his office, where he served coffee and cake and pitched his proposal.

Rhonen's interest in Islamic and Arab history had grown considerably during his year of command while knowing the Grand Mufti of Jerusalem, Haj Mohammad Amin al-Husayni. The Grand Mufti had helped the general recruit his Muslim troops.

As cleric in charge of Jerusalem's holy Muslim sites such as the Dome of the Rock and Al-Aqsa Mosque, Al-Husayni, an Arab nationalist, collaborated with the Nazis who allied with his cause to stop Jewish immigration to Palestine and to end British rule there.

When Hitler took power in 1933, the Grand Mufti sent a telegram to Berlin expressing his desire to see the National Socialist ideology spread to the Middle East and offering help in the Nazis' war against Jews, an offer the German regime welcomed.

Al-Husayni would become a Nazi propagandist and recruiter of Muslim soldiers and in return he received financial and military assistance for his battle against Britain and the Jewish effort to create a homeland in Palestine.

Rhonen, though, was interested in Arabic history – not Al-Husayni's anti-Semitism. He wanted to apply their cultural and religious disciplines in training espionage agents, another of his avid interests.

With cold detachment Himmler listened to his idea of training elite units to assimilate – *gleichschaltung* – into Allied countries to become respected members of society and gain power and influence.

The Reichsfuehrer was intrigued. "And what would be their purpose?"

"To introduce National Socialism," Rhonen said. "The English and the Americans don't entirely disagree with our philosophy of governing."

Himmler sipped his coffee and mulled it over. "What you propose would take years. We don't have years, I'm afraid. We need decisive actions now."

Rhonen anticipated Himmler's response. "Then what if I were to tell you I know how to put an assassin in America to kill that Jew Roosevelt."

Himmler shrugged. "That's been tried, badly. However, you have a better idea?"

Rhonen thought a moment before answering. "In past attempts unreliable people were used; American expatriates, German expatriates – they didn't hold to themselves the spirit of National Socialism and German supremacy."

Rhonen could see interest dawning in the Reichsfuhrer's expression.

He continued. "In the Third Reich's eleven years, we have produced and trained youth strictly devoted to the cause – to the Fuhrer and to the Fatherland. They think and behave very much like our Muslim troops."

Rhonen paused for affect. "Give me one of these boys – and not just any boy, but a boy who is exceptional, who can speak English, who has demonstrated leadership skills – and I can train him to infiltrate America undetected and carry out his assignment."

Himmler frowned. "We no longer have a network of agents in that country."

"Yes, *Reichsfuhrer*, it's true that Admiral Canaris and the Abwher no longer have spies there, but *I* do."

Frustrated the last year at being unable to get Gerhard to consider his idea, Rhonen took utmost satisfaction in the surprised look on the SS leader's face; like a chicken ready to cluck.

The Reichsfuehrer looked expectantly at Rhonen. "How have you managed this?"

Rhonen explained that in early summer 1939, before war in Europe broke out, he visited the United States, where he attended a German-American Bund gathering on New York's Long Island. There, he befriended Bund leaders who supported Hitler.

"They were prepared to help Germany," Rhonen told Himmler.

Fritz Kuhn, the national leader of the Bund, helped Rhonen establish contact with seven Americans of German descent, eager to play a role in the National Socialism cause and to work for its embodiment – Adolf Hitler.

Rhonen had built an elaborate communications system with these individuals, maintained through telegrams and mail via diplomatic pouches of neutral embassies.

Rhonen sent them money and contributions for political candidates they believed supported the cause. They sent him information on coastal defenses and war production – information the general passed on to military intelligence.

"They're waiting for an assignment," Rhonen said.

Himmler was hesitant. Like Hitler, Himmler considered the Bund ineffective and Kuhn clownish. New York District Attorney Tom Dewey convicted Kuhn of embezzling Bund funds six months after Rhonen had met him.

The American fascist movement's leader was sitting out the war with other Bund leaders at a Texas internment camp.

"Are they reliable?" Himmler asked.

"They've been waiting for four years, *Herr Reichsfuhrer*," Rhonen said. "Yes, I believe they are reliable."

Himmler stared through his spectacles, his eyes searching the floor. He recalled the group of espionage agents the Abwher sent in June 1942 to blow up railway lines and dams in America.

Two U-boats landed eight agents carrying explosives and $175,000 in cash on the night-time beaches of Long Island, New York, and Ponte Vedra, Florida. But the agents' training had been haphazard and they were caught almost immediately, one of their leaders turned traitor.

Six of the saboteurs went to the electric chair; the other two were imprisoned. The failed mission had so shook the confident German intelligence, and angered naval command at having risked the U-boats, that no more were attempted.

Himmler knew the Abwher and Kriegsmarine had no appetite for another adventure, but the times were desperate and this would be an SS operation. Why not, he thought; it's no worse – perhaps better thought out – than the Abwher's failed saboteurs.

In the silence, the ticking wall clock grew louder as Rhonen waited for the Reichsfuhrer's answer. Himmler finally sighed. "Very well, then, proceed."

Rhonen congratulated himself after Hahn left his office.

After months of bureaucratic ineptitude – he often wondered whether the Reich was ever efficient beyond its program to eliminate Jews – he would launch his long-sought plan.

Hahn was the best young man they could find, he assured himself, pouring a brandy.

He sat down and started laughing. He knew better. Since June, when the Allies landed in France, Berlin had been sending every available boy, including the Hitler Youth, off to the front, many of them into Waffen SS units.

Hahn wasn't the best they could find; he was the only one they thought to send.

Chapter 3

Dover, Delaware

"The U-boats would form 'wolf packs' to hunt and torpedo allied supply convoys." Sam Grey studied the sentence in a book on submarine warfare and wondered: Did "wolf pack" have a connection with "little wolf," the notation he found at the murder scene?

He read on, unbuttoning his collar and loosening his tie, as he sat at his desk, piled with books on the U-boat campaign in the North Atlantic during World War II, a subject Grey never studied in depth.

As he culled his own book collection and combed the university's library for material, he thought he would use the opportunity to work on his thesis but instead found himself focused on the murdered U-boat captain.

Grey leafed through a bound volume containing old black-and-white photographs of U-boat crews and their boats. The grainy depictions of extreme close quarters, of men working on top of each other while submerged underwater for days at a time, left him claustrophobic.

Turning a page he read a passage about American U-boat hunters. They called the black, cigar-shaped submarines *hearses* and described how U-boat crews were trapped like rats under a successful depth-charge attack.

Grey flipped the page back to study the photos again. The thought of dying in a flooded, narrow steel hull with no way to escape terrified him.

"You got a second?"

Startled by the gravelly sounding voice, he glanced up at a gnomish figure looming over his shoulder. "Yeah, Hank," he said, catching his breath and closing the book. "What is it?"

Rare was the case that brought Henry Kay to an investigator's desk, but when the state's forensic specialist appeared outside his lab, it signaled his interest in evidence he found unusual. Kay picked up a book from the pile on the desk.

"What's all this?" he grumbled. "Are you writing a dissertation or something?"

Grey laughed.

The 71-year-old specialist was well past retirement, but thrived in his work and earned a reputation for noting obscure details that kept him in demand.

His slightly stooped, gray, thinning figure and his wrinkled, thought-worn face enhanced his cantankerous reputation. Intolerant of fools – and he thought most people were foolish – Kay sought comfort and satisfaction in his cluttered lab, immersed in forensics or paging through the latest crime science journals.

Kay dropped two plastic bags on Grey's desk. One contained shell casings found in the old U-boat captain's bungalow, the other the smashed slugs removed from the corpse.

"What've we got here?" Grey said, picking up the bags and peering at them.

Kay sighed. "First, take out one of the casings."

Grey held one between thumb and forefinger. Kay breathed heavily as he leaned down to study the casing through a pair of thick black-frame glasses. Grey smelled stale coffee and cigars on his breath.

"Now," Kay began, "the numbers – one, nine, four, four – are the year the casings were made – 1944. The letters DWM are the *Deutsche Waffen und Munitionsfabriken* monogram."

Grey looked at the old man with disbelief. "Are you telling me the bullets were made in World War II by a German arms maker?"

"That's what I'm telling you."

"What kind of gun were they fired from?"

"Take out one of the slugs that killed your U-boat captain."

Grey complied.

"Now, since what I told you about the casing surprised you – and you seem like an easy fellow to surprise – you're going to be amazed when I tell you about the slug."

"Go ahead, amaze me."

"It was, or rather both bullets were, fired from a nine millimeter parabellum pistol that ejects spent casings when it recoils."

"Which means what?"

"The weapon was most likely a Luger."

"You say most likely?"

"Well, it could also have been fired from a similar pistol type like a Walther P-38."

"But you think it's a Luger?"

"A Luger P dash zero eight."

Grey, surprised, mulled it over: "A German Luger, World War II, hmmm."

Kay glanced at the books on Grey's desk. "I've done a little research of my own. It may or may not bear on your case, but prior to the war the German navy armed U-boat officers with this type of Luger."

Grey considered the information. "So, what are you saying?"

"Your suspect – and his motive – may be in the victim's past, but who knows."

Grey leaned back and clasped his hands behind his head, unsure how to respond. "Well, thanks, Hank. This is helpful – I think."

Kay grumbled and started to leave. He stopped and handed Grey another bag containing the newspaper clipping found near Hoest's body.

"Oh, almost forgot this. Couldn't get any prints off it; interesting story, though."

"Wait a minute, did you get *any* prints?"

"Couple off of the casings; they're fairly clear. I'll send them up to you."

Kay shuffled off. Grey watched his stooped frame disappear out the door before turning his eyes to the clipping.

Newspapers write the first draft of history.

As he ran the sentence through his mind, Grey recalled his Yale undergraduate days and the history professor from whom he first heard it and who often repeated it.

"Of course, the first draft of history is written by newspapers – Yes, a question?"

Professor Edward Witherton nodded perfunctorily to a young Kenyan with a raised hand who asked in a heavy accent, "Sir, how do we trust such vital responsibilities to newspapers that are either government-run or adhere to certain political agendas?"

Witherton sounded offended as he upbraided the student, accusing him of failing to grasp western culture and media, and questioning his academic ability.

"I suggest you reconsider continuing my course," the professor said.

The young man sat uncomfortably as Witherton gazed unsympathetically at him before returning to his lecture. Appalled at such treatment, Grey used the opportunity of a meeting on his term paper he had the next day in the professor's office to confront him about it.

Witherton scolded Grey. "My academic relationships with other students are no matter for you or anyone else to be concerned about."

"I thought it inappropriate and unfair," Grey said. "It was a good question; I wanted to hear an answer."

Witherton became angry. "Well, then, maybe *you* should reconsider this course, if you think such questions need answers and are worthy of your time."

"What's wrong with the question?" Grey demanded.

"Nothing, other than it's a question that you and the other black gentleman should have asked yourselves well before ever entering my class."

The mention of his skin color angered Grey. "What does my race have to do with it?"

Witherton looked sharply at his student. "Don't make accusations, Mr. Grey, and don't read anything more into what I said. This discussion is over."

It had been years since he thought about the incident and why it came to mind he wasn't sure as he re-read the article:

FORMER U-BOAT CAPTAIN FINDS HOME IN AMERICA

Associated Press

LEWES, Del. Aug. 9 (AP) – If it wasn't for his accent, Eric Hoest would pass for just another fisherman on the Atlantic, not a former captain of a German U-boat that used to patrol off the Delaware shores during World War II.

More than 30 years ago, Hoest left his homeland to live along the same coast where he and his crew had sunk several merchant marine ships. The United States, he said, had always been a place he wanted to visit.

"Even during the war, I never considered America my enemy, but as a sailor I had my duty," said the 82-year-old resident of this beach town on the Delaware Bay.

Hoest left Kiel, Germany, in 1968 and moved to Lewes, where he started a deep-sea fishing business that had become one of the more popular excursions for tourists. The former submariner has long been shy about discussing his war experience.

"That's the past," he said with a shrug. "I like to live in the present."

While on a recent fishing excursion off Cape Henlopen, Hoest pointed out to a reporter the sandy shoreline and said that during the war his U-boat had passed by this way at night on several missions. Though the submarine was miles off shore, he could see from the conning tower the distant lights of beach homes.

"As a sailor in the Germany Navy, I fought for my country, not for Hitler," Hoest said. "The Nazis ruined my old country."

Hoest was among a group of immigrants who recently became American citizens at the Sussex County Courthouse. "America," he said, "is my new country."

Grey set the clipping aside and leaned back to consider his investigation. The Sussex County coroner said Hoest had been dead for about three days. He died from the two bullets, fired at close range. There are no suspects, no witnesses and no way to know a motive.

A check on calls to the bungalow two weeks prior to the murder found nothing unusual. Several were out of state, but the phone company believed most of those were telemarketers.

Hoest made few calls during this time period. Most were to his neighbor, Oskar Franks.

Two slugs from World War II, possibly fired from a pistol made back then were Grey's only lead, but he was encouraged. He smiled to himself. Kay had no idea how he confirmed his hunch about searching the past. Where else could he go in this case?

"You want to know why I think Franks killed Hoest?"

Grey had returned to Lewes, not sure what he expected to find. He went to the police station off tree-shaded Main Street and picked up Christopher, who entertained him with *his* murder theory.

Grey nodded as he steered the car over the green-mesh draw-bridge that spanned the canal. "Yes, I want to know why you think Franks is our suspect."

"He's a Jew; probably came to resent Hoest and his Nazi past."

Grey shook his head. "I don't know, Chris; that seems hardly a motive."

"Look, he's a Jew and Jews hate Germans for the Holocaust and all that other crap."

"You're saying Franks killed Hoest because he's German?"

"Yeah, that's what I'm saying."

"But Franks is German," Grey said, patiently. "I can't imagine that's a plausible motive."

Christopher shrugged. "Yeah, what the hell do I know, you're the expert."

Grey gave him a sidelong glance. "Are we going to start that again?"

Christopher was annoyed. "Look, at least ask him if he owns a Luger. Okay?"

Grey glared at him as he negotiated the car along the narrow shore road and said, quietly, "I intend to, so ease up."

The car rolled to a stop outside the Franks' home. Grey shoved the gear shift into park, pulled the key from the ignition and angrily tossed the jangling chain on the dash. Christopher looked at him, but said nothing.

"Let's be clear, because I'm tired of the nastiness," Grey said. "For whatever financial or political reasons, this town decided with the state's blessing that it can't afford a homicide squad – that's why I'm here."

Christopher sputtered, "I know why you're here, goddammit."

"No, I don't think you do." Grey spoke sternly. "I don't want to be here, but it's my job, and there's nothing else I can do about it. And if you won't work with me then I'll work around you because I have no time for this."

Grey turned and looked out the car's window. Oskar Franks stood on his porch, watching them. "Our suspect is on his porch, wondering, I'm sure, what the hell we're doing. Now, are we going to get along on this investigation?"

Christopher grudgingly nodded. Grey held out his hand to the wary looking police chief who paused before shaking it. The two men opened their doors and stepped out of the car. They greeted Oskar Franks who looked surprised to see them.

"We weren't expecting you."

Grey spoke reassuringly. "We're going back into Mr. Hoest's house so we decided to stop by and see how you were doing."

"Come in, gentlemen."

Franks led them inside. A young man around Grey's age rose from the sofa with a look of concern. Franks introduced him as his nephew, Herman, an adjunct college professor from Staten Island, New York, who now lived just across the bay in Cape May.

"Herman teaches history," Franks said. "He takes the ferry over once a week to visit."

Lean with dark, curly hair, Herman skeptically appraised the officers. He started to ask a question when Rosemary emerged from the kitchen and greeted them. Grey went to the point.

"Mr. Franks, do you own a gun?"

"A gun?" he said, confused. "No, why?"

"It's just routine," Christopher said. "We ask anyone involved these questions."

Franks was taken aback. He glanced at his wife. "Am I – am I a suspect?"

Grey reassured him. "Mr. Franks, at this point in the investigation, everyone is a potential suspect, but no, you are not under investigation."

"Then why are you here?" Herman demanded, angrily.

Grey ignored him, his eyes focused on Franks.

"Oskar would never do such a thing," Rosemary said. "He's never owned a gun."

"I understand," Grey said, glancing at a now subdued Christopher.

As Grey interviewed the couple, Christopher wondered whether he was too hard on the corporal. He was, the police chief reluctantly acknowledged to himself, just doing his job.

Grey reassured the Franks once more and asked about friends and acquaintances Hoest had, more to ensure that Oskar Franks understood he wasn't a suspect than to learn anything.

With a sense of relief Oskar relaxed and said, "He had acquaintances in town, but really, we were his closest friends."

They left the Franks and the nephew and walked to Hoest's house under a hot sun. Ocean winds carried sounds of buoy horns, motor boats and children's laughter over the grassy dunes.

Christopher tried to make amends. "How did you get picked to play football for Yale?"

"How do you know where I went to college?" Grey said, surprised the police chief had become interested enough to learn his background.

"Somebody in Dover told me."

Grey nodded, glancing at the sparkling waters of the bay as he tried to decide whether or not he wanted to like the police chief. "Academic and a needs-based scholarship," he said. "Ivy League colleges don't give athletic scholarships."

"What'd you study?"

"History and pre-law," Grey said.

"You wanted to be a lawyer?" Christopher said.

"My father wanted me to be a lawyer. I'm more interested in history."

"Hell, what do you do with history?"

"Teach," Grey said. "I'm working on my doctorate so I can do just that."

"What're you doing in the state police?"

"I guess it was a compromise of sorts, an effort to please my father, but I do enjoy criminology work."

"You're one of those intellectual types, aren't you?" Christopher said.

Grey laughed. "Not really." He stopped on the sand-dusted road outside Hoest's house. "I'm just curious about things."

Christopher grunted as they ducked under the yellow CRIME SCENE tape. They climbed the porch stair, unlocked the door, and entered the house.

Inside, Grey went to the study and began going through desk drawers.

Christopher watched him. "What exactly are we looking for?"

"Not sure really, but I think I'll know when I find it."

Grey carefully perused the book-laden shelves and the room's belongings once more, but found nothing of interest. "Let's go to the second floor."

Christopher led the way up a narrow stairway. Grey noticed simple furnishings in the upstairs rooms. Of the three, one was small and narrow with enough space for a bed, a small dresser and desk. It had a low ceiling and a single, large window.

He studied the room and realized it was actually a large dormer. He went over and drew back the window curtains to see white boats with wind-filled sails slicing through the waters of the Delaware Bay.

On the desk, Grey lifted up a worn, cloth-bound book with *Schiffs-journal* in faded gold lettering. He listened as Christopher wandered toward him from the other bedroom. He opened the book's yellowed pages. The second page listed a dozen names.

"This is a pretty tight room," Christopher said, standing in the doorway.

"It was Hoest's room," Grey said, staring at the page.

"How do you know that?"

"This is his captain's log and I believe this list of names were his crew members."

"What's that got to do with anything?"

"Just a hunch, but the clues to this case might be in Hoest's past."

"Sounds far fetched," Christopher said. "I still think the Jew killed him."

Grey closed the book and put it under his arm. "I'm done here."

The two men went downstairs and outside. Grey waited as Christopher locked the door. They descended the porch steps, ducked under the police tape and started down the shore road. As they walked, Grey looked back at the house and stopped.

"What's wrong?" Christopher said.

"Curtains in the dormer."

"What about 'em?"

"They're drawn. Did you close them?"

"I never went past the doorway in that room."

The two men looked at each other knowingly.

"Okay," Grey said. "How do you want to do this?"

Christopher handed him the key to the house. "I'll go 'round the rear."

Grey nodded and they headed back. As they closed in, Christopher dashed his heavy set frame toward the backyard. Grey hurried up the porch steps and inserted the key in the lock. He heard footsteps pounding down the stairwell. In quick succession he dropped the book, drew his service pistol and turned the key. He gripped the door knob and burst in just as a blurry figure in dark clothes headed into the kitchen.

"Hey! Hold it!" Grey ordered.

He heard a door bang open and Christopher shout. A moment later he reached the back door in the kitchen and found the police chief in the yard, in a stance with his legs spread wide apart and his gun aimed at a gaunt-looking figure in black T-shirt, black jeans and heavy black boots. His tattooed arms raised above his shaved head.

Grey approached the man. He looked young, but lines at the corners of his darting brown eyes hinted he was older than his effeminate appearance; his long, bony arms were covered in an odd mix of tattoos – birds, butterflies, snakes and a swastika.

"And what do we have here?" Grey said, eyeing the man closely. "What were you doing in that house?"

Christopher nodded at a smashed basement window. "That's how he got inside."

The man remained silent, staring angrily at Grey.

"Come on, you can do it," Grey said. "Tell us what you were doing in there?"

The man's eyes turned to slits as he stared at Grey.

"Answer him," Christopher ordered.

The man looked at the police chief. *"Ich spreche nicht mit scheisekopfe!"*

Christopher looked at Grey. "What did he say?"

Grey smiled. "He called us, in well-spoken German, shit heads."

Christopher walked up to the man and struck him hard in the head, knocking him to the ground. Grey interceded. "Whoa, let's take it easy." He helped the man to his feet, searched his pockets, but found no identification. "Let's get him out of here."

"Who do you think this skinhead is?"

"I don't know," said Grey, a little exasperated. "Let's get him into a cell and we'll worry about that later."

Christopher handcuffed the man as Grey locked up the house and retrieved the book from the porch. The suspect did not say a word as they took him to the police station and put him in an overnight holding cell.

Grey watched him through the bars and sensed something odd about the man, but what he couldn't determine. The man gave him a less angry glance, prompting Grey: "You'll have to talk sooner or later, why not now?" The man lay on the cell's steel-framed bed and closed his eyes.

Christopher stood, hands shoved in his pockets, excited by the break in the case. He used an arm to nudge Grey. They went back to his office.

"Now, what do we do with him?" he said, as he sat behind a clean desk that caused Grey to raise a mischievous eyebrow.

"Keep him here overnight and we'll talk to him in the morning," Grey said. "You got him on enough charges."

"What if he calls his lawyer?"

"I doubt that'll happen, but if so get him arraigned on breaking and entering and whatever else you can find, then ask the judge to deny bail."

"What are you going to do?"

"I'll be back in the morning," Grey said. "Right now I want to get back to Dover."

"Are you going to get the book analyzed?"

"No, I've got a dinner date," Grey said.

Christopher began to object, but Grey assured him. "I'm going to analyze the book, but first I'm going to my father's for dinner."

After steamed shrimp and New York strips chased with Yuengling lagers, Grey sat with his aging father on the screened porch, catching the steady breeze while watching the day's light drain into a crimson sky.

Short, plump and gray around the temples, Woodrow Wilson Grey's baritone voice and broad smile always reassured his son. His military career began in the infantry in World War II and ended as an Air Force military policeman at Dover Air Force Base.

Woody had a good pension, but he spent the early part of his retirement as a cook at the American Legion hall near the base. A widower, he lost his wife, Antonella, a Nicaraguan who he met while stationed at Bolling Air Base in Washington, D.C., to a drunk driver in 1962.

Sam was their first and, as it turned out, only child. The morning she was killed, she was on her way home from the doctor with the happy announcement of her second pregnancy.

The remorseless driver and the apologetic prosecutor who told Woody the man had been cited over the years for numerous drunk-driving violations left a lasting impression on Sam, who was five years old at the time.

Woody was beyond anger. "How can the law allow a man like that to be on the road?"

The prosecutor sympathized, telling him Maryland's drunk-driving laws were weak and poorly enforced. "Mr. Grey, cases like this man's fall through the cracks way too often."

The memory of standing in the district attorney's office, watching his father pound on the desk, rattling an ashtray on which a cigarette lay burning, never left Sam. "You're telling me that if someone had done their job my wife and child would not be dead right now?"

The prosecutor nodded.

Grey filled the emotional void left by his mother's death with school work, earning entry into Yale, where he ran track and played football. Following college, he took a two-year stint as a military policeman at U.S. Army Headquarters in Heidelberg, Germany, in the mid-1980s.

Memories of his military service returned as he sat on the porch sipping beer. He looked at his father. "Dad, what do you remember from the war?"

Woody sat comfortably in the brown wicker chair and stared out past the porch, enjoying a warm, westerly breeze before answering. "You haven't asked me that in a long time."

"I know; tell me what the Germans were like as fighters."

"Why you asking now?"

"Just interested, that's all. I served in peace time so I don't know what war is like, though I've tried at times to imagine it."

Woody sighed. He had few good memories, but he understood what his son was asking him. "The Germans were tough fighters, even the kids fought hard; fanatics, you know, driven by loyalty to Hitler."

"What drove you to fight?"

"Not wanting to be killed, that's what."

Grey started to laugh.

"No, it's just that we were motivated to fight for different reasons, son."

"Are we, really, or does killing just become a function of the soldier's job?"

Woody mulled the question. "War does weird things to people."

"What kind of weird things?"

"Well," Woody's voice trailed off. "I don't know, I guess I can't explain it."

Father and son sat quietly for a moment before the father began a story he never wanted to tell, but for some reason felt now was the time.

On a snowy day in Bavaria, Woody crouched behind the ruins of an old farmhouse, firing at an unseen sniper who had been picking off his helpless platoon.

"That's a mean sum bitch out there," he said, breathing hard from fear as a fellow soldier listened. The sniper had had them pinned down for more than an hour; blood splattered over the snow. One squad member was dead, three wounded. Woody was getting his combat baptism.

He peered over a broken stone wall as the sniper's gun fired from a cluster of buildings. He watched until finally he pinpointed the gunman's position. Just as he did, a bullet exploded into the wall near his head, spraying fragments into his eyes.

"Damn!" Woody threw himself down, and with his gloved hand frantically wiped white mortar dust and stone shards off his young brown face. "What the hell's going on? I thought we mopped this place up."

"Apparently this guy didn't hear the news," said his fellow soldier.

Woody laughed nervously and quickly peered over the wall, drawing fire again. "He's in the barn's hayloft over on the right. We can swing around this way and get behind him."

The two soldiers stayed down as they hurried around the edge of the barnyard, ducked along a stone wall and crawled to the barn. The sniper's continued firing from the hayloft was greeted by sporadic return fire.

They reached the barn, opened the back door slowly and slipped inside. At the front of the building, dust and straw drifted down from above. They crept forward until Woody looked up and, through gaps between the floorboards, could see the sniper, firing.

He grabbed his fellow soldiers' arm, used his thumb to point up, and motioned with his machine gun.

The sniper fired once more before the soldiers sprayed the floorboards in an emotional release of pent up frustration, having felt helpless behind the stone wall. Shouting curses, they fired until they spent their ammunition and could hear their lieutenant – who followed them inside after they entered – shouting at them to stop and relax.

Woody, shaking, looked fearful. The lieutenant glared at him. "I think you got him. Now go up and check it out."

They carefully climbed into the hayloft and made their way over the piles of straw to the sniper's riddled body. Woody gasped. The boy couldn't have been more than 12 or 13 years old.

Woody looked at his son. "You know what was weird about that?"

Grey shook his head.

"The war had been over for eight months."

Grey thought about the story while feeling the breeze on his face. Woody watched his son until he finished his beer. It was late, Grey said, kissing his father on the forehead. "Work calls."

"Let me ask you something before you go?" Woody said.

"Sure."

"When're you going to find a nice woman and settle down?"

"I don't know, Dad. I'm just too busy right now."

"What about that young lady you brought over a few weeks ago?"

"Alicia? She's as busy as I am."

Woody shook his head. "I don't understand young people today, you all so busy. What're you so busy about?"

"Living."

Woody snorted. "All I got to say is it sure would be nice to have grandchildren around before I'm too old."

His son smiled. "I'll work on it."

His father's expression became serious. Grey knew what he was about to say and over the years learned to stop arguing about it and just listen, hoping his father would forget.

"You know son, I wonder sometimes whether you are afraid to get serious with a woman; you were so young when your mother was killed."

"I know, Dad," he said. "I gotta go."

Grey returned to his Dover townhouse. He dropped into an overstuffed chair in his book-lined study and examined Hoest's log book, wondering how he would go about locating the men whose names were listed in it. He read the first few entries when the word 'wolf' jumped off the page at him. He sat up and read further.

After about an hour, Grey decided he needed help translating. He e-mailed his longtime friend in Heidelberg, Germany, who he would be visiting in a few days. The log book appeared crucial. The idea of pursuing this case through historical research excited him.

Grey arrived at Lewes around eight o'clock the next morning to find Christopher joking with an officer in the lobby of the old brick station. The chief took him to his office and closed the door, offering him a cup of coffee.

"That skinhead ain't doing any talking this morning," Christopher said.

"You've been to the cell already?" Grey asked.

"Yeah, but I don't think he plans on talking, least not for awhile."

"Let me go in and see what I can do."

"Sure, but if there ain't no cooperation I'm having him arraigned this morning and I'm going to have the prosecutor ask the judge to deny bail and put him into county. As far as I'm concerned, he's a murder suspect."

"What makes you so sure?"

"We processed him last night, after you left. His prints match some found in the house."

Grey nodded. He wanted to see the suspect. Christopher led him to the cell, called out "visitor," and left him. The man sat on the bed, staring off. He ignored Grey's greeting.

"They're going to put you in prison unless you talk," Grey said. "They may find enough evidence to prove you're a murderer, though I have my doubts."

The man looked at Grey and turned away. Grey watched him for a moment more before returning to the police chief's office. He sat down, frustrated.

"Okay," Christopher said. He went to the doorway and called down the hall, "Hey, Joe?"

A voice replied, "Yes sir!"

"Get the skinhead ready."

Christopher returned to his desk and called the prosecutor.

When he finished, he turned to Grey with a tone of annoyance. "I get the impression you don't think this guy killed Hoest either."

Grey sighed and nodded.

"And why's that?" Christopher said.

"First, we don't know who he is so we can't suspect motive. Second, and this may not be important, but why is he back visiting the scene of the crime? It doesn't make sense."

"Criminals have a habit of returning to the crime scene."

"If I'd murdered Hoest, I wouldn't return several days later and hang out."

"We've got one dead Nazi and two suspects who couldn't be more obvious – a Jew and a skinhead."

"Uh huh, and what's the skinhead's motive?" Grey asked.

"How the hell should I know? He's not talking, but I'm going to find out."

Grey began to wonder how Christopher ever became a police chief. He spoke quietly. "Maybe that's my problem, Chris, they're too obvious."

"Sometimes the guilty party is the most obvious."

"And sometimes the person you least suspect is the guilty one."

The exasperated police chief exhaled deeply. "What other leads do we have?"

"The log book, I think one or some of those names may be a lead for us."

Christopher shook his head, annoyed. "This sounds like one of your school assignments." He stood and said, "I'm getting the skinhead arraigned."

Grey watched the chief and an officer put the suspect into Christopher's police cruiser.

"I'm going to get the log book translated, Chris; I'll let you know what I find."

"You do that."

The police chief slammed shut the car door just before the cruiser drove off.

Grey received a reply to his e-mail that evening from his friend in Heidelberg, who told him to send the list of names in the log book and he would research German military records to determine their whereabouts. He promised to have the information when Grey arrived.

At state police headquarters the next morning, Grey updated his supervisor. A decorated veteran of Vietnam, Davis appreciated the instincts of his favorite subordinate; Grey was taking a night flight that evening for Germany. He planned to pursue a lead.

Davis chuckled at Grey's enthusiasm. "What makes you think going over there is going to lead to anything?"

"Just a hunch, but the evidence we've found so far points in that direction."

Davis nodded as he shifted some papers on his desk and leaned back in his chair. "You're one of the few guys around here whose hunches are pretty good," he said. "Who are you visiting over there?"

"An old friend, he's a bit of Bohemian who hates to leave a party."

"Oh?"

"Don't worry, Jack, he's no commie," Grey said, half-jokingly. He knew the ex-Marine's aversion to communists, borne fighting Viet Cong in Southeast Asia. "He teaches literature at the University of Heidelberg. He's helping me translate the log book."

Davis nodded his consent and dismissed him, but as Grey started to leave, he inquired in a casual way, "You were stationed in Heidelberg, weren't you?"

"Yes sir," Grey said.

"You liked it over there?"

"I did, very much, but I haven't seen Germany or my friend in sixteen years."

"Okay," Davis said. "Don't forget to let Lewes police know what you're doing."

On the telephone, Christopher reacted to Grey's trip with silence.

"Chris?" Grey spoke into the receiver. "Are you still with me?"

"Why are you going over there when we have a murder suspect in custody?"

"Look, I scheduled this vacation months ago and besides, we have no evidence linking the guy to the murder."

Frustrated, Christopher dismissed Grey. "If you want to waste your time, be my guest, but when you get back, we'll still have a murder suspect in custody."

Grey decided he could longer argue. Less than twenty hours later, he was in Germany.

Chapter 4

Heidelberg, Germany

October, 1944

Lieutenant-General Joachim von Rhonen, wearing his SS uniform, rose from his desk to greet the man who was his superior in Yugoslavia.

General Walther Gerhard, his billed cap a bit too large for his head, was several years younger than Rhonen. He was short, slender with wavy blond hair, brown eyes and a face of delicate, soft features. He was one of Himmler's favorites.

His boyish features, to which those who worked for him knew he was sensitive, belied his reputation in the SS hierarchy as an ambitious, ruthless administrator.

As the Allies closed in on Germany – British and Americans advancing from the west; Russians from the east – Himmler, like many in the army high command, was desperate for a strike to demoralize the Allies. Rhonen's assassin could certainly deal the Americans a severe blow, he told Gerhard before sending him to Heidelberg to evaluate Martin Hahn's training.

"*Herr General*," Rhonen said, smiling pleasantly, although suspicious about Gerhard's arrival, considering the man had no interest in his work. "I did not expect to see you."

Gerhard wore a sour expression as he sat in a chair and deftly slid a hand inside his tunic to remove a gold cigarette case. "The *Reichsfuhrer* wants a progress report on your" – he paused for effect – "project."

Rhonen nodded. "Fine, Hahn should be ready in another month."

Gerhard frowned as he lit a cigarette that he let dangle from his lips. "A month," he said, sharply. "What about sooner?"

Rhonen sensed interference from Berlin's bureaucracy, but only shrugged. "The mental preparation takes time, but I assure you he'll be on his way before November ends."

Agitated, Gerhard demanded, "Hahn did exceptionally well under me infiltrating student traitors in Munich. What more does he need?"

"Time," Rhonen said, firmly. "Besides, I'm also preparing his transportation."

Gerhard spoke sarcastically. "And how do you propose to get him to America?"

Rhonen ignored the tone and spoke confidently. "U-boat, naturally; a Commander Hoest is arriving later today."

Gerhard scoffed. "He won't make it across the Atlantic. The British and Americans are catching and killing anything that moves in those waters."

"Maybe," Rhonen said, "but is there any other way? This commander believes he can do it and I need believers, if this mission is to succeed."

Gerhard laughed at Rhonen's argument. "You'll forgive me, general, for not believing in this absurd mission of yours – boy assassin; delusional U-boat commander. But, it is not for me to care. I'm just here to get a progress report and prod you on."

"Then your assignment is complete," Rhonen said.

"You don't really believe this can succeed, do you?"

"Why should I doubt my efforts," Rhonen replied. "The young man has the will, a strong will, and I'm confident of success."

Gerhard shrugged, dismissively. "You're fortunate, Rhonen, the *Reichsfuhrer* believes in your crazy plan; otherwise you would be back in the Balkans with your fez-wearing troops." He stood, impatient. "As you said, my assignment is complete. I want to see him before I leave."

Rhonen was only too happy to hurry Gerhard's departure. "He's at the castle, training in self-defense and weaponry. We'll go together."

The staff-car ride up the steep, winding road to *Der Schloss* was short in the cool autumn morning. The Mercedes stopped at a black-and-white striped sentry box, where the armed guard saluted and waved the vehicle into the graveled courtyard.

Inside the imposing red-stone medieval fortress, a young lieutenant escorted them into a large hall, its walls hung with enormous embroidered tapestries.

Hahn sat at a long table with two instructors when the generals entered. He almost leapt to attention at the sight of Gerhard, a sudden deluge of memories – the student movement, where he made friends only to betray them to the Gestapo.

The experience in Munich left him confused emotionally; the students were traitors, but he came to like them, to almost understand their argument. They opposed Hitler, but they loved the Fatherland. Was it possible, he wondered, to do both?

Whenever Hahn showed any doubts, Gerhard would call him into his office, reminding him of Hamburg's fiery destruction. He could hear the general's voice: "Their action indirectly supports the very criminal acts such as the bombing that destroyed your family."

Now, with the two generals standing before him, Hahn clicked his heels, thrust out his arm, and nervously greeted them with, "*Heil Hitler.*"

"Don't be so formal, Hahn," Gerhard said, studying the young man who was more than a foot taller than him. "Are you ready for this assignment?"

"*Ja, Herr General.*"

Rhonen nodded to one of the instructors, who spoke to Gerhard. "Martin is most adept in weapon-training, particularly knives." Gerhard ignored the instructor and said to Hahn, "What is your mission, Hahn? Can you tell me?"

Hahn paused before responding. "To strike at the enemy's heart; to keep alive the spirit of the Furhrer and National Socialism."

Gerhard looked wistful at him and recalled his lost opportunity when Hahn served under his supervision. He tried to embrace the young man in his Munich office. They had just returned from the student beheadings – a scene Gerhard insisted Hahn observe.

"What's wrong, Martin?" The general's voice became seductive as he lifted a soft hand to caress Hahn's smooth, rugged face as he tried to offer him a glass of brandy.

Gerhard ordered the executions and pulled the guillotine's lever for the first student. The exhilaration he felt from killing always left the general amorous, and he was eager to quench his desire with this boy.

"Nothing, *Herr General*," He sat stiffly on the couch before rising and going to the door.

"Martin?" Gerhard called.

Hahn walked out without answering him. The aroused general seethed, but didn't bother to pursue him. He had other young men willing to attend his needs.

In an act of retribution, Gerhard had Hahn sent to Rhonen. Looking back, he wished he had not reacted so harshly. He could have persuaded Hahn, as he had other boys, and he might now be enjoying a romp in a warm bed, instead of standing in a cold, dark castle.

Gerhard took a long last look at Hahn before turning to Rhonen. "Things are in order."

"Very good, *Herr General*," Rhonen said.

"Hahn," Gerhard said, turning to the blond-haired youth. "Good luck."

The generals spoke little on the return drive to Rhonen's office. Gerhard, eager to leave, climbed into his staff car. "I shall tell the *Reichsfurhrer* you'll be ready in a few weeks. What a waste of a fine young man. I can think of much better assignments for him."

Rhonen saluted, relieved at Gerhard's departure. He never had much tolerance for Reich bureaucracy politics. When he needed to, though, he could play the game quite well.

"*Herr General*," Rhonen said. "Please visit again to see the progress of our efforts."

Gerhard smirked. "General, I have no desire to return. If you never launch this mission, I would not care. I have absolutely no confidence in its success. *Auf weidershen*."

He ordered his driver on and the car rolled forward, accelerating to the sounds of shifting gears. Rhonen checked his watch; the U-boat commander was due to arrive soon.

Cold rain from dark, overcast skies splattered drops against Rhonen's office window as the door opened and his adjutant entered, clicking his heels and announcing U-boat Commander Eric Hoest.

Rhonen, who had shed his SS uniform for a gray suit, greeted the blue-uniformed officer warmly. They sat facing each other in chairs that had been arranged by the unlit fireplace.

Admiral Donitz' staff at the *Kriegsmarine* recommended Hoest when Rhonen sought a crew. He would only describe it to them as secret; he insisted on limiting the number of people who knew the exact nature of Hahn's assignment.

Hoest was a lean, rugged-looking sailor with chestnut-brown hair and a light beard. He was 26 years old, relatively young for a commander. He proudly joined U-boat service in 1940, following his father who served on a battleship in World War I.

In the last year, Hoest had become a bitter critic of the admiralty's conduct of the war in the Atlantic. Between 1943 and 1944 the U-boats went from near domination of the seas to near decimation by Allied naval forces.

U-boat Command dutifully noted Hoest's theories behind this change in fortune, but they refused to either acknowledge or believe.

He was a skillful commander and had beaten the odds at getting killed in a naval service where most failed to return from the sea. After nearly three years, an incident of insubordination landed him behind a desk at U-boat Command.

Hoest was unhappy there and longed to return to active duty, and to the sea.

His criticisms, and his complaints about his assignments, only irritated his superiors, who welcomed Rhonen's request for a commander as an opportunity to dispose of Hoest.

Rhonen knew this and much more about Hoest. As he offered him a cigarette, the general said, "You're somewhat of an upstart, aren't you?"

Hoest, who, like most Germans, always dealt cautiously with the SS, raised his eyebrows and flashed a what-is-this-going-to-be-about look.

"I'm not sure what you mean?"

"Of course you do," Rhonen said, as he lit Hoest's cigarette. "You come from a family of upstarts; your father was among those in the naval mutinies of 1918, wasn't he?"

Hoest laughed to himself, but he worried. The mutinies in the last war had helped seal the former German Empire's fate. The ultra-patriotic Nazi leaders cited this as reason enough to stay wary of the *Kriegsmarine*.

Many young sailors swore undying allegiance to the party to demonstrate their loyalty to Hitler, but not Hoest; he became a Nazi only to ensure his entry into the navy. He had no interest in politics. As war destroyed Germany's cities, he grew disillusioned with Hitler.

Hoest allowed a contemptuous tone in his voice. "*Herr General*, are you trying to indict me for something my father did more than twenty years ago?"

"It wasn't just some 'thing,' commander; it was mutiny – he participated in a treasonous act that helped lead to the fall of the Empire."

Hoest became angry. "He was no traitor; he was a loyal German and a sailor."

Rhonen stood and went to his desk where he picked up a file from the blotter and opened it. "Your father served on the *Kronprinz Wilhelm*. Correct?"

"Yes," Hoest answered, quietly.

"The crew mutinied believing the officers were trying to disrupt armistice negotiations, negotiations that weakened and humiliated Germany," Rhonen said, tossing the file on his desk for effect and returning to his chair. "What's loyal about that?"

"I thought you had an assignment for me?"

"I want an answer," the general demanded, in a flare of temper. "What was loyal about your father's mutinous actions?"

"The war was over. My father and the other sailors believed the officers were preparing to risk their lives for a lost cause; they only wanted to avoid a needless loss of life."

Rhonen relaxed. "Lost cause? Do you think we're fighting a lost cause?"

Hoest, growing more uneasy with the conversation, shrugged.

Rhonen discerned his reluctance. "You may speak freely."

Hoest gave a dry laugh. "Before the SS? I'd lose my head; others certainly have."

Rhonen spoke calmly. "I'm an SS officer, commander, not a fanatical fool. I have my doubts about the war's progress, too. Now, I would like to hear your answer."

"What is it you want to know?"

"Why are you so disagreeable with the admiralty?"

"They're wearing blinders and it's costing us the war," Hoest said.

"Tell me how?"

Hoest refused to answer, wanting to know the point of his interview. "Is this why you brought me down here, to get my opinions on how to run the war?"

Rhonen smiled. "I'll explain shortly. Answer my question."

"They show no interest in understanding why we are being defeated."

"And you know the reason, yes?"

"I have a suspicion, but I'm certain it's true."

"What is it?"

Hoest paused, to collect his thoughts. "It's quite simple, really. They've broken our codes and so they know where we are and where we are going."

"That's an interesting theory, though I'm not sure I'm ready to subscribe to it."

"I don't see how else we could have lost so many boats so systematically in the last year; it's been like shooting fish in a barrel. The Allies must have learned our codes."

"Perhaps, but what do you suggest?"

"I wouldn't start a mutiny, if that's what you want to know."

Rhonen did not laugh at the remark, but waited for the answer.

Hoest said, "I would send out boats with a single order: sink Allied shipping. Halt ship-to-shore communications, so we no longer broadcast our whereabouts."

The room fell silent except for the patter of rain against the window. Rhonen decided he was confident in Hoest. "Would you like to prove your theory in an assignment that would take you to the American shores?"

Hoest shrugged, still suspicious of the general, but excited by an opportunity to return to sea. "Considering that I haven't much choice in the matter, certainly."

"I can't divulge much about what's involved; your mission will be to get an agent ashore, as close to Washington as possible."

"A spy?"

"Yes, but that's about all you will know," the general said. "Your mission is to get him to America and return to Germany."

Hoest was intrigued. "And I will be permitted to conduct the mission as I see fit?"

"Certainly," Rhonen said. "No radio contact, if that's what you wish."

"Why, *Herr General*? If you don't believe my theory, why allow me to pursue it?"

"It has nothing to do with you," Rhonen said. "It has everything to do with putting my agent in America."

"No radio contact means you won't know whether we succeeded," Hoest said.

"Understood," Rhonen said. "I expect a report from you when you return."

"What if we don't make it back?"

Rhonen spoke firmly. "Commander, I did not make it this far in my life expecting failure. I expect success, as you should. Is that clear?"

"Quite clear."

"You will succeed because you don't follow conventions," Rhonen said.

A rap on the door interrupted their conversation. Rhonen answered with a command and his adjutant appeared, Hahn behind him. The general introduced Hahn to Hoest.

To the U-boat commander, Hahn appeared much too young for whatever assignment the general was planning. After a few pleasantries were exchanged, Rhonen dismissed Hahn.

Alone again, Hoest accepted the mission, but gave the general two additional conditions:

"First: no political officer."

Rhonen smiled knowingly. "I suppose that's about your insubordinate conduct?"

Surprised by the remark, Hoest wondered why the general had not broached the incident with him earlier. It had occurred in late 1942 while prowling off North Carolina's coast. The U-boat he commanded fired two torpedoes into an Esso oil tanker. When the boat surfaced, Hoest found the sinking ship ablaze and seamen with no life preservers floating in an oil-covered sea.

He ordered two life rafts dropped for the dozen survivors, but the political officer whose duty was to ensure constant adherence to Nazi party ideals, adamantly warned the crew against such action.

"Stay at your stations," the officer ordered. "You would be aiding the enemy; in direct violation of Admiral Donitz' instructions to rescue no one."

The crew stopped. Hoest became enraged and countermanded the officer. "Follow my order, immediately!"

"Nein!" the political officer barked, looking at the crew. "Any man who acts will be reported as a traitor."

Hoest shouted. "I take responsibility for my orders, now follow them."

"Nein!"

The crew did not move. Hoest could see the political officer intimidated them and that, Hoest always believed, was the real intention of the officer.

Hoest stormed out of the control room and the political officer began to issue orders, but Hoest returned moments later with a pistol in hand. He shoved the gun barrel against the officer's temple and pulled the trigger back.

"By God, Herr Leutnant, I will put a bullet in your head."

Sweat began to bead on the political officer's face. His eyes darted nervously around to each man to see whether he had support, but the crew stood by their commander. He glared at Hoest and said to the crew, "Do as he says."

The memory remained fresh for Hoest as he said to Rhonen, "Is that what all the mutiny talk was about? Why did you not ask me directly?"

Rhonen shook his head. "You have a commendable service record. I'm sure you had valid reason to disobey an order and threaten an officer. My only interest is whether you can handle the mission."

"The man was countermanding my orders," Hoest said.

"Understood, commander, no political officer," Rhonen said. "And what is your other condition?"

"Since we will have no rendezvous with a supply boat, I will take a scaled-down crew of nine so food provisions will last longer."

Rhonen agreed and presented his condition: "No attacks."

Hoest opposed the idea, but Rhonen insisted he obey his orders.

"Why?" Hoest demanded. "The crew is trained for battle, not milk deliveries."

"It increases risk of capture and jeopardizes the mission. Your torpedoes should only be used as defensive measures." The general smiled at him. "It also won't put you in a position of having to aid the enemy again."

Reluctantly, Hoest agreed, if only because he was eager to command again. He inquired about the landing. "You said as close to Washington as possible?"

"That's right," the general said.

"Do you have a specific location in mind?"

"What do you suggest?"

Hoest went over in his mind the charts and maps he studied of that region of the United States. "It's risky, and would be quite a feat if we were successful, but I would try for the upper Chesapeake Bay."

"Why there?"

"It's about eighty kilometers from Washington."

"How risky is such a voyage?"

The commander explained they would have to get past a large naval base near the mouth of the bay, where shallow waters required surface sailing. However, the bay was the largest inlet on America's east coast. Its entrance was about 12 miles wide. With luck, and cover of darkness, they could slip past the American navy.

Such a dangerous feat, in fact, was accomplished more than a year ago, he said. A U-boat had laid mines just inside the bay.

"The Americans have mined part of the approach to the bay, but I know that field and it's easy to navigate around," Hoest told the general.

"What about anti-sub nets?"

"Not across the bay," the commander said, shaking his head. "Too large and the shipping channels to Baltimore are much too busy. Inlets and harbors with naval installations have netting, but we're staying in the bay."

Hoest paused a moment. "I have to check my charts, but there are a couple of tiny islands in the bay and not too far from shore that would allow for a landing."

The idea impressed Rhonen. "You have my confidence, commander."

As he mulled over the details of such a dangerous mission, he realized one potential way to reduce the risk. They could use the Walter Boat; the prototype Navy High Command shelved three years earlier because of the demand for more of the U-boat types already in service.

Named for Hellmuth Walter, the rocket engineer, the boat was smaller and sleeker than the Type VIIC, the most commonly built and used U-boat. At half the Type VIIC's weight and size, the Walter Boat could submerge entirely in the Chesapeake's relatively shallow depths.

An airless propulsion system using hydrogen peroxide and diesel fuel negated any need to surface while in the bay. The boat could submerge hours longer, and travel three times faster, than the Type VIIC because it didn't need to surface as often to re-charge batteries.

Hoest's chief concern and the primary reason the navy set aside the prototype was its fuel, Perhydrol, a volatile mixture of hydrogen peroxide and diesel. But tests showed careful monitoring and proper handling avoided the chance of an explosion.

Walter adapted his propulsion system to a standard U-boat diesel engine, allowing crews to switch to conventional power when desired. Hoest believed limited use of Perhyrdol reduced the risk significantly enough to make it relatively safe.

He recommended the boat, moored at the base in Kiel. The idea intrigued Rhonen, but he worried about it limiting the mission's chance of success until the commander convinced him the prototype would likely be easier to acquire for the mission.

"You're correct," the general sighed. "Donitz does hate to part with his boats, but why do you want to risk a boat with an engine that could explode?"

Hoest said the high risk for an explosion came during extended use and combat. "There's a greater risk we won't make it out of the bay with a boat we can't submerge."

Rhonen acknowledged the commander's reasoning with a reluctant nod.

"Now a question for you, *Herr General*," Hoest said.

"I imagine you have many."

"Do you think the war is a lost cause?"

Rhonen smiled. "Perhaps, commander, but the National Socialist German Workers Party will never be."

Under a cold, leaden sky, the *Reichsfuhrer's* mud-splattered black Mercedes staff car lumbered down the road to the double-fenced gates of Wolf's Lair. An SS guard followed by several more wielding submachine guns held up a hand to halt the vehicle.

The black-helmeted guard, his face hollow-cheeked, peered through the driver's window to verify the car's backseat occupants. Gerhard sat next to Himmler, who had been engrossed in the report on Hahn's progress since they left the railway station at Goerlitz.

Gerhard last visited Hitler's tree-shrouded headquarters in the damp East Prussian forest in early spring. As the guard waved the car through, the general noticed the compound was now even more heavily fortified since the assassination attempt on Hitler in July.

How, Gerhard wondered, did von Stauffenberg, the one-armed army officer who planted the bomb in the conference room, believe he could get away with it? The German army colonel and his conspirators were summarily arrested and executed.

"*Sehr gut.*" Himmler's voice interrupted his thoughts. Gerhard turned to the *Reichsfuhrer* who patted the manila file confidently. "The Fuhrer should be pleased."

Gerhard was unsure how Hitler would respond, but he knew Himmler was one of the few people the Fuhrer trusted. He also knew Himmler was ever eager to win favor.

The staff car lurched to a stop at a thick-walled, concrete and wooden bunker where the conference was scheduled on further planning of the Ardennes offensive – what the Americans would come to call the Battle of the Bulge. After the conference, Gerhard waited outside while Himmler met privately with Hitler.

Inside the Furhrer's office a servant had brought in coffee and cream cakes. Hitler paused in his monologue about how the new offensive he was planning in the west would drive a wedge in the Allied advance and push their armies into the English Channel.

Himmler took this chance to brief him on Rhonen's plan and request the Walter boat.

Hitler rubbed his right arm, badly injured in the explosion from the assassin's bomb, and listened carefully until Himmler finished.

"You are certain this can work, Heinrich?" Hitler said.

Himmler nodded, expecting to have to defend the plan's use of resources because the Fuhrer's focus was on assembling forces for the Ardennes offensive. "Quite certain."

Hitler said nothing as he dumped several heaping spoonfuls of sugar into his coffee cup and sipped. Finally, after several moments, he nodded to himself.

"Yes! Yes! Yes! Yes!" The Fuhrer excitedly rocked in his chair. "This could be a double blow to the Americans – their army defeated in battle, that

Jew Roosevelt, dead. The Americans would not recover and we would secure the advantage and victory. Yes!"

"Then I have your approval for the U-boat?" Himmler asked.

Hitler paused. He expressed concerns about relinquishing even a single boat because of limited production inflicted by Allied bombing raids. Himmler suggested the prototype Walter Boat was available and the Fuhrer looked relieved at the easy solution.

"I will have Donitz informed immediately," he said.

Himmler left feeling confident about getting the Walter Boat. Donitz jealously guarded all of them, but the prototype was inconsequential to the fleet.

Though pleased at having won Hitler's approval, the *Reichsfuhrer* had serious doubts about Germany winning the war. He had started to plot deals with the British and Americans while at the same time he wanted to help the cause, in case Hitler's offensive succeeded.

Gerhard watched as the *Reichsfuhrer* emerged from the building, buttoning his leather greatcoat. Himmler nodded, approvingly. "It's done. He was most impressed."

Gerhard was secretly surprised. Surely, he had thought, Hitler would dismiss such a crazy plan, but then these were desperate times.

"Very good, *Reichsfuhrer*," Gerhard said.

As they climbed into the staff car to return to the railway station, Himmler told his general, "Please inform Rhonen and '*der Wolf*.'"

Chapter 5

Heidelberg, Germany

The mid-morning sun burned the blanket of fog off the lush countryside as the train screamed into Heidelberg station. Grey, whose plane landed in Frankfurt three hours earlier, turned away from the window as the compartment door slid open.

A conductor stood in the doorway and said in thick German, "*Heidelberg*." Grey nodded and collected his bag and briefcase while listening as the conductor moved down the car calling, "*Heidelberg! Heidelberg*!"

Outside the station, Grey caught a taxi into the old town and wandered the *Hauptstrasse* to the *Café Journal*, his old haunt from his military police days. The cafe was around the corner from Heidelberg University.

He ordered breakfast and read the *International Herald Tribune.* At eleven o'clock, when he knew his friend would be finished with his classes, he left the café for the university. Grey had last visited Wolfram Geiser nine years earlier. They had stayed in contact by letter and e-mail since their MP days at the U.S. Army's European headquarters in Heidelberg.

As military policemen they worked as American and German soldiers did, in the same detachments. In those days, the Cold War was on, Russia was a sprawling communist empire, and Germany was divided between communist East German and democratic West Germany.

The U.S. military had hundreds of thousands of troops stationed in Germany to serve as the first line of defense against communist expansion into the west. Americans soldiers and air crews had been there since the end of World War II in 1945.

Grey and Wolfram became friends while working a case in which factional remnants of the violent left-wing terrorist group Baader-Meinhof had unsuccessfully tried to assassinate the commanding American general by firing a U.S. military bazooka at his staff car.

Assigned to determine how the terrorists acquired the bazooka, they traced the weapon to the army depot in Darmstadt. They arrested a supply sergeant who set out to build a comfortable retirement selling arms on the black market.

It was Grey who suggested their suspect was a corrupt soldier at the depot, but Wolfram was skeptical because his partner had no evidence to support his theory.

"How do you know it isn't a corrupt general?"

"Maybe," Grey said. "But I'm betting it's a low-paid soldier."

Wolfram looked at him in disbelief. "How are you so sure?"

"It's just a hunch."

"What kind of hunch?"

Grey produced a sheet of paper listing weapons and ammunition the depot had reported missing during a recent inventory.

"So?" Wolfram said.

"Two points: first, all of these weapons are small, portable, easy to get out of the depot," Grey said. "I'm betting a general would sell intelligence, information about troop movements."

"Perhaps it's true, but doubtful; and your second point?"

Grey smiled and produced another sheet with a list of names. He pointed to one and said, "The last time the depot did inventory was more than a year ago, shortly before this sergeant was assigned to supply."

Wolfram remained uncertain until the sergeant confessed. He learned to appreciate his friend's investigative instincts.

Grey walked the cobblestone streets until he came to an ornate 18th century baroque style building with a large, heavy wood door and tall windows. Inside, the cavernous cobblestone hall led into a spacious courtyard with a fountain trickling water.

He stepped into the courtyard and a voice echoing from somewhere greeted him.

"Gut morgen, Sam! Wie geht es?"

Grey looked up to see Wolfram on the second floor balcony, smiling at him. He returned the smile to the small, thin goateed man who wore his hair long and scraggly, reminding Grey of a 1970s rock musician. Wolfram directed him. "Stairs are on your left."

The two men greeted each other with handshakes. Wolfram pulled him close and threw his wiry arms around his friend. They laughed. Wolfram guided him to a small, neatly arranged office with a courtyard balcony.

"You've done well for yourself, I see," Grey said, taking a seat.

"And you, my friend, look wonderful," Wolfram said, beaming.

Grey admired the bookcase-lined room. "What are you teaching these days?"

"Ah! I'm trying to start a literature in cinema course."

"Interesting?"

"Not really, but I'm sure it will help bring in the pretty students. Brecht doesn't arouse lust as much as *sin-e-ma*."

Grey laughed at his friend.

Wolfram turned to business, sitting at his desk and removing a notebook from the drawer. "I have accomplished the tasks you sent me, *meine freunde*," he said.

"And?"

"First, I checked with the military archives in Aachen and located one of the nine names you sent me from that *Unterseeboot* captain's logbook."

Grey sighed. "And?"

Wolfram leafed through his notebook. "*Ja*, I'm afraid everyone else on the list is dead."

"Who's the survivor?"

"The guy is *Kriegsmarine* Lieutenant Rolf Krug." Wolfram read off his notebook. "Lives in Berlin, is in his late seventies, sounded healthy when we spoke."

"Is he willing to talk to me?" Grey asked.

Wolfram nodded. "Yes, though he's not sure he can tell you anything."

"Well, it's a start," Grey said. "I'll go up in a couple of days."

"There's something else, though, and I'm not sure what it means."

"What's that?"

"This U-boat you gave me, U-812, is that right?"

Grey nodded.

"It doesn't exist."

"What do you mean?"

"U-812 was never built," Wolfram said. "I checked and found U-812 was planned for, but for some reason never commissioned."

The information confused Grey. "How is that possible?" he said.

"Maybe the old boy made it up; maybe the log *ist falsch*, a fake."

"Come on, let's be serious."

"Perhaps they re-numbered an existing boat," Wolfram said.

Grey pondered the suggestion. "Why would they do that?"

Wolfram shrugged and turned a page in his notebook.

"Did you ask this Krug about it?"

"No, I thought you should," Wolfram said. "Now, on the word 'wolf.'"

"Okay."

"I found someone who will lead us to someone who may have some answers."

"I just want to know the significance of the word."

"I'm afraid this is more complex than you may have realized," Wolfram said. He sat forward in his chair and fished a cigarette from a pack lying on the desk. "We have a history professor here; he's related to the Speer family."

"Albert Speer? The Nazi architect?"

"*Ja*. He studies and writes on the Third Reich and the war so when I went to him with your inquiry. He offered to help."

Grey looked at his friend. "What does he know?"

"Would you like to meet *Herr Professor Heinz Manfred?*"

Grey nodded. Wolfram stood, checked his watch and said, "Then come."

They walked downstairs and through the courtyard, their footsteps echoing off the walls. They exited the back, crossed a cobblestone alley and entered another old building that dated to the early 19th century. Up two flights and Wolfram rapped on a door.

A moment passed before the door opened. A tall, angular man in his early sixties stood in the doorway, wearing a white, open-collar shirt and dark trousers. Age had left wisps of hair. His earnest eyes peered through thick, square-framed glasses.

"*Heinz!*" Wolfram said. "*Gut morgen.*"

"*Morgen,*" Manfred replied, quietly, studying the two of them.

Wolfram motioned to Grey and said, "*Meine freunde*, Sam."

"Oh! Please come in." Manfred waved them inside a cluttered office much larger than Wolfram's with a sofa and two chairs. "I forgot I was expecting you."

Grey sat on a chair and Wolfram plopped down on the sofa as Manfred wandered behind the desk, removing his glasses as he looked for something.

"Any coffee, Heinz?" Wolfram asked.

"No," Manfred said, searching through paper piles littering his desk. Grey noticed the man spoke English deliberately. "No coffee, but I do have for Herr Grey something he – " his voice trailed off for a moment before he exclaimed, "Ah!"

Manfred removed a sheet of paper from a book and carried it over to Grey and handed it to him. In neat, bold-face type across the top of the sheet was the name, Walther Gerhard, with a short biography underneath.

Manfred said, "I wrote this up for you because this man you may want to talk to."

"Who is he?" Grey said.

"You are the man with the question about the 'wolf,' yes?"

Grey nodded.

"Then I think Gerhard is the man to talk to," Manfred said, nodding to himself. "He is a former SS general who ran a spy ring for Hitler in the last years of the war."

"What's the connection?" Grey said.

"In the last months of the war, Gerhard assembled teams of young soldiers, boys from the Hitler Youth. They roamed villages and cities in the paths of advancing Allied troops; they set up explosive traps and sniper nests. They also intimidated the local population to keep them in line."

"I don't understand – " Grey began before Manfred impatiently interrupted him: "They were called "werewolves," but more importantly many of them continued to fight months after the war, acting like a minor insurgency, terrorists, actually."

"What makes you think "wolf" is related to these werewolves?"

"You said the initials HJ were on the notepad next to the word 'wolf,'" Manfred said. "I believe that's for *Hitler Jungen* – Hitler Youth. Many of the werewolves were Hitler Youth."

Grey thought for a moment, running the information through his mind. "You think the U-boat captain's murderer may be one of these terrorists?"

"I don't know," Manfred said. "War breeds contemptible things that hang around forever and perhaps this 'wolf' was a Gerhard creation."

Grey shared with the professor his father's post-war experiences and wondered whether the boy sniper in the barn loft was a werewolf.

Manfred shrugged. "Who knows, but you should talk to Gerhard."

"Where is this general?"

"In an Alpine village in Switzerland, a place called Adleboden."

Grey looked at Wolfram. "Maybe we could take a drive down there."

His friend nodded.

Manfred said, "Meeting Gerhard is difficult. He likes seclusion and he's ninety."

"Ninety? Is the guy coherent?" Grey asked.

Manfred nodded. "Quite so. I've been desperately attempting to interview him, but he has so far refused my requests."

"Why do you want to interview him?"

"A book I'm working on concerning former Reich officers' roles in the western counter-intelligence efforts against the Soviets."

"Was this general's role significant?"

"To call it significant would be an understatement. He long helped Americans catch spies and foment dissent in East Europe and Central Asia."

"Why haven't you been able to get an interview with him?" Grey asked.

"He's a suspicious man. I've been able to get this close to him because of my contacts in western intelligence agencies."

"And how close is that?"

"I've never met the man, but my German intelligence friends relay messages to him for me and keep me informed about his infrequent appearances in public."

"I'm only here for a week; I would need to meet him as soon as possible."

The skeptical look on Manfred's face told Grey this would be difficult, but the professor nodded after a moment. "Let me try to find out his whereabouts. I'll call you tomorrow."

Having returned to Wolfram's office, Grey relaxed while his friend made coffee.

"Damn inconsiderate of Heinz not to have had coffee for us," Wolfram muttered.

"Can he really arrange a meeting with this old Nazi?" Grey asked.

"I don't know," Wolfram said, carefully pouring water into a Krups coffee maker. "He has maintained his contacts from his military intelligence days."

"When was that?"

"Oh, I think back in the seventies."

"What kind of work did he do?"

"What else," Wolfram said, "data analysis."

Grey decided to show Wolfram the ship's log belonging to Hoest. He took the faded blue cloth-bound volume from his briefcase and handed it to his friend.

"I think it's time you read the captain's journal," he said.

Wolfram opened the book and briefly scanned the pages as Grey left his chair to pour a cup of coffee. "I'll read it tonight, after dinner and drinks and debauchery since it seems you're not going to take vacation."

"I'm trying to," Grey said.

Wolfram shook his head. "Sam, you haven't changed."

At breakfast the next morning, Wolfram, bleary-eyed from lack of sleep and too many beers, poured coffee and set out a plate of sliced cheese and meat along with thick bread and soft butter. "I found something in the log book last night," he said, sleepily.

Grey stopped reading the *Suddeutsche Zeitung* and looked sharply at his friend. "I'm glad you're not waiting until lunch to tell me."

"Sorry, but I was up very late reading and I did not think it was necessary to wake you," Wolfram said. He set the log book on the table and opened to a certain page. "The entry date is January 9, 1945, and he writes what sounds like a joke: 'We are preparing to drop off our 'little wolf.' He's a child in need of a mother.'"

Wolfram repeated the passage and stared at Grey. "What the hell is that?"

Grey shook his head, "Does he mention where they dropped him?" Wolfram shook his head. Frustrated, Grey said, "Does it say anything else?"

"No, not really." Wolfram shook his head and thumbed several pages before he stopped to compare each of them. "Wait," he said, slowly. "Under the date of each entry, there's written what I assume is the longitude and latitude of the U-boat's location at the time."

Grey examined the coordinates for the entry dated January 9, which read, 38°20 11 N, 76°27 51 W. He looked up from the page. "Do you have a world atlas around?"

Wolfram fetched one from his living room bookshelf, but it was not detailed enough. He snapped his fingers, suddenly remembering a navigational map in one of the university's lecture halls. "It's just a short walk from here," he said.

They left their breakfast and hurried to the large room. Wolfram switched on the light, his footsteps echoing in the amphitheater as he walked over to the front, picked up a long pole with a steel hook and pulled down an enormous map of the eastern United States. They stood, searching for the captain's coordinates from January 9th.

"There," Wolfram said, "in the Chesapeake Bay, near a place called Solomons."

Grey studied the map, nodding to himself. "Well, this is a start; now what?"

They returned to Wolfram's flat. The phone was ringing. Wolfram answered and listened. He turned and handed the receiver to Grey. "It's Heinz," he said.

Manfred learned that late every afternoon Gerhard had lunch at Adleboden's Hotel Baren and offered to drive Grey and Wolfram there. He said it was his chance to meet the old general.

Grey accepted and when he hung up the receiver, Wolfram said "Adleboden, translated, is 'eagles nest.'"

The state trooper shrugged. "So?"

"Have you forgotten your Hitler trivia?"

He then remembered the dictator's alpine retreat house, now a tourist attraction he and Wolfram visited in their army days. His mind, though, was somewhere else. His friend sensed this. "What are you thinking?"

"I think I've found a better subject for my doctoral thesis," Grey said.

He considered his information – The U-boat mission occurred late '44 and early '45 and on American soil, but according to books he researched the chance of that happening late in the war was slim, if not impossible. The Allies broke the German naval codes and knew when a U-boat headed to sea and where it was going.

"So how could they have made it?" Grey mused.

"Under those conditions," Wolfram said, "I would think by not sending codes."

Grey snapped his fingers. "Exactly. Now, how do I prove that in a thesis paper?"

Early the next morning Manfred arrived outside Wolfram's apartment house in a 20 year-old black Mercedes sedan to begin the four-hour drive to Adelboden. On the first leg of their trip they discussed American and German politics. The two Germans were interested in Grey's views of the upcoming American presidential election.

"It is quite interesting that there is a Jewish candidate for vice president," Manfred said.

"Why?" Grey said.

"Because he is Jewish and because American liberals make so much of him," Manfred said. "I don't see why that's important."

Wolfram, sitting in the back seat, called to Grey, "Sam, as a black American, does the man's religious background impress you?"

Grey spoke over his shoulder, "What's my skin color got to do with it?"

"Blacks struggle in your country for elected office. I think the highest they have reached is the mayor's office in the big cities, yes?"

"We have a governor in Virginia and a U.S. senator in Massachusetts," he said. "But you know, I don't see many blacks holding high office in Germany."

"Yes," Wolfram conceded. "We are a long way from that occurring."

Grey inquired about Manfred's relationship with Albert Speer.

"It's just by marriage," Manfred said. "I married a distant cousin."

"Ever meet him?"

"A few times," Manfred said. "He lived in Heidelberg."

Yawning, Wolfram said, "Heinz even has a connection to the 'Little Corporal.'"

Grey looked at Manfred.

"*Ach*!" Manfred said. He waved a dismissive hand while giving Wolfram a sharp look in the rear view mirror. "During World War I my grandfather served in the same Bavarian regiment as Hitler," he told Grey. "That is all."

The conversation lulled as Grey admired the Alps looming ahead of them. The majestic beauty of the snow-capped jagged peaks was punctuated by snoring. Wolfram had fallen asleep in the backseat. The Mercedes sped along the ascending highway.

"Gerhard sounds like an obscure figure," Grey said.

"He was to some extent," Manfred said, "but there was a controversy in the early 1970s. The press learned he worked for the CIA and there was rumor he had allegedly committed war crimes."

"Did he?" Grey asked.

Manfred shrugged "No one could find any evidence, but the Americans, at least publicly, disowned him, and the scandal passed."

"What kind of man is he?" Grey said.

"Ruthless," Manfred said.

"Heinz!" Wolfram, now awake, called from the back. "Stop at the restaurant up ahead. I need to piss."

Clouds blocked the early afternoon sun as the Mercedes pulled up the steep, narrow road into Adelboden, a Swiss village built on the mountainside. Manfred steered down winding streets of clustered homes and shops until they came to the Hotel Baren.

They checked into their rooms. Manfred volunteered to wait in the lobby until Gerhard arrived, at which time he would call Grey. Two hours later the phone rang in Grey's room and Manfred's hushed voice was tense. "He is here, *Herr Grey*."

Wolfram went to his room and Grey went downstairs.

Gerhard was seated at a table tucked away in an alcove off the dining room. For as old as he was, he had a commanding presence, the wait staff busily hovering over him, ensuring his orders for lunch were carried out promptly and efficiently.

The old general nodded to the waiter who brought him a glass of white wine. It was late afternoon. The dining room was empty but for him, the waiter and Paul, a strapping young man who served as his assistant. Paul stood sentinel at the doorway. He was tall, muscular with dark hair and eyes.

Paul provided comfort to the general; protecting him from intrusion, for which Gerhard gave thanks as he broke bread over his soup. As he counted his blessings he looked up and was startled to see Paul in conversation with a black man. Paul was shaking his head.

A moment later, leaving the man standing at the doorway, Paul approached the general, apologetically. "I'm sorry, but this American insists I give you a message."

"What is it, Paul?"

"He said he's a police officer and he has some questions about '*der Wolf*' and U-812's mission in 1944."

Grey stood in the doorway, watching shock and puzzlement register on the old general's face. Gerhard's mouth opened slightly as he listened and nodded. His eyes darted at Grey. Paul returned. "Your identification card, please?"

As Grey reached into his jacket to remove his badge and identification, Paul said, "Your name and affiliation?"

"Corporal Sam Grey, Delaware State Police." Grey handed him his badge.

Paul studied Grey's laminated ID card for a moment. "Come with me."

A perturbed Gerhard scowled as he examined the identification card and badge.

Grey looked at the old general; he was slight and bald and reminded Grey of a little boy in his white, open collar shirt with an olive-colored V-neck sweater. The old general nodded at Paul who handed Grey back his ID and badge.

Gerhard offered the state trooper a seat across from where he was sitting.

"Why did you come here?" Gerhard said, dismissing Paul with a wave.

"I'm trying to solve a murder."

Mild amusement crossed the old general's face. "Whose?"

"The commander of U-812," Grey said.

A cold stare hardened Gerhard's face. Grey briefly explained the case. "Does the word, 'wolf,' mean anything to you?"

"I haven't heard it in more than fifty years."

"Do you know anything about U-812's mission in late '44 and early '45?"

The general's facial features softened as he closed his eyes and nodded. "Yes, I know something about it, but it's been a long time."

Grey tensed. "What can you tell me?"

Gerhard considered the question. He thought that absurd affair had ended with the defeat, though at times he did wonder what became of Hahn. But now an American – and a black one no less – was interrogating him and this annoyed him.

"How long have you been a police officer?"

"Eighteen years," Grey said.

Gerhard smiled. "And you're still just a corporal?"

Grey shrugged off the taunt. "It's an insignificant ranking. Delaware State Police identify homicide investigators as corporals, not detectives." He tried to return to the matter, but Gerhard held up a hand with a mocking laugh. "Insignificant? Please, corporal, you must realize there *is* a reason whites are running the world."

Not sure whether he heard the old general correctly, Grey paused before saying anything, trying to determine whether the man was baiting him.

"I'm sorry, I didn't hear what you said."

"I just wanted to see whether you were really listening and apparently you were not. And I thought American police officers were better trained. Apparently everyone can't be trained."

Grey smiled knowingly. "My apologies, now, please, go ahead, repeat what you said."

"I was just sympathizing with you over your country's unwillingness to give blacks the opportunity to hold meaningful positions in society."

"I see." Grey was getting tired of the game. "You're concerned with the plight of black Americans?"

Gerhard spoke coyly. "I was just saying – "

Grey became impatient. "I want to know about the U-boat mission."

Offended by the corporal's rude interruption, the old general scowled. Grey sat patiently, unperturbed, waiting for his response.

Gerhard's expression suddenly relaxed. He spoke softly. "My apologies, corporal, I had thought you might be one of those so called Nazi hunters looking for a military officer from the Reich to arrest, which is most unjust. The few of us left are persecuted for who we are – simple soldiers who did their duty."

Grey shook his head at the man's audacity. "It never occurred to me that ex-Nazis were an oppressed minority." He leaned forward and demanded, "What about the boat's mission?"

The scowl momentarily returned to Gerhard's face before he spoke haltingly. "There was a fantastic plan to send an agent to America late in the war to kill Roosevelt, but I had nothing to do with any of it."

"Who did?"

"General Rhonen."

"Who's he?"

"An eccentric rogue."

"Is he around, maybe I could talk to him?"

Gerhard shook his head and pointed at his mouth. "Crushed a cyanide capsule between his teeth when he realized Himmler no longer had any faith in his plan."

"Is there anyone around who knows something about the mission?"

Gerhard gave Grey a sympathetic smile. "I'm sorry, corporal, but there is nothing more."

Grey began to ask another question when Paul appeared at the table. Gerhard rose slowly and said, bowing slightly, "*Auf wiedersehn*, corporal."

They started to leave and Grey spoke rapidly. "In his log, the U-boat captain says he had delivered the 'wolf' to American shores."

Gerhard stopped and gripped Paul's arm tightly. *I struck a nerve*, Grey thought, but the old general answered only with a grin before letting Paul escort him from the dining room. At the hotel bar, Grey joined Manfred.

"Well, you're right about war breeding contemptible things."

"Were you successful?" Manfred asked.

"Somewhat," Grey said. "I thought you wanted to meet him?"

"I don't think the time is right," Manfred said. "Was he helpful?"

"I think he knows more than he's telling."

"*Ja*? And why do you believe this?"

"Just a hunch."

The next morning, as Grey finished dressing, Paul knocked on his door and asked that he accompany him. Grey followed the bodyguard outside the hotel, to a beige-colored BMW sedan idling at the curb. The old general sat comfortably in the back. Grey stepped in while Paul stood outside and waited.

Gerhard spoke: "Rhonen had led a division of Bosnian Muslims in Yugoslavia, where he came to know the Grand Mufti of Jerusalem who helped in troop recruitment. The Mufti regaled Rhonen about Hasan-i-Sabbah. Have you ever heard of Hasan-i-Sabbah?"

Grey shook his head, listening intently.

"He was born in the eleventh century, in Iran; started a group known as the 'assassins.' They were a secret sect of Ismaili Shia Muslims and they used terrorism to oppose the ruling Sunni Muslims."

Grey became impatient. "What's this all about?"

The old general smiled. "Rhonen tried to emulate Hasan-i-Sabbah and his practice of dispatching '*schlafen*' or 'sleeper' agents to carry out sabotage or assassinations, years after locating in a country. Some were suicidal; all were devout believers in their cause."

"So what are you telling me, general?"

"There was an agent sent to America."

"For what reason?"

A tone of annoyance crept into Gerhard's voice. "With Rhonen you never really knew."

"You called Rhonen a rogue, but no one could have authorized such a mission without Hitler's consent," said Grey, appreciating his recent study of U-boat history.

The old general nodded. "You are correct. Hitler did approve the U-boat mission."

"Why? It was so late in the war."

"These were desperate times."

"So what happened to this agent?"

"He was never heard from once he landed on shore," Gerhard said.

"What are you saying, he's alive and well in the United States?"

"That's a possibility."

"Sounds like a probability."

The old general shrugged.

Grey thought for a moment. "This guy isn't still fighting World War II?"

"That's also possible. Only Rhonen believed his plan would succeed."

"So the idea of assassinating Roosevelt wasn't his mission?"

"It may have been *part* of his mission," the old general said.

"What was the other part?"

"As I told you before, corporal, I don't know."

"I don't understand why this agent wouldn't have returned to Germany after the war?"

"If they trained him as a sleeper his assignment may have been anything. Rhonen was a strong believer in the National Socialist cause – he believed it would never die."

"Weren't you a believer, general?"

"I was neither believer nor fanatic," Gerhard said, glancing out the window. "What I've always been is a realist who recognizes opportunities."

Grey returned to his original line of questioning. "What's this agent's name?"

Gerhard sighed. "I believe it may have been Hahn, but it has been so long.

"Have any idea why he'd kill the captain of the U-boat that dropped him off?"

Gerhard shook his head. "None." The old general tapped on the window at Paul. "Let's hope you find him, if he exists."

The door opened. Grey climbed out, but turned and asked the old general, "I'm curious, why did you come back to talk to me?"

Gerhard smiled as Paul closed the door. Grey stood and watched Paul climb behind the wheel of the sedan and drive off. Something was not right, he thought. There is more about the agent than the old general had shared.

As the car picked up speed heading out of the Alpine village, Paul listened to Gerhard sigh. He glanced into the rear view mirror. *"Herr General, was ist los?"*

Gerhard stared out the window as he answered. "We have another little corporal stirring up trouble in the world."

Chapter 6

Kiel, Germany

November 30, 1944

Kriegsmarine Kapitanlieutenant Eric Hoest stood on the quay, admiring his moored U-boat and the conning tower with its insignia, Hermes, the Greek gods' winged-cap messenger, painted in a light blue. Fitting, he thought, for this voyage.

Cold winds blowing off Kieler Bay's dark-gray waters whipped at the strands of brown hair protruding under his cap. He checked his watch then turned to see the young man arriving on time, approaching in the late afternoon light.

Behind Hoest, Lieutenant Krug, standing in the conning tower, watched as Martin Hahn came toward them. He grunted sarcastically: "Christ, Eric, what're they sending us?"

Hoest said nothing as Hahn, dressed in a wool suit and fedora and carrying a tan leather suitcase, marched up and gave him a stiff-armed salute.

"*Heil Hitler*," Hahn said. He removed a document from his coat and handed it to Hoest. "My papers."

Hoest looked over the youth while glancing disinterestedly at the documents. "Let's get aboard," he said. "We have a long trip ahead of us."

Hahn followed Hoest onto the sub's deck and to a hatch. The captain took his suitcase as Hahn descended the steel-rung ladder. As he came down the ladder behind him, Hoest called out to his crew: "Prepare to set sail!"

Hatches slammed, men shouted, and the diesel engines kicked in with a loud hum. Hahn felt the boat moving under his feet as Hoest led him through the control room. Smoked sausage dangled from overhead pipes and loaves of dark bread stuffed into nets hung from hooks. Hahn commented on the food.

"Space is limited and we have a long voyage ahead," the captain replied.

Part way down a narrow passage off the control room, Hoest stopped.

"You will share my quarters," he said.

He parted a curtain to reveal a narrow, wood-paneled space: two narrow bunks, a cabinet, writing desk with the ship's log laying on it, and a small lamp above the desk.

Hahn nodded matter-of-factly as he stepped inside. He tried to act familiar and shake the sudden feeling of claustrophobia. Hoest concealed a grin when Hahn suddenly turned to him and said earnestly, "I need to use the toilet."

Hoest stepped out and pointed down the passageway. "Second door on the right, you may have to move a block of cheese off the seat."

Hahn looked uneasy as he started down. Hoest called after him, "Stay in my quarters; I'll be back once we're out to sea."

Hoest returned to the control room and climbed up the ladder to join Krug on the conning tower, where a brutally cold wind blew. He flipped up his leather coat collar, put his hands in his pockets and took a last look at Kiel. Krug stood next to him, peering through binoculars.

"So," the lieutenant said. "That's our spy, huh?"

"Yes." Hoest cupped his hand and lit a cigarette in the indigo twilight.

"He looks like a believer, Eric, and a young one at that."

"Sure, the young are the only ones capable of believing anymore."

"What's his mission?"

"Who knows, Krug, just be careful about asking questions. SS, you know."

"How about our mission, *Kayleu?*" Krug said, using the endearing term U-boat crews gave their commander, but using it sardonically.

"What about it?"

Krug put down his binoculars and confronted Hoest. "What the hell are we doing?"

Hoest gave his officer a scowl. "We're fighting a war."

"What war? Your war against U-boat Command?"

Hoest was surprised at his lieutenant's attitude. Weeks before, when he briefed the crew on the mission and sought volunteers, Krug was first to step up. He knew the danger and knew they were to avoid the enemy, not engage except to defend themselves.

"The odds are against us on this," Hoest told his crew as they gathered around a table in his naval base quarters. "We'll carry only a couple of torpedoes for defensive measures; there'll be no attacking convoys or enemy ships."

The volunteers nodded and murmured their "yes, sirs." Hoest studied the men, all able submariners, most of them he had served with before. He had their trust and confidence, which for a commander was essential to a successful mission.

He told them the type of ship they would be on. "We're sailing the Walter Boat."

The Walter Boat's shape, more fish-like than the typical cigar design of U-boats, made for swifter speeds and reduced detection by radar or sonar. Constructed without deck guns, the boat's conning tower rose low and ran narrow. Its deck could accommodate two persons. This prototype was built more for stealth than combat.

To reduce risk of disastrous engine problems, Hoest decided to operate the Perhydrol-fueled propulsion system only when they were in the Chesapeake Bay. The boat would sail on diesel the rest the journey.

Everyone appeared to appreciate the stakes. Still, Hoest offered anyone having second thoughts the chance to back out. No one did. Now perturbed, he spoke sharply to Krug: "Why are you bringing this up?"

"Because after seeing the little believer I can tell his mission has nothing to do with this war; you're risking lives to make a point with U-boat Command, and they don't give a damn."

Hoest took the binoculars and searched the horizon. Krug was a loyal sailor and a dear friend who spoke his mind, a trait Hoest did not always appreciate.

"What you say may be true," Hoest said. "But the point I intend to make is about returning home alive." He put down the binoculars, looked at his officer and said, firmly, "*Verstanden?*"

Krug understood the tone in Hoest's voice. His commander had heard his concerns and noted them. Now he was expected as an officer to obey orders. He nodded. "*Jawohl, Kayleu.* I understand."

"Good," Hoest said, pressing the binoculars against his eyes. "Let's concentrate on our mission; we're going to be sneaking around a hornet's nest the next two months."

Hahn stumbled out of the head feeling queasy. As he found his way back to the captain's quarters he covered his nose with a handkerchief to block the stench of diesel fuel, fried cooking and sweaty, unwashed bodies.

He entered the quarters and sat on the bunk and wondered for a moment whether he could make the voyage. The long night's journey by train from Heidelberg was more than tiring; it was harrowing, passing through two burning cities that were torn apart by incendiary bombs dropped less than an hour before.

Removing the black-and-white photograph of his parents from his jacket, he undid his tie and lay on the bunk. He missed them. His mind wandered over the last few months spent training in espionage and assassination.

He showed his teachers he was highly proficient in this work, but longed for the days before the state required all children to join the Hitler Youth; days when he would help at his father's *schokolade* factory in Hamburg.

Hahn hung onto his prosperous father's hand as Klaus Hahn brought his son to work in the rapidly growing dark-brick factory. Hahn Chocolates had become popular in Hamburg and its suburbs. Klaus developed his own candy recipes that his son memorized as a teenager.

Klaus let his curious son roam the factory as long as he didn't interfere with the workers or the production of chocolate. Hahn often accompanied his father, as Klaus inspected the plant machinery or tasted the latest batch of chocolate to ensure consistent quality.

As Hahn came into his teenage years he showed an aptitude for making chocolate and for running a business, often making suggestions, though minor, on ways to increase efficiency or to promote the candy. Klaus was deeply proud of his son. Hahn loved his father.

His father began to change when Hitler took power. Klaus talked about a fever gripping the people, blinding them. Hahn didn't understand what his father meant. His mother disagreed with her husband, gently reminding him how well he benefited by the prosperity Hitler brought Germany. His mother could subdue his father in a way he did not understand.

Hahn would come to see things as his mother did, and though he questioned his father's views at times, particularly about Jews, he remained devoted to him. They often spoke of Hahn one day taking over the *schokolade* factory, once the war ended and Hahn finished university.

War destroyed his father and the chocolate factory. It replaced both with a mission.

"Hahn! Never forget your duty to the Fatherland or National Socialism," Rhonen would declare. "Never forget!"

It was late November when Hahn departed for Kiel. Snow flakes pelted the *Schloss* as the general's staff car sped out of the gravel courtyard and headed to Heidelberg station. Rhonen was chattering nervously – *"I'm not letting the Russians get me and I'm not letting the Americans and British put me on trial. Don't forget your duty to the party."*

Hoest entered his quarters to find Hahn dozing. He was struck by how young the 19-year-old looked. He himself was only a few years older, but war aged him; he looked more like thirty-six than twenty-six.

Hoest removed his cap and coat and sat down on the chair by the writing desk. He opened his ship's log, lit a cigarette and spent a few minutes making an initial entry. When he finished he put down his pen and said, loudly, "Hahn!"

Hahn's eyes popped open and he jerked himself up to see Hoest watching him.

"Want some coffee?"

Hahn nodded and ran his fingers through his hair. Hoest disappeared only to return a moment later with a stainless-steel pot with hot coffee and two cups. They sipped ersatz and smoked and talked.

"You seem so young to be in espionage," Hoest said.

"The Fuhrer needs every able German. I am nineteen years old and quite able."

"*Ja, ja*, I'm sure you are."

Hahn looked at Hoest and said, "You've been in the *Kriegsmarine* long, yes?"

"Since '39, when war broke out." Hoest smiled. "I'm not much older than you, actually."

Hahn looked surprised as Hoest nodded, "True. Fighting takes a toll."

"You must be very proud to have served Germany and the Fuhrer for so long."

Hoest shrugged, dragged off his cigarette and leaned back in his chair, studying Hahn. He had a sense that behind the deep-set blue eyes, the serious mindedness and the earnest expression swirled a sea of emotions the young man dared not navigate himself, let alone with others.

"May I ask what you will do in America?"

Hahn shrugged and sipped coffee. "I'm instructed not to divulge such information, but I can tell you I will be away from the Fatherland a long time."

An officer appeared in his quarters and announced the boat was prepared to submerge. The commander excused himself and went into the control room. He circled the room, eyeing each crew station as he rapidly relayed orders that the sailors echoed back.

Hahn felt a gliding motion as the boat slipped beneath the whitecaps of the frigid North Sea and headed toward the North Atlantic. He wanted to see what was going on and entered the control room. He watched Hoest who stood in the dimly lit interior with Krug by his side.

For the next several hours, the boat would pass under waters heavily patrolled by British naval and air forces. Hoest gave orders to run silent and deep until they reached Atlantic waters, far off the coast of Ireland.

Noticing Hahn, Hoest said to Krug, "I'll be in my quarters until time to surface."

"*Jawohl, Kayleu.*" Krug watched as Hahn followed Hoest like an eager puppy.

Back in his quarters, Hoest climbed into his bunk, exhausted. Hahn questioned him more about the boat. He was particularly curious about the symbol painted on the conning tower.

"What's the reason for choosing Mercury?"

"It's Hermes, the Greek god," Hoest said, sitting on the bunk. "Mercury was the *Roman* messenger of the gods. Do you know your mythology, Hahn?"

"Some, yes."

"In the Iliad, Hermes led Priam behind the battle lines during the Trojan War to retrieve the body of his dead son."

"This is how you see your mission?"

"This is not just about you, Hahn. Hermes returned Priam safely to Troy."

The U-boat commander lay down and closed his eyes. "I suggest you sleep. This may be the only chance you have until we reach the Atlantic. Things may get rough."

Hahn felt a moment of awkwardness with the commander, but climbed into his bunk. The nervous energy he had when he first came aboard was fading and he drifted into sleep.

Allied bombers filled the skies over Hamburg and soon an iron rain poured down, smashing and setting fire to everything. Thousands of droning airplane engines faded as explosions rocked the cellar in which Hahn and his parents took refuge.

As the explosions diminished, the sound of a fast-moving freight train filled the cellar, becoming louder and louder as Hahn rushed to a corner, turning to see his parents burst into flames.

"Mutter!"

The cellar doors blew open and outside a tornado of fire with dark eyes danced on the street, sucking people up and beckoning him to step outside in the rain of flames.

"Mutter!"

"Hahn! Hahn!"

He woke to Hoest, in his white cap and leather coat, shaking him. Hahn sat up and looked at him wild-eyed then fell back on the bunk, shaking.

"A nightmare," Hoest said, staring at him intently. "You were screaming."

Hahn nodded, sat up and mumbled, *"Es tut mir leid."*

"No need to apologize, come on." Hoest handed him a heavy leather coat. "We surfaced a little while ago. Come up to the conning tower and get some air."

On the tower, Hoest lit two cigarettes and handed one to Hahn. It was cold and wet and the waters dark; the inky blue, starry sky enveloped them. The wind whipped about. Hahn tried to relax and shake off his dream.

"What was I screaming?"

"You were calling for your parents. Are you worried about them?"

Hahn shook his head. "No, not anymore."

"Did you lose them?"

Hahn nodded. "Last summer, in Hamburg."

"My God! The bombing raid?"

Hahn's body heaved as he spun around, vomiting over the conning-tower railing. "Shit!" he said. "It smells like shit down there!" He vomited once more, dropping his lit cigarette and clinging to the railing.

Hoest stepped over and crushed the dropped cigarette with his boot. After a moment's silence he said to Hahn, "Are you better?"

Hahn moved his head weakly to nod. *"Ja."* He appeared pale even in the darkness. When he regained some composure, Hoest spoke sympathetically. "Hamburg was such a horrible thing to happen your family, to those people. I'm sorry."

"Yes, well, Roosevelt will pay for such things," Hahn said, wiping off his mouth with the sleeve of his coat and spitting over the side.

Hoest said nothing. Hahn began to boast the way scared boys do. "And if the *Wehrmacht* fails to eliminate him, then *'der Wolf'* will."

"Wolf?"

"My code name."

"What's it mean?" Hoest offered him another cigarette, lighting it.

Hahn started to speak, but caught himself. "I'm sorry, no more information."

Hoest shrugged and scanned the horizon. Hahn finished his cigarette and bid him good night. He returned to his bunk, angry he had said as much as he did.

Hoest searched across the rolling seas and questioned, after five years of war, the point of it all when boys were being sent to do what sounded like jobs men wouldn't do.

The boat sailed for nearly two weeks without encountering enemy ships, though late one afternoon an officer on watch spotted through binoculars several merchant ships in the distance, heading east. The crew, out of boredom more than anything, urged an attack regardless of risk. Hoest remained steadfast against it, saying the ships were not worth getting sidetracked from their course.

While his decision disappointed the crew, he worried U-812 might have been sighted and had the boat submerge. From now on, he ordered, they would surface only at night, which meant using the snorkel during the day to bring in air.

He took advantage of this opportunity to test the propulsion system using the Perhydrol, a volatile mixture of hydrogen peroxide and diesel fuel. Hoest was relieved each time it performed without any problems, but still he worried.

After the final test, the chief engineer inspected the system and assured Hoest he had little to fear from an explosion as long as the system wasn't used longer than eight hours.

"Risk of overheating becomes increasingly greater then, *Kayleu*."

Meanwhile, Hahn kept close to the captain. He avoided the crew whose hearty attitude and salty submariner sensibility had intimidated him. He spent much of his time reading in his bunk or in the radio room, trying to catch news of the war.

Hoest sensed Hahn's unease with the crew and tried to reassure him. "They live on the edge in this service, knowing death is out there waiting, so they approach life with gusto."

Max Gelb, the radioman, was the only member of the crew who befriended him; most of the others considered him an oddity.

"Martin?" Hahn looked up as he stepped from the captain's quarters one morning to see Gelb waving him over to the radio room. *"Radio Berlin! Kommen!"*

Hahn hurried to the closet-sized room, took the headset handed him, and eagerly listened to crackling airwaves and a dim German voice reading the news. Hahn's brow furrowed and his eyes turned intense, his hands gripping the headset.

"What is it?" Gelb said.

"Good news. Our soldiers are on the offensive in the west … broke through the American lines in the Ardennes forest … they are pushing them back toward the coast."

"Mein Gott," Gelb said. He looked at the calendar – it was December 21st – then noticed the engines' droning had stopped. The boat began to slope downward.

"Alarm!" The shout was made throughout the ship. Hoest was at the radio room. "Cut the radio, Max. An allied patrol is on the surface."

Hahn followed Hoest to the control room. "Who is it? The British?"

"An American destroyer, I think, but I have no interest in finding out – Krug, take us down fifty meters."

"Jawohl, Kayleu," Krug replied, ordering, *"Fuenfzig Meter unten!"*

The boat descended into the cold black depths. Hahn searched for guidance in the control room's anxious faces. Everyone silent, tense, listening to the hull groan from squeezing pressure; waiting to hear the destroyer's sonar "ping;" bracing for boat-shaking depth-charges, threatening to sink the sub.

As the hydrophone operator listened intently through headsets Hoest demanded, "Well?" The sailor held up a finger and shook his head. Hoest began to sweat, he hated the waiting more than he hated the depth charges knocking the boat about.

Several minutes passed and Hoest looked at the hydrophone man again. "Helmut? Are they coming or not?"

Helmut started to nod his head. He looked at Hoest. "They're moving off. I think they were trying to hone in on us and lost the signal."

A loudly indignant Krug demanded. "What signal?"

"Quiet!" Hoest ordered, looking at the hydrophone operator. "Are they coming?"

The operator, sweat beading on his upper lip, listened intently before tentatively shaking his head. Hoest decided to wait and the boat sat silently below. Two hours passed and no sound of sonar. Again he asked the hydrophone operator, "Are they coming?"

Hearing no propellers or "pings," the operator shook his head, a little more confident, but Hoest wanted a visual confirmation, a risky move because the enemy could be lying in wait. The commander decided to take the chance.

He ordered the boat to periscope depth. A breathless crew riveted their eyes on him as he turned his billed cap around. "Up scope!" he barked.

He grabbed the handles and peered through the eye piece, slowly scanning the green choppy waters. He covered about one hundred and eight degrees when he spotted smoke on the distant horizon.

"*Kayleu*," the hydrophone operator said, quietly. "I believe he's gone."

Hoest nodded, watching with relief as the smoke disappeared over the horizon. "Clear!" he slapped the handles back in place as the periscope dropped down into its housing.

As the crew relaxed, Krug again demanded, "What signal?"

"The radio," Hoest said. "Max had a broadcast on for Hahn."

"How stupid!" Krug blurted, glancing at Hahn.

The crew turned silent. They looked to Hoest, who snapped at the lieutenant. "It was an error! We will be sure it doesn't happen again. Get us back on course. I'll be in my quarters."

He hurried out of the control room toward his quarters and the radio room, where Gelb stood in the hatchway, pleading: "*Kayleu*, I'm sorry. I didn't – "

"It's all right, Max," Hoest said, waving him off and entering his quarters.

Krug watched Hahn follow after Hoest before he turned and issued orders. The electric engines kicked in and the boat began to move.

In his quarters, Hoest fell into his chair and removed his cap. He looked tired. His face was expressionless as he looked at Hahn. "No more radio. It's too dangerous."

"I'm sorry," Hahn said. "I didn't mean to put the crew in jeopardy."

Hoest waved his hand. "You didn't. Krug's a bit high-strung." He started to laugh as he leaned back in his chair.

Hahn watched him intently. "Is everything all right?"

"What mission could you be on when it looks like we are losing this war?"

"I can't discuss it, but I assure you the tide is changing favorably for Germany."

Hoest gave him a weary look. "Oh? How is this possible?"

"On the radio, Berlin reported a new offensive in the west has taken the Americans by surprise and broken their lines."

Hoest shrugged, knowing what came out of Berlin was mostly propaganda.

"What is the matter?" Hahn demanded.

"You worry me." Hoest lit a cigarette.

"Why?"

"I think you're risking your life for a pointless mission. We may be winning an offensive somewhere, but it won't last long. I'm afraid the war is lost."

Hahn became angry. "Is it not more accurate to say *you* fear risking your life?"

"No," Hoest said, coolly. "It is not more accurate."

"Why should you care about me, when it's the greater cause of Germany that we should be concerned about, not the individual."

"Without the individual there wouldn't have been and won't *be* a Germany," Hoest said. "You should be out getting laid, Hahn, not sitting underwater waiting to explode."

Hahn looked at Hoest curiously. "You know nothing about me or my mission."

"Then tell me about your mission."

"*Nein*!"

"Then tell me about you, Hahn. I know you lost your parents in the war, but what about yourself? What have you been doing since they died?"

"Working for the greater good of Germany."

Hoest laughed.

"What's so humorous?" Hahn demanded.

"Can't you talk to me without spouting a line from the Hitler Youth manual?"

Hahn remembered his father saying those very words to him and suddenly found himself laughing. The reaction surprised him because HJ instilled in young men the importance of taking seriously oneself and one's duty to the Fatherland.

"God, it's like talking to a parrot," Hoest said. "If I asked what time of day it is, you'd tell me it's all for the greater good of Germany."

Krug entered, giving them an odd look. Hoest stopped laughing. "Yes?"

"We're back on course, *Kayleu*, with plans to surface in about two hours."

"*Sehr gut, dank.*" Hoest dismissed his lieutenant and opened the half-empty bottle of schnapps he kept in his desk drawer and offered Hahn a swig. Hahn happily sipped from the bottle.

"Okay," Hoest said, sharing his schnapps. "I'll ask an easy question: Did you have a girl in Heidelberg?"

Hahn sat quietly, staring off. "There was a *fraulein* in Munich, I still see her when I close my eyes at night … ." He sounded distant, his voice trailing off.

"What'd she look like?"

Hahn, distracted, didn't hear the question. Hoest repeated it.

"What?"

"The *fraulein* in Munich, what'd she look like?"

"Oh, beautiful; blond hair, blue eyes … "

"And you left her to sit on this tub? You are too serious."

Hahn sobered up. "I have an important mission and I may never return to Germany."

Hoest sat quietly and stared at Hahn's tan-leather suitcase. "Did they supply you with a weapon?" Hahn removed a switchblade from his coat pocket. "The safe house will provide me with whatever else I may need for my assignment."

Hoest felt uncomfortable sending him into enemy territory without more of a weapon. He finished his schnapps and reached into his bunk, removing a pistol and handing it to him. "Here," he said. "In case you need it before you get to the safe house."

"A Luger?"

"My father's gift to me when I entered the service; you know how to use it?"

Hahn nodded, holding the weapon admiringly. "Yes, I've had pistol training."

"It's loaded," Hoest said, climbing into his bunk and closing his eyes, exhausted from the day's trials.

"Don't you need it?"

"I have my requisitioned P-38," Hoest said, sighing. "And I've only once needed that; to convince an officer under my last command to stop challenging my orders."

"Why did he do that?"

"He was like you in a way, too serious about his job. I wanted to provide life rafts to the survivors of an oil tanker we torpedoed and he thought that was traitorous."

"You wanted to help the enemy?"

The question annoyed Hoest. "No, I wanted to help fellow sailors from burning to death. There was no need to let them die, they no longer threatened us."

"I don't understand."

Hoest told him how months prior to the political officer incident his U-boat slammed two torpedoes into a tanker off Morocco's coast. They surfaced and he emerged on the conning tower to fire a *coup de grace*, but was horrified by the scene that greeted him – a fiery oil slick and men in life preservers unable to stop the ocean from floating them into the flames.

They screamed as they burned alive. For Hoest, the sight and sound of the men burning to death had never left him.

"Donitz' had ordered us never to assist the enemy, which I dutifully followed that day," Hoest said. "But I could never forget those men burning. When we sunk another oil tanker off the American coast months later, I was determined to help the survivors."

Hahn lay quietly, unsure how to respond. Finally, he said, "Thank you for the pistol."

But Hoest was already asleep.

Nearly three weeks later the boat surfaced at night in the cold waters off the mid-Atlantic coast of the United States.

Under a canopy of stars, Hoest watched a harvest moon rise over Delaware's distant shoreline as the lights in its towns twinkled. A bitter wind snapped at his face as he worried about a patrol spotting them in the moon's brightness.

He kept a watchful eye on the sea as Hahn emerged from the tower hatch.

"Take a look, Hahn. America."

Hahn looked silently at the distant shoreline and nervously realized he would soon be well beyond the beaches, deep inside enemy territory. His body shuddered from the cold, but Hoest, watching him, could sense his fears.

"Don't worry," the commander said, quietly. "You'll do fine."

Several hours later, having submerged as the gray dawn approached, the U-812 reached the mouth of the Chesapeake Bay, turned eastward and headed out to sea for an hour, putting it about 15 miles offshore. The boat stopped and rested on the sandy ocean floor until nightfall.

As dusk descended, Hoest ordered a course for the mouth of the bay. He stood at the map table, studying charts, when Hahn, having woken, wandered into the control room and stood next to him.

"We should have you on land in the next few hours," Hoest said, glancing at his watch.

"Where are we?" Hahn asked.

"Near Norfolk, Virginia, at the mouth of the Chesapeake," the captain said. "It's going to be a little difficult entering the bay."

"Why?"

Norfolk was a major naval base with patrolling ships and planes. Getting past the fleet undetected was hard but not impossible. The mouth of the bay was 12 miles wide. Fortunately, they could travel submerged to their destination in the upper reaches of the Chesapeake.

"Pray we're not spotted," Hoest said.

He raised the periscope to check the weather and was pleased to find a heavily overcast sky and a choppy ocean. U-812 approached the coast. Hoest sighted a few ships – none naval – at the bay's entrance. He could see no planes. This limited activity surprised him. Dropping the periscope down, he went back to his charts.

Twenty minutes later he checked his watch and peered through the periscope once more. Lights flashed from the Cape Charles and Cape Henry lighthouses that guarded the northern and southern points of the bay's entrance.

"Night's fallen and the overcast sky blocks the moon," Hoest told Krug. "We may have good luck tonight; there's little traffic."

He peered into the periscope and marked bearings for the main shipping channel. It was not mined and its 40-foot depths would allow U-812 to remain submerged to the landing.

Hoest called the engine room, ordering the switch to Walter's propulsion system, which ran efficiently and safely in tests conducted on the voyage. The engine chief's voice crackled in the control room's speaker, reporting it operational.

"Ahead fourteen knots," the commander ordered quietly. "We want to get past the naval base quickly."

Krug gave the order. The boat gradually picked up speed. Tense silence filled the control room as U-812 moved faster through the murky depths. The boat shot into the bay. Hoest risked the periscope to glimpse the number of surface ships, but to his surprise spotted none.

Where was the navy? He took comfort in the fact America focused coastal defenses on an invasion force – not a lone submarine's audacious attempt to penetrate the inland waterways. At least that's what he hoped.

U-812 sped northward, its periscope slicing the water. Hoest turned the scope left; bright, white lights silhouetted Norfolk. Americans are too confident in their defenses, he surmised, and let the periscope down.

A half hour later, as the dark shores slipped past, Hoest raised the periscope and surveyed the waters behind the U-boat. He relaxed. While still cautious about the lack of naval activity, he said to Krug, "No ships in pursuit."

Hoest went to the chart table and examined the map. They had to pass one more military base, a naval air station at the mouth of the Patuxent River, which emptied into the bay and was two miles south of where they would land Hahn.

He worried about what to expect. He never told the crew he was relying on five-year-old intelligence.

The boat pushed up the Chesapeake to an island less than a mile off the shores of Calvert County, Maryland. Hoest had calculated the journey from the bay to the landing then back to the mouth of the bay to take roughly six hours.

"We should be well away from America before the dawn," he told Krug.

Three hours later, Hoest, back on the periscope, spied lights on the few ships anchored at the mouth of the Patuxent. No patrol in sight. Everything appeared peaceful.

Despite his crew's skill, Hoest knew luck was helping them avoid detection. He checked the waters behind them, where the night was specked by lights from distant ships. Krug called to him from the other side of the control room.

"*Kayleu*, we will reach our coordinates in fifteen minutes."

"Very good," Hoest said. "I want you and Helmut to take him ashore."

Ten minutes later, he ordered the engines stopped and went to his quarters to assist Hahn, who was checking his suitcase. When he entered, he noticed the money, thousands of dollars, in fifty and one hundred denominations. It had been sewn inside the suitcase lining.

Hahn, who had shaved what little beard he had grown in the month-long trip, removed a few bills and put them in his wallet. Hoest asked, "How much have you there?"

"About twenty-five thousand."

Hoest noticed that in the open suitcase on top of the clothes lay a large manila envelope, unclasped, with documents stamped with the official Reich seal partly removed. Hahn had been examining them.

Odd, thought the commander. *Why is a spy carrying official government documents?*

Realizing what caught Hoest's attention, Hahn moved abruptly without a word, sliding the documents back inside the envelope and snapping shut the suitcase. Hoest knew the signal not to inquire. He said nothing about the papers.

Hahn slipped on his dark wool coat and fedora, nervously gripping the suitcase handle.

"You look like an American," Hoest said. "Can you sound like one?"

Hahn said in a nondescript accent, "Yeah, what's it to ya, pal?"

Hoest's face broke into a broad smile.

Hahn said, "My mother was an American." He shook Hoest's hand. "Thank you."

"Good luck, Hahn."

Hoest reminded him of the procedures they discussed: They would take him to an island, where he's to wait for a contact. Rhonen's agents in the United States were alerted about Hahn's arrival via coded message through the diplomatic mail, which ensured it could not be intercepted by the Allies. Hahn's arrival date was based upon an estimated time Hoest calculated.

They met the arrival time. Now, hopefully, Hoest told Hahn, the contact should meet him on the island in the next few hours, if not already waiting.

Hoest stood in the conning tower watching Krug and Helmut help Hahn into an inflatable raft. They rowed about a hundred yards to the island. Hoest could not see them once the raft had moved a few yards from the boat. In the darkness, he could hear paddles dipping into water.

At the tiny island, Krug jumped into shallow, lapping waters and hauled the raft ashore. Hahn, shoes off and pant legs rolled up, hugged his suitcase as he carefully waded through the icy water onto shore, the cold, gritty sand oozing between his toes.

Krug and Helmut wished him luck and hurriedly shoved the raft back into the water and began to row. Krug glanced behind and laughed hysterically; there Hahn stood, water lapping at his feet, giving a stiff-arm Hitler salute.

Hahn watched them disappear into the darkness until he could no longer hear the paddles beating the water. His eyes adjusted to the darkness and he made out the island. It was small with few trees and mostly scrub pine.

A bitter cold wind picked up. He sat on the shore, opened his suitcase and used a shirt to dry his feet. He put on his socks and shoes, stood, and walked around to warm up. Sudden panic seized him. He worried the contact would never arrive, he would be left alone on the island with no way to get off; he would die here. He calmed down, assuring himself that wouldn't happen.

He found a large log and sat and waited and wondered: *What am I doing here?*

When Krug and Helmut returned Hoest immediately ordered U-812 to retrace its course, but half way down the bay they found themselves in the wake of a slow-moving freighter. Hoest ordered the engines stopped. At their present speed they would run into the ship.

He then gave the order to proceed, only slower and cursed the reduced speed they had to assume as they followed well behind the ship. He feared less about getting seen and more about the propulsion system overheating and exploding.

The boat reached the mouth of the bay around three a.m., an hour later than he planned, and passed undetected. Yet, Hoest worried. The propulsion system had been running for nearly seven hours and the engine chief had warned against it running any more than eight because of the increasing risk of explosion.

Still, they needed to put more distance between the boat and the American coast. Hoest pushed on, knowing the risk.

Almost an hour off the coast, with the engine chief warning Hoest about the danger, the commander decided to press his luck no more and ordered the boat's high submerged speed of 19 knots reduced. Several minutes passed. Finally the engine room reported the switch back to conventional power. Hoest sighed, relieved. Risk of explosion was now minimal.

By dawn they were hours away. Hoest ordered Gelb to tune into an American broadcast for war news. He had it piped through the sound system. The broadcaster's voice crackled while reporting defeat was near for Germany.

Hoest and most of the crew did not doubt the accuracy of the reports. After a few minutes he went to the radio room and gently ordered Gelb to turn off the broadcast. As Hoest returned to the control room, Krug sidled up to him and whispered, "Eric, what do you think?"

"American propaganda," he said, loud enough for the crew to hear. "Everyone knows we have at least a year in which to lose this shitty war."

The crew laughed. Hoest called "beer for everyone" as he ordered, "Let's go home."

Across the Atlantic, U-812 encountered no enemy ships or aircraft. A week from Kiel, supplies ran low because of spoiled food. Meals were rationed. The crew was fighting hunger pangs between meals while hearing American broadcasts. The news was bad for Germany.

Hoest began to worry about the crew's morale.

Mercifully, U-812 reached Kiel without an incident. An hour before reaching the harbor, Hoest for the first time since the mission began used the Enigma, the cipher machine, and sent a coded message to Rhonen that he believed would be read by the Allies – "package delivered."

Certain the Allies would disregard the message because it lacked context, he retired to his quarters for sleep, but lay restless. His confidence at having proved his theory about Allied code-breaking was displaced by an unsatisfied feeling.

The boat now moored, Hoest was in his quarters, packing his belongings and the logbook into a duffle bag. Krug stood in the doorway, watching his captain. He noticed the unsettledness.

"Kayleu, was ist los?"

"I don't know."

"You should be happy, we're home, and you proved U-boat Command inept," Krug said.

"Ja! Proving Command inept – now there's something not done before."

"You succeeded; what more could you hope for?"

Hoest shook his head. "Perhaps nothing, I don't know."

"Well, now you can make your case that our codes have been broken."

Hoest looked contemplative as he sat on his bunk and lit a cigarette. "Unlikely," he said. "I don't see the point."

Krug was astonished. "After all we went through to prove it and now you are just going to abandon your case?"

"You were right, they don't give a damn and they don't give a damn because they already know what we just spent nearly two months trying to prove."

Krug started to speak, but Hoest interrupted him. "Go home to your family, Krug. You heard the broadcast; the Americans and Russians are at the gates, the war is over so what's the point? Go home."

Hoest thanked Krug for his service. He followed his lieutenant onto the deck of the boat to watch him disembark with the rest of the crew. When they left, Hoest sat on his duffle bag in the gray light of late day and took one more look at the Walter Boat.

It was his ship now; he proved it could sail successfully, although its propulsion system needed more work. That was an accomplishment he could cheer about. Perhaps after the war – he dismissed the thought. No one would have any use for such a boat.

He glanced across the harbor at a busy shipyard, the name KRUPP hung in huge letters on the face of the massive main building. Beyond wide open doors bursts of sparks danced off the welding torches workers were using to construct more U-boats.

He knew they would never sail.

Over the sounds of shouting men and clanking machinery came distant sirens, but Hoest paid no heed. A staff car arrived for him, he climbed in, and the vehicle drove from the quay as air raid sirens wailed at the thundering approach of planes.

The car lurched to a stop. Hoest ordered the driver on despite the bombers, but the driver fled the car. Bombs fell and the boat works around the harbor began to explode in flames.

Hoest jumped from the car and ran for a ditch. A nearby explosion threw him into it and he landed hard on his side. He curled into the fetal position as explosions and the "ack-ack-ack" of anti-aircraft fire went on for what seemed endlessly.

The raid ended twenty minutes later. Hoest rose from the ditch, unhurt but for a bruised side. Across the harbor the boat works was in flames. He could see dead workers who failed to escape. Black smoke hung in the air. Destruction and death was everywhere he looked.

Hoest turned to where U-812 was moored; it floated along the quay, undamaged except for shrapnel tears in the profile of Hermes on the conning tower.

He smiled.

Hermes wasn't just the messenger of the gods.

He was also the god of luck.

Chapter 7

En route to Berlin

Manfred swung the Mercedes down a narrow cobblestone street, tires rumbling over the uneven roadway. He stopped outside an imposing old baroque-styled apartment house of brown stone where Wolfram had his second-floor flat.

It was early afternoon, and cool for late summer in central Germany. Grey spent much of the four-hour trip from Switzerland pondering troubling questions, particularly one Wolfram had raised: "With no evidence how are you sure this assassin is the guy you're looking for?"

"I don't know. It's just a hunch."

"Ach!" Manfred said. "It's fantastic to believe the man would exist after all these years."

The case challenged Grey's instinct, motivating him, but Manfred's assessment tempered his enthusiasm. He asked rhetorically, "How *do* you pick up a man's trail half-a-century later?"

"What are you going to do, my friend?" Wolfram asked.

"Go to Berlin, talk to this Lieutenant Krug. Maybe he knows something."

Wolfram sighed. "So much for your vacation."

Late the following afternoon the two friends rode the tram to Heidelberg station, where Grey caught the overnight train to Germany's capital. After bidding one another farewell Grey started to climb onto the train when Wolfram stopped him with a tone of concern.

"Sam?"

Grey turned. His friend looked uncertain and appeared at a loss for words.

"What is it?"

Wolfram sighed. "Just be careful with these old Nazis; they don't stop believing."

Grey laughed. "Since when did you become so motherly?"

Wolfram smiled sheepishly and waved for him to get on the train.

A few minutes later a whistle screamed and Wolfram watched the red-and-cream colored DeutscheBahn chug slowly from the station in the soft fading summer light.

The train gained speed at the twinkling city's outskirts, heading northward. Grey sat alone in the compartment, watching evening fall on a landscape slipping away. A conductor poked his head in to announce the dining car was open.

"What time tomorrow morning do we arrive in Berlin?" Grey asked.

"Eight o'clock," the conductor said, closing the door.

Grey noted the fourteen-hour trip ahead as he entered the crowded dining car. He glanced down the long, narrow interior elegantly decorated with fine white-linen covered tables that were lit by small lamps and set with glass goblets and gleaming silverware.

At a table for four at the end of the car sat two men with their backs to the wall. One was big, fat and smoking a cigarette; the other young, blond and gaunt-faced.

The fat man caught Grey's eye and motioned to one of the two empty chairs at their table. Grey went over and sat down. "Thanks. Wasn't sure I'd get a seat."

"My pleasure," the man said, his accent distinctive.

"American?" Grey said.

"Expatriate, but still an American."

For some reason his features caught the trooper's attention; mustache draped over heavy jowls; gray speckled hair kept closely cropped; and thick fingers on large beefy hands made the cigarette he held look dainty. Grey thought he detected a light western twang in his deep voice.

"Bill Smith." He offered a meaty paw Grey tried to grip as he introduced himself.

Smith smiled and nodded at the blond man. "This is Gunter. Doesn't speak English."

Grey greeted the man with a nod. He appeared older than he did from across the dining car, probably in his mid-thirties. Up close, Grey noticed he had hawk-like features; a beak of a nose on a narrow face, eyes close together, and hair brushed back to a peak.

"You two friends?" Grey asked.

"No, we just met. We're having a couple of beers and waiting for our meals."

A waiter appeared at the table and handed Grey a menu. He ordered a beer as he studied the selections. Smith said something in German and the waiter walked away.

"Where's he going? I want to order," Grey said.

"It's OK, I told him to bring you your beer. He'll be right back. They have a pretty good schnitzel this time of night. I recommend it."

When the waiter returned with his beer, Grey ordered the schnitzel. Smith made a request to the waiter and when he left to place the order, Smith said, "I asked him to hold our dinner and bring it out when yours is ready."

"Oh, that's not necessary; I don't want to hold up your meal."

Smith laughed. "You won't. They'll prepare yours quicker. It'll be a couple of minutes."

Grey sipped his beer. "You seem to know the staff here pretty well?"

"Oh, I make this trip often," Smith said, raising his beer glass. "*Prosit*!" Gunter and Grey lifted their glasses in return. "*Prosit*!"

Grey looked at Gunter. He seemed uninterested in conversing, but Smith was chatty. "So, where you from in the states?"

"Dover, Delaware. You?"

"Out west, but I've been living in Europe nearly thirty years."

"Where in the west?"

Smith spoke German to Gunter, his words slipping off his tongue too rapidly for Grey to understand, and the blond laughed derisively as he sipped his beer.

"I told him some people are never satisfied with simple answers," Smith said.

Grey smiled, politely. "I didn't realize the question was complicated."

"It's not." Smith smiled. He called the waiter and ordered a Scotch, straight.

"What do you do for a living?" Grey said.

Smith grunted as he finished his cigarette with a puff. "Businessman. And you?"

"State trooper."

"Well – " Smith began, but was interrupted by the arrival of their meals.

Smith chortled while they ate. "You certainly are an interesting dinner companion. What brings you to Germany, work or pleasure?"

Grey sliced his veal. "Unfortunately, work, though it was supposed to be pleasure."

Gunter ate quietly and appeared to Grey to be following the conversation.

Smith said, "What's a Delaware trooper doing here in *mittle Europa?* Chasing down an unpaid speeding ticket?"

"I'm not a highway patrolman."

"What's your line of work?"

"Homicide investigator," Grey said.

"Oh, I think we would be very interested in your mission."

"I can't discuss it."

"At least give us a general idea? Is it extradition? An escaped prisoner?"

"I'm sorry."

"Of course, but I can't help but wonder what kind of case would lead you across an ocean and a continent?" Smith said.

Grey shrugged and ate his dinner.

"Well, you've left me intrigued, sir. Where you going or is that also confidential?"

"Berlin," Grey said. "Where are you headed?"

"Warsaw."

"Business or pleasure?"

"Business, of course."

"What kind of business do you do in Poland?"

"Exports," Smith said, finishing his meal and lighting a cigarette.

"What kind of exports?"

"My, I feel like I'm being interrogated."

Grey took his turn at sardonic replies. "My, I didn't realize I was being interrogatory."

Smith laughed and drained his glass of Scotch. "You sound like a detective."

"You sound like you're evading questions."

"I am." Smith glanced at Gunter, who was concentrating on his meal. "I live in Europe because people mind their own business."

"Or they're hiding from the law."

"You think I'm a fugitive, Sam?"

"I don't know, are you, Bill?"

"My, you are a detective." Smith offered an appreciative smile. "I think you should have no problem solving your murder case."

Grey did not answer. Smith prodded. "That's what you're working on, isn't it?"

"Who are you?"

Smith laughed. "Please, don't start seeing conspiracies; I'm just a businessman."

Grey let the conversation lull, tired of Smith's un-amusing games. The waiter appeared to remove dishes and take orders for dessert. Smith and Gunter asked for coffee and cake, but Grey declined, deciding to retire for the night.

"I thought you'd make for interesting conversation." Smith spoke condescendingly. "And I was right."

Grey paid his fare and bid good night.

An hour before the train reached Berlin, Grey rose, washed his face and had breakfast in his compartment, where he remained until arriving at the station.

Onto the crowded platform he made his way, listening as loudspeakers announced train departures and arrivals. He passed the dining car and glanced up to see Smith at the same table he was the night before, sipping coffee and reading the *International Herald Tribune.*

Gunter was nowhere to be seen.

Outside the station near the center of the bustling German capital, Polizei Lieutenant Max Lehmann waited for him. He had notified Interpol of his visit and Berlin police arranged to have an escort officer.

"Herr Grey, willkommen." Lehmann, tall and intense, reached out to shake Grey's hand. "I've reserved a room for you at Hotel Europa, off the *Ku'damm."*

Grey had not expected the hospitality and thanked the officer, who only shrugged. "It's no problem." Lehmann handed him a slip of paper. "Here's the address."

They walked to a green-and-white police sedan as Grey described his investigation. He asked whether the officer had heard of Gerhard. Lehmann shook his head. "Who is he?" Grey explained, but the name meant nothing to the lieutenant.

"There are many officers from the war still living," he said.

Lehmann drove a couple of blocks before stopping along a narrow street outside a brick-and-glass post-modern apartment house where former Kriegsmarine lieutenant Rolf Krug of U-812 had lived the last twenty-five years.

"Call if you need assistance," Lehmann said.

Grey climbed out of the sedan and stood on the sidewalk in front of the building, located a few blocks from Berlin's station. He could hear train whistles echo loudly as he entered, taking a small elevator to the second floor apartment.

Krug greeted Grey at the door. He had a slight build, a shock of white hair, and an easy smile on a face beaten from years of sun and wind. He kept his dark shirt buttoned to the collar; wore a sweater vest and corduroy pants and padded around in socks.

He warmly insisted they have coffee.

"My wife died several years ago and other than my daughter and her children, I don't get visitors too often," Krug explained. "So, please, sit."

The place was modestly furnished. A framed sepia-toned photograph on a dining room wall depicted Krug and other sailors on a dock by a U-boat with Hermes' winged cap profile on the conning tower. Grey recognized Hoest in the picture.

"When was that taken?"

Krug squinted at the picture for a moment and replied flatly, "Late '44."

"Was that before your last mission?"

Krug did not answer, but went about pouring dark coffee into cups of white china and putting out an apple crumb cake.

The two men talked about the new Germany. Grey wondered whether Krug was avoiding the topic he came to discuss. When they finished cake and coffee, Krug said, "Why do you come to Berlin for Eric's murder? Do you think the murderer is here?"

"No, well … I don't know. I came because I think his murder has something to do with his past, his years in the war."

"For what reason do you think this?"

Grey shifted uneasily in his chair. "It's the only lead I have."

Krug stood and slipped on his shoes. "I'm not sure I can help you." He started to leave the room. "I am happy to try. *Eine Minute, bitte.*"

He returned a moment later with a light jacket. "Let's take a walk, yes?"

They strolled down a busy sidewalk. Grey marveled at the change occurring over the city, marked by giant cranes looming across the skyline. Krug noted Grey's expression.

"So, we are a united country once again, but still struggling with our past."

"By the looks of things, you seem to be succeeding in correcting that, too."

"Perhaps; it will be some time before we really know. The easterners have a difficult time with unification. I wonder if we can make it."

They came to a broad intersection, where the train station stood and where Grey had been more than an hour earlier. He pointed at the station across the way. "The wall wasn't too far from here, if I remember correctly."

"You have been to Berlin before, corporal?"

"Years ago, when I was stationed in the army. Doesn't look at all as I remember."

"We do well at removing physical reminders of our past, but memories remain; at least for my generation, they are ever present," Krug said.

"Can you remember the mission you had in December 1944?"

Krug looked reflective as he stared at the sidewalk for a moment. "Yes," he said, smiling. "You are the first person to ever ask me about it."

"Really?"

"Not even the admiralty knew what we were doing; we had been ordered never to discuss it, even after the war, or we would face death, but I think such an order is no longer relevant."

"A secret mission?" Grey said. "Is that why there's no record of U-812?"

Krug nodded.

Grey tensed with anticipation. "What was the mission?"

"We were to land an agent in America."

"Where?"

"On an island, somewhere in the Chesapeake Bay."

"Were you successful?"

"Yes, which is another reason why there's no record of U-812. It was a prototype and it allowed us to submerge in the shallow bay."

"What happened to the agent?"

The old sailor shrugged. *"Ich weiss nicht.* I never saw him again."

"Do you know what his mission was?"

Krug shook his head. "We knew nothing about the man, only Eric. He spent many hours with him, in his quarters talking."

"Did the captain know the agent's mission?"

"Perhaps; only Eric dealt with the general who assigned the mission."

"What general?"

"I don't recall his name, he was SS."

"This agent – can you remember his name and where he was going?"

Krug thought for a moment and chuckled.

"What?" Grey asked.

"He was a boy, a bit fanatical, always giving the Hitler salute. God, he was damn pitiful."

"Why do you say that?"

"He was one of the believers."

"Were you?"

"No," Krug said, shaking his head. "And by then neither were most of the crew."

"What about Hoest?"

"No, never."

"Did you keep in contact with Hoest after the war?"

"Not really, though I think in the 1960s he called on me. It was a brief visit."

"What was he here for?"

"I don't remember, but I believe he had been visiting family in the south."

Grey stared at the busy city. Krug sensed his frustration. "Have you tried any of the other crew members?"

"You're the only one living."

Krug smiled, ruefully. "The past is slipping away from you."

Grey was desperate. "It there anything you can remember about this agent?"

Krug frowned and shook his head. "I'm sorry."

A cool breeze blew through Berlin. Krug felt a chill and wanted to return home. As they headed back, Grey asked about the U-boat's Atlantic voyage in 1944.

"How did you manage to get across the ocean without being detected?"

Krug answered matter-of-factly. "We never made radio contact. Eric suspected the Allies knew our codes; he managed to convince someone in authority we had a much better chance not reporting in."

"You never made radio contact because you suspected your codes had been broken?"

"Yes."

Grey could not conceal a satisfying smile; he had found the subject for his doctoral thesis.

"What is it?" Krug asked.

"You've confirmed my theory."

"Oh?"

He briefly explained. Krug, now realizing U-812's accomplishment, only nodded, too old to feel pride in his service to the navy or to even care.

Grey asked, "I take it, then, you never encountered the enemy?"

"We came close, but I'm amazed we made it with the U-boat prototype."

Grey looked quizzical and Krug started to explain the Walter boat's volatile fuel before he suddenly stopped and grabbed Grey's arm. "I remember something about the boy; Eric told me his parents had been killed in the bombing raid on Hamburg."

"Why is that important?"

"I'm not sure, but the bombing raid caught my interest because thousands burned alive," he said. "You've heard about it I'm sure, corporal. It happened in 1943."

They walked in silence as Grey considered Krug's information, wondering whether this was another part to his case. As they approached the apartment house, Krug said to Grey, "I'm sorry I could not have been more help to you."

Grey smiled. "I'm flying home day after tomorrow; if you can remember anything else, I'm staying at the Hotel Europa."

Outside Krug's apartment house, Grey thanked the old sailor and started off. Krug called after him, "Corporal, you should read about the Hamburg firebombing."

It was nearly noon when he left Krug. Grey found a café where he spent a leisurely lunch reading the *Times of London*. Afterwards, he decided to vacation a little and toured the city.

As night enveloped Berlin, he returned to the hotel, where he had checked in after lunch to deposit his suitcase. He washed up and set out for dinner at the Dancing Bear, a restaurant on the *Kurfurstendamm*, a bustling boulevard of shops and eateries. The concierge recommended it.

He walked a couple of blocks when he sensed someone following him, a figure he caught out of the corner of his eye, darting amid the crowds, but focused on him. Grey stopped outside a restaurant and casually glanced down the sidewalk for a look. Nothing, he thought.

In the smoke-filled restaurant, he was provided a small corner table that gave him a view of the entrance. He sat nursing a beer and waiting for his meal when a blond woman entered. He caught his breath and his heart pounded at the possibility, but as she stood there in the blue haze, glancing around, he realized it wasn't her. It could never be her; too many years had passed for her to look as she did those months they had in Heidelberg.

He watched the blond, gauging her age around thirty six, a few years younger than Sana would now be. She directed her gaze at him, her oval face expressed recognition as she stepped off the landing and walked to his table and stood there, smiling at him.

She was thin, attractive, the color of youth hardly faded in her fresh-looking complexion; her soft green eyes captured his attention. She wore black jeans and a white sweater.

"Might I speak with you?" she asked.

Surprised at her approach, but attracted to her, he pulled out a chair. She slipped into the seat and spoke softly but urgently. He listened, detecting a lilt in her accent. He guessed she was from southern Germany.

"I understand you have come from Switzerland recently, yes?"

"Yes." Grey was now suspicious. "And how do you understand that?"

She spoke deliberately. "It's not important, but what is quite important is the man whom you were seen talking to at the Hotel Baren."

"And who the hell are you?"

The woman blushed. "I am sorry." She reached into her black leather purse, removed a card and handed it to Grey. "Marta Toth. I'm an attorney for *La ligue des défenseurs d'enfant*."

"The League of Child Defenders?" Grey asked, testing his college French.

"Yes, that is correct; you speak French?"

"Not really, just a lucky guess," he wisecracked. Toth seemed not to notice. "What kind of organization is this?"

"We are an international group, based in Luzerne, and we are trying to put an end to the practice of using children as soldiers and slave laborers."

"So what does that have to do with me?"

"Not you, the man you met at the hotel."

"And what man was that?"

"Please, Mr. Grey," Toth implored. "You know General Gerhard."

"What about him?"

"He holds controlling interests in a West African cocoa plantation enslaving children to harvest cocoa beans."

Toth's information stunned him, but he was skeptical. Grey was becoming annoyed with these chance encounters – first Smith, now her; it seemed every time he wanted a meal he faced interrogation by someone with a hidden agenda.

He spoke tersely. "So what do you want me to do about it?"

"We would like your help – " Toth began.

Grey interrupted her. "Why don't you tell me just how you know my business?"

She started to, but he would not let her finish.

"Look," he said, angrily. "I'm sorry about children in slavery, but I don't know who you are or why you are here and frankly, I don't care."

Grey's voice rose. Patrons at other tables glanced over as Toth tried to calm him.

"I am sorry, Mr. Grey, I'm very sorry, and I will explain, just give me a chance."

"How do you know my business?" he demanded.

A waiter appeared, inquiring whether there was a problem. Grey realized he had become loud and disruptive. He settled down and apologized. He sent the waiter away with a drink order for them. They sat quietly, making small talk until the waiter returned with a glass of white wine for her and another beer for him.

Grey said, softly, "Okay. Explain."

When Toth told him how she came to sharing a drink at his table, Grey loudly responded, "Wolfram! Wolfram sent you to me?"

"Please, Mr. Grey, your voice," Toth pleaded, stealing an embarrassed glance at the other diners who were again looking at them.

Grey again settled down, realizing Wolfram had always liked to send attractive women to him, although he was disturbed his friend had shared with her information about his case. He had asked him to keep the matter confidential.

"I'm sorry," he said to Toth. "Go ahead."

The League was certain Gerhard owned the plantation, she said, but they had no evidence to proceed with legal action. Corrupt Ivory Coast officials protected him. When Toth learned that the old general frequented Hotel Baren, she staked it out, hoping for a lead to help her case.

After Grey's dining room meeting with Gerhard, Toth's associate, who was watching the old general, obtained Grey's and his two companions' names from the hotel manager. Manfred's address was gleaned from his car's license plate.

"And that's how you traced me?" Grey said.

"Yes, I spoke to *Herr Manfred*, who referred me to Wolfram." Toth smiled. "He's a flirt, but he was sure you would want to speak to me."

"He owes me one," Grey said, as the waiter brought his meal.

"I'm sorry, what?" Toth said.

"Never mind," he said, stealing another glance into her eyes and finding an enchantment he had not felt in such a long time. "Would you like to have dinner?"

Toth happily accepted. The waiter left with her order and his sauerbraten, which the cook kept warm for him until her meal was ready. Grey relaxed. She was intriguing and attractive, but her purpose for approaching him was vague and he wanted more answers.

"I don't understand what you think I can do," he said, watching her green eyes.

"You are a police officer in Delaware; you are here because of a murder case," she said, matter-of-factly. "I think there is much you can do."

Grey frowned and shook his head. "Wolfram likes to talk to pretty women."

She shook her head. "Your friend only told me I might find you in Berlin, Mr. Grey; my Interpol sources gave me your profile; *Herr Krug* told me about your case; and most Americans come to this restaurant to eat when they visit Berlin."

"You guessed I was at this restaurant?"

Toth smiled. "Actually, no; the hotel doorman told me he directed you here."

"You've gone to a lot of effort to hunt me down; what do you think I can do?"

"I would like to know what your meeting was about."

He shook his head. "Nothing to do with child slavery; it's really none of your business."

Toth pensively fingered her wine glass stem. Their meals arrived and over dinner she told him about Gerhard's plantation.

The men who run the plantation for the general lure boys as young as ten years old from villages. They offer bicycles for a day's work picking cocoa beans, but once a boy arrives, he is prevented from leaving; forced to work every day in the fields, and in searing heat.

The boys' meals are few and meager; they get little medical care; no toilets; and a bed is the dirt floor. Parents who find their sons can usually free them with bribes to local officials and Gerhard's men. Some boys escape; some are sent to fight in someone's army; some die.

"We hear horrible stories about a foreman the boys call *Le gros homme*, 'the fat man.' He beats and starves children he believes don't work hard enough," Toth said. "All this is carried out with Gerhard's knowledge and we're sure his blessing."

When she finished, Grey, pushed away his mostly uneaten meal. "That's a sad story, and of course it ruined my appetite, but I still don't know how I can be of any help."

Toth hardly touched her meal. She spoke to Grey patiently. "Ivory Coast authorities can only free those children if the corrupt government officials protecting Gerhard no longer protect him from the international community."

"And for that to happen, Gerhard would have to stop paying them off, correct?"

"Exactly."

"And the only way that's going to happen is what?"

"He's arrested and convicted, or ... " Her voiced trailed off.

"Or what?"

"He dies."

Grey digested her remark as the waiter came and removed their plates.

"So where do I figure in all this?" Grey asked.

"If he is your murder suspect we would like to help; it's one way of getting him."

"Well, he's not a suspect and I don't know how you can help me."

He was not unsympathetic to her cause and was in fact trying to resist the urge to ask her out, but he did not see how they had anything professionally to offer one another.

"Look," he said. "The guy's ninety; death can't be too far away."

Toth became angry. "If such an event was a day away it's still too long for the children who suffer on his plantation."

Grey found her more alluring angry, but he harbored suspicions about her motives and he was tired from his day traipsing around the city. "I'm sorry, but I can't help you."

His answer disappointed her, but she brightened. "Maybe I could help you on your case."

"I don't see how – " Grey began.

"I have many contacts in German law enforcement," she said.

Her offer sounded like an opportunity to combine work with pleasure. Krug's remark on the Hamburg bombing aroused his curiosity, and Berlin was his for one more day before he had to return home.

"Actually, you could help me with a research project," he said.

Toth smiled. She, too, found herself enchanted for the first time in many years. There was something about this American man she liked.

"Can you take me to a book store that carries English titles? I need information about the bombing of Hamburg during the war."

They agreed to meet in front of the U-Bahn station at Berlin's Wittembergplatz the next afternoon. Toth took him to a nearby book store and café, where Grey found historical accounts of the July 1943 bombing written by a British author.

After he purchased the paperback they sipped coffee at a table outside, where she asked about his interest in the subject.

"It may be a link in my investigation," Grey said.

"You've made me curious."

"A possible suspect I'm looking for lost his family in the bombing."

"What does that have to do with your case?"

"I don't know; I'm wondering whether researching the bombing will tell me anything."

"Germans, the older ones, don't like to think of the war; it's too painful for them."

"It's painful for Americans, too," he said.

"Oh? I thought it was your country's 'good war?'"

Her acid comment irritated him. "Yeah, for those who didn't fight in it or live through it."

Awkward silence fell between them. Toth sensed his anger and decided to leave. As she thanked him for a pleasant afternoon, he stopped her with a request.

"I was wondering whether you'd like to have dinner this evening."

Toth smiled. "I thought after last night you wouldn't care to dine with me again."

"As long as you don't bring up Gerhard, I'd love to have dinner with you."

He returned to his hotel room to a waiting message from Krug. Grey called the old sailor who sounded like he wanted just to talk. He had remembered Hoest almost fired a bullet through the head of a political officer because the man countermanded his orders.

Grey listened politely and inquired about a name, but Krug's memory failed. He thanked the man, although he doubted the information's relevance. Krug sounded lonely when Grey said goodbye.

He rang room service for a pot of coffee. He settled into the room's overstuffed chair and opened the book on the Allied firebombing of Hamburg in the summer of 1943:

It was called Operation Gomorrah, a British plan formulated by Prime Minister Winston Churchill and Air Chief Marshal Arthur Harris and finalized in May of that year. The first in a series of bombing raids on the city occurred the night of July 24. The Royal Air Force struck with 740 bombers, which reached their target with only a loss of 12 bombers.

The following day, 68 American flying fortress bombers, B-17s, hit Hamburg's shipyards including the Blohm and Voss U-boat yards. The Americans returned on July 26 and bombed the city power plant. This was followed the night of July 27 with another British raid of more than 700 bombers.

The bombers with their thousands of tons of iron and ordnance ignited a firestorm with 150-mile per hour winds that sucked up people off the streets and temperatures that soared to at least 1,500 degrees Fahrenheit. The intense heat caused asphalt to burst into flames. Air raid shelters became ovens, cooking the people huddled inside. The storm so crippled the city and its support systems and services that fire crews were unable to contain the raging fire; flames engulfed entire neighborhoods and the inhuman heat left the dead desiccated, depleted of all moisture.

The Allies, though, were not through with Hamburg. Night raids by the British went on for a week, concluding on August 3. The American bombing effort ceased after those first two days because the smoke from the night raids obscured their targets in and around the city. In all, about 9,000 tons of bombs were dropped on the city.

Estimates of the dead caused by the raids range from 40,000 to 50,000; more than 16,000 buildings and 250,000 houses were destroyed, leaving 1 million people homeless. Approximately ten-square miles of Hamburg was reduced to rubble.

In the aftermath of the raids, two-thirds of the city's residents fled. The bombing was so awesome in its destruction and effect that it shook Hitler and his command. They worried other such attacks on German cities could bring defeat.

At the time, it was the heaviest air assault in history. British officials would later refer to it as the Hiroshima of Germany. It was later determined that what helped to create the firestorm was a large concentration of bombs in one area of the city; unusually warm, dry weather; and firefighters unable to reach the initial fires because of the high explosives used in the bombs.

Grey closed the book and took a last sip of coffee that had long gone cold. War makes criminals out of everyone, he decided, no matter what side you're on. Why Krug thought it important for him to read about the bombing, he wasn't sure, other than to make a point, perhaps. He doubted the bombing was a motivation for his elusive suspect, yet knowing your parents died in such a tragedy had to do something to a person.

He met Toth, who had spent her afternoon collecting legal documents for a client, at a small restaurant near Wittembergplatz. They kept their dinner conversation to light topics.

When they finished, Grey surprised her by suggesting they find another place for after dinner drinks. She found the American attractive and wondered where this was leading. It was unlike her to impulsively set aside work and agree eagerly to dinner and drinks.

Grey had similar thoughts. He expected an evening alone, but Toth intrigued him. They strolled down the *Kurfurstendamm* to an intimate old café she suggested for its soft jazz combo that played there each night.

They took a dimly lit corner table, ordered a bottle of white wine, and shared their life's stories, finding similarities in their hectic professional lives, in which they had so little time for meeting people and building relationships.

"It's been so long since I've spent time with someone like this," Marta said. "My staff says I need a personal life."

Grey laughed. "They sound like my father," he said. "Do your parents give you a hard time about not getting married and settling down?"

"They're both gone now," she said. "Father passed away when I was at university, my mother died two years ago."

Grey nodded sympathetically. Marta asked, "You still have both your parents?"

He shook his head. "My mother died when I was five; a drunk driver killed her. My dad worries that it left some deep psychological scar, making me fearful of commitments."

"Has it?"

"No, I just haven't found anyone I want to make a life with."

That wasn't true, but he didn't want to share everything; some things people needed to keep for themselves. Sometimes holding a piece of the past was just as important as leaving it behind.

They met riding the tram between Neuenheim, where she worked at a restaurant, and Heidelberg. Grey fell fast for Sana, wanted a life with her, but her parents smashed any such hope and dream when she told them he was black – not just black, but also Hispanic. "Mixed breed, a mongrel!" her father viciously spat at Wolfram who attempted to intercede.

Sana bowed to her parents without an argument, meeting Sam at a Heidelberg café to tell him she couldn't disrespect their wishes. He tried to convince her otherwise, telling her what the last few weeks with her meant to him; but she was unmoved.

She stood abruptly from the table. "Aufwiedersehn, Sam."

He watched her slim figure in boots and jeans hurry across the cobblestone square; he felt hollow. For a few weeks he called and wrote, but she never answered. Wolfram tried to show his deeply hurt friend what he could not see – Sana never loved him; she just wanted the passage out of Germany, away from her family that an American soldier – any American soldier – can provide with a wedding ring.

Months later Grey learned Sana had found another soldier while they had been dating. A handsome white army captain from Texas who was stationed in Mannheim. They married before he was sent back to the states for a new assignment at Fort Sam Houston.

Wolfram tried to console his friend.

"She was no good, Sam," he said, as Grey plied himself with drink. "She was looking for a plane ticket. I've seen it before; German girls willing to do anything to live in America."

"How can someone do that?" he demanded, in drunken anger. "It's so goddamn cruel."

"As it is my friend, in love and in war."

Grey's failure to recognize or perhaps his willingness to ignore the racist attitude toward him impressed Wolfram, but Grey told him racism was other people's problem, not his.

"I don't live based on what others think about the color of my skin," he said. "Naïve as it may be, I've led a fuller life because of that attitude."

Grey gently entwined his fingers with Marta's as the night melted away. He could hear a distant clock tower chiming midnight.

"I don't want this to end," he said.

She shook her head, not wanting to hear what she knew he would say next.

"Unfortunately, I have an early flight."

Marta didn't move. She felt warm and comfortable. She smiled as she held Grey's strong hand. "Can I walk you back to your hotel?" she said.

Grey smiled as he hailed the waiter.

As the door to his room closed behind them they faced each other immediately with deep longings. They embraced passionately, their bodies warming, turning liquid. They removed each others' clothes between hot kisses, their garments slipped off easily as they made their way to the bed, where they remained for what seemed hours.

Marta felt natural and comfortable in his arms, as if that's where she belonged, and Grey held her warm, lithe figure and never wanted to let go. Later, lying contented amid rumpled bed sheets and diffused light, Grey watched an odd expression cross Marta's face.

"What is it?" he whispered.

With an impish look Marta whispered: "I can't believe I've made love to a man I met only yesterday." He wrapped his arms around her, nuzzling her neck, and listened to her sigh. They held each other, not wanting to let go, and drifted off to sleep.

In the morning, as the cab driver loaded his bags into the car, the two lovers embraced and promised to see each other again, soon.

"I'll e-mail you as soon as I'm back in the states," he said, wrapping his big arms around her waist and looking into those green alluring eyes. "This is very strange and very wonderful."

Marta smiled. "Yes," she said. "Now go, you will miss your plane."

Chapter 8

Washington D.C.
January 10, 1944

Fiery hands reached out of the smoldering pyre that his neighborhood had become and grabbed maniacally at him. He stumbled backward and fell. He yelled for his parents, but only the dead responded; desiccated corpses struggling to rise from ashes of flesh and bone.

Hahn screamed, jolting awake on an early evening train bound for the American capital.

"Hey! Easy there, fella, easy."

Hahn turned violently toward the voice and a gaunt, unshaven face in short stringy black hair appeared before him. The man, peering curiously at him now, had leaned over to shake him awake. They were alone in the dimly lit compartment.

"What?" Hahn sat up, rubbing his face. "What is it?"

"Washington," the man said. "We'll be in the station in a few minutes."

Hahn stared out the compartment window at the red and white lights of traffic as homes, tall apartment houses and neon lights flashed past. It looked so peaceful. He tried to get a sense of his whereabouts.

"Where is the Capitol building and the White House?"

"Can't see 'em from the train," said the man, tapping a cigarette out of a pack of Camels.

As the train rocked lightly, Hahn studied Marc Volker, who wore a wool overcoat and dark trousers. He guessed late thirties for his age. Volker was a Baltimore factory worker and local German-American Bund member.

Fifteen hours earlier, he fetched Hahn off an island on the Chesapeake Bay in a skiff equipped with an outboard motor.

They had identified themselves with code words: "north" and "cross."

Volker was a first-generation German-American, a fervent Nazi before the war, but in the last year, as Germany's power waned, his enthusiasm receded into sympathy for the cause.

The day before his rendezvous, Volker was contacted by the agent to whom Hahn shortly would meet – Emil Baum, a small, middle-aged dealer of used and rare books who left Germany in 1929 to become a United States citizen.

Family connections brought the diminutive Baum and Rhonen together when the general visited the country in 1939.

Stirred by the Fatherland's might and the handsome salary the wealthy general paid out of his own pockets, Baum agreed to become Rhonen's personal espionage agent, reading every U.S. government publication he could find and summarizing them in coded, monthly letters.

Baum communicated through Mustafa, a pro-Nazi Turkish diplomat whose own nation was neutral. Thin with ink-dark hair and mustache, Mustafa belonged to a dwindling society of bureaucrats and businessmen who longed for Turkey's return as the Ottoman Empire. Imperial Turkey had supported Germany during World War I.

Mustafa was one of the Sultan's generals before joining the Foreign Service, assigned to Berlin where he met Rhonen. Their friendship began at a diplomatic reception for Hitler, having found they shared similar ideas about empire – Rhonen's Darwinian view that German National Socialists were Europe's rightful rulers and Mustafa's belief in the Turks reclaiming the Middle East, where they reigned for centuries until the end of the First World War.

In the winter of 1943, when Rhonen commanded the SS division of Bosnian Muslims in Yugoslavia, Mustafa stopped at the Turkish consulate in Sarajevo. He wanted to visit the general and inform him of his diplomatic post in Washington.

Rhonen, by then formulating his espionage schemes, considered Mustafa an opportunity and proposed they stay in contact. "I need eyes and ears in America," Rhonen told him. Mustafa bowed slightly and smiled. "Rhonen *Bey*, I accept with honor."

The general's messages increased significantly the last few months, compelling Baum and Mustafa to meet regularly at a Connecticut Avenue café, near Dupont Circle. Over coffee, they exchanged books with messages Mustafa routed to and from Turkey's embassy in neutral Switzerland.

For the unassuming Baum – pudgy and unmarried with only few he could call friends – meetings with the erudite diplomat invigorated a comfortably mundane life as owner of a small, but profitable book shop. Castle Books stood in tree-lined Northeast Washington, near Catholic University. It was a long, narrow shop, lined with book-burdened, floor-to-ceiling shelves.

Early in December, Mustafa handed him the message of an agent's pending arrival and Baum's life accelerated. The idea of entertaining a spy excited him, but as he rode the streetcar home, he recalled another message the Turkish attaché conveyed that disturbed him.

As Mustafa sipped his coffee and lit one of his scented cigarettes, he said quietly, "This may be our last meeting for awhile; my country expects to declare war on Germany soon."

Baum lamented losing his favorite past-time. Mustafa only smiled at the man's pathetic sounds. The book shop owner bored him. If not for his duty to Rhonen (and a lucrative fee the general deposited in a Swiss bank account for him) he would not choose to meet with the little man who was so child-like at times.

Mustafa gently reminded him: "If Turkey declares war its embassy in Switzerland will not tolerate a German attaché collecting the general's mail."

"But why can't we at least still meet? Don't you like our conversations?"

Mustafa shook his head. "My immediate concern is the embassy's security officer."

Apprehension gripped Baum, who always worried his treasonous, clandestine activities would be discovered. "What about him?"

"The man has suddenly shown an interest in where I am going and who I am talking to," the diplomat said. He tried to allay the book shop owner's fears. "It's probably nothing."

Baum shrugged off his worry as he opened the door to his shop. From a filing cabinet he fetched a list of Bund contacts and went upstairs to his apartment. He scanned names, noting the Bund leaders who had been jailed for pro-Nazi sentiments since America entered the war.

He examined the names of the loyal rank-and-file. The highly recommended had stars by their name. Volker's name had two stars.

Five hundred dollars, more than devotion to the cause, had motivated Volker to accept Baum's assignment. He kissed his wife goodbye with a phony excuse about a fishing trip and climbed into his dusty '38 Plymouth coupe with his pole and creel and drove several hours to Solomons Island, a small Chesapeake community at the tip of Calvert County, Maryland.

He arrived late in the afternoon under an overcast sky. An icy wind blew over the island, stationed at the confluence of the bay and Patuxent River. A creek, spanned by a rickety wooden bridge, kept separated Solomons from the mainland.

Volker had visited the sandy, scrub-brush island many times before to fish. The scraggly old man with a ruddy complexion at the rental cabin was familiar with him.

"A little cold to go fishing today," the man said as Volker rented a skiff. Volker nodded and laughed. "Taking it out in the morning," he said. "Things should be calmer then."

After securing the skiff, Volker drove through Solomons, a quiet fishing village thriving on oyster packing and ship building. He passed sailors and marines on leave from the air station or the amphibious training base, both of which were across the river.

He took a room at a boarding house near Our Lady Star of the Sea, a weathered church of white stone and blue trim, and waited until early morning to travel to the landing point. He knew neither the agent's name nor his mission, only that he would be waiting.

Four-thirty the next morning he returned to the dock with pole and creel. A gentle breeze blew away the rain clouds, uncovering a bright moon. He set off in the skiff, headed for the bay, wondering whether the agent would be waiting for him.

He glanced casually over his shoulder and was startled to find himself fifty yards ahead of a chugging flotilla of white-sailed skipjacks – watermen sailing out for oyster harvesting. He momentarily panicked then calmly mulled his course of action if the boats were to go north into the bay, where he was headed.

At the river's mouth the fleet slowly veered southward, to his relief.

Volker sped his boat into the bay and looked toward the island's passing shipyard where workers were building landing craft. He turned his eyes to the naval base, on the opposite shore of the Patuxent, where big gray ships anchored around the mouth of the river.

Clever spot to land an agent, he thought; last place anyone would think to look. On deck of a naval ship he was passing, a sailor in silhouette raised an arm and waved. He waved back.

Fifteen minutes later he approached the island. He circled the small land mass looking for the agent and making sure he wasn't sailing into a trap. The first time around the island appeared deserted. On his second lap a young, blond-haired man in a hat and coat stepped from a clump of trees and stood watching him.

He's a boy, Volker said to himself.

They exchanged their code words, though each man felt silly about it. Who else but them would be on the cold island just before dawn? Hahn climbed into the skiff and they headed to the mainland. Volker navigated the boat into shallow waters by an old abandoned, lighthouse along a sandy, pine scrub beach, where he often fished.

He instructed Hahn to wade ashore and walk up to the lighthouse. "Wait by the door."

Light streaked the morning sky as Volker approached Solomons' docks. He tied the boat to a pier near the rental cabin. He calmly carried his gear across the empty parking lot to the car, placing the fishing rod and creel in the trunk.

He was not one who easily rattled, which was why the Bund recommended him to Baum. Volker's cool demeanor even impressed his boss at the engine factory.

Hahn heard crunching and snapping before he saw the car, its tires rolling over a crushed oyster-shell roadbed. Volker sat behind the wheel and waved for him. Hahn climbed in and they began a long drive through rural Maryland.

At Annapolis they followed a concrete state road to a highway that led them to downtown Baltimore. They did not, as ordered, exchange names, and spoke little. Hahn mostly slept. Volker drove and thought about ways he could spend the money Baum paid him.

Volker parked near the city's Penn Station. Their circuitous route was a precaution that Baum had insisted on, but which Volker considered not necessary. It was mid-afternoon when they entered a diner on Charles Street. They took a smooth red-leather booth.

Famished, they ordered eggs, ham, toast and coffee. Having long rationed food – he had rarely smelled, let alone sipped, real coffee or tasted butter – Hahn couldn't suppress his delight at the portion size and quality of their meals when the waitress set them on the Formica table.

He vanquished his meal. The last time he had eaten, which was some sausage on the U-boat, was nearly nine hours earlier.

Volker attempted conversation, mentioning the news accounts of the war going badly for Germany and wondering whether Hahn's mission was relevant anymore. He shoveled a fork-full of egg into his mouth and said nonchalantly, "Just what're you planning on doing?"

The factory worker's inability to be discrete astonished Hahn who believed the man was putting them both in jeopardy by talking. He scowled at him over his plate, his tone tense. "*Not* now," he hushed.

Volker shrugged. They finished eating in silence. When they left the diner for the station, Hahn admonished him. Volker hung his head in silence. He did not care for this young man, but he had his assignment to keep. They entered the marble-walled station and bought tickets for the five-fifteen to Washington.

With a couple of hours before departure Volker suggested a movie at a cinema around the corner. Inside the theater, Hahn began to relax, but when the newsreels flickered on screen showing Wehrmacht troops beaten or retreating under Allied advances, he became tense, then distraught.

NAZI TROOPS ON THE RUN – Images of captured German soldiers as a confident-sounding narrator intoned: *After smashing Hitler's Ardennes' offensive, the Allies roll on into Germany with Patton's 3rd Army leading the way.* RED ARMY PUSHES INTO POLAND – Cold and hungry German infantry fight snowy weather as the narrator blurts, *After throwing the Nazi invaders out of the Soviet Union, Commander Zhukov's army is closing in on Warsaw.*

Shaken, Hahn left his seat and went to the restroom at the rear of the theater. He splashed his face with cold water. He felt anxious, breathing heavily. He leaned over the porcelain sink and calmed down, assuring himself he lost his perspective over American propaganda. *Germany was on the march.*

Hahn returned to his seat and watched the feature, *Keeper of the Flame*, a drama about a journalist investigating a national hero's death only to uncover his plot to overthrow the country in a fascist coup using his Forward America movement.

Spencer Tracy plays the journalist, Steve O'Malley, and one scene resonated with Hahn; when O'Malley asks a friendly cab driver in the hero's hometown about the group.

"Did you belong to that Forward America Association of Mr. Forrest's?"

"They asked me to join. Guess it's a good notion, but I'm no joiner. When I march, I like to march at my own pace. And when I fight, have to fight, I like to pick it."

"You said you had no wars."

"Not in a manner of speaking, but there's always good and evil up against one another. A man's got to take sides sooner or later."

Hahn considered the scene as they walked out of the theater and in an excited, expansive moment he said to Volker, "That was a swell flick."

The factory worker glanced at him. "You sound like an American."

Hahn liked hearing that. Truth was, although he was only starting to admit it to himself, he liked the country whose leader he came to kill and whose political structure and ideology he was to help rebuild into National Socialism.

He said in a bragging tone, "I was born in Chicago," then caught himself, putting his guard up once more. "Let's hurry. I don't want to miss the train."

"Union Station! Union Station! Washington, D.C.!" The train slowed to almost a crawl as the conductor wobbled past their compartment. Volker crushed out his cigarette in an ashtray and Hahn grabbed his bag as the train came to a stop along the platform.

They stepped off the train into a sea of dark suits and military uniforms, which swept them down the platform and through the granite station's cavernous noisy concourse and out double doors to a wide portico with soaring archways. Beyond, the street teemed with traffic.

Compared to Germany's bomb-ruined cities, the war hardly showed here. Its only sign in Washington was the thousands of men and women walking around in uniform.

They walked down the portico, crossed the busy street and walked past the city's main post office to the corner of Massachusetts Avenue and North Capitol Street, where Volker bid Hahn goodbye.

"This is where I leave you," he said, as the green-and-white trolley rolled toward them, down North Capitol. "You'll take this to the Brookland stop. When you get off, go up Newton Street for about two blocks and look for Castle Books."

Hahn repeated the instructions as the trolley slowed to a stop. He nodded thanks and climbed aboard. Volker watched sparks dancing off overhead wires as the trolley headed on down the street, picking up speed.

As he sat on a worn cushioned seat, Hahn looked out the windows, glimpsing buildings along the nighttime street, but the interior light's glare made it difficult. He turned his attention to the advertisements above the windows.

He studied a war production poster of a soldier aiming a machine gun: "Your IDEAS are on the attack – KEEP 'EM COMING! This is YOUR WAR ... FIGHT IT!" It reminded him of one on a Munich kiosk that depicted a soldier in battle: *So wie wir kampfen Arbeite Du fur Den Sieg!* "This is how we fight. You too must work for victory!"

The trolley car stopped. "Brookland," the conductor called in monotone. Hahn stepped off and looked at the street signs: Michigan Avenue and Newton Street. He gripped tightly the handle on his suitcase as he nervously examined his surroundings; homes with yards and trees while up one block he could see a cluster of shops.

He walked to a corner store with "People's Drugs" in brilliant red neon above the door. Impulsively, he went inside.

At the counter, he asked for chocolate. The clerk went over to a rack and grabbed a bar wrapped in brown paper. Hahn examined the label – "Hershey's Chocolate."

"That'll be five cents."

Hahn pulled out a fifty dollar bill. The clerk grumbled. "That the smallest ya got?" Hahn nodded and the clerk shook his head. "I don't have change to break that, pal, sorry."

"Keep the change," Hahn said, walking away from the counter.

"Keep it? This is fifty bucks!"

Hahn slipped the candy bar in his pocket and left the store, leaving the clerk shaking his head. He walked along the street until he spotted the shop window with the name Castle Books in gold-lettering. He stopped. The shop was dark except for a light in the back.

Hahn started moving toward it when the doors of two large sedans opened and men in suits climbed out and converged on the shop. The door was smashed open, there was shouting from inside; more men in suits appeared in the alleyway beside the shop.

For a moment, Hahn froze in panic. He turned around and headed back down the street, trying not to hurry, trying not to let fear overwhelm him. He headed to the trolley stop. He slid his hand inside his coat pocket and gripped his switchblade, preparing, as he had been trained, for an attack. Near Michigan Avenue he heard someone shout to him.

He looked around furiously, spotted an alleyway and hurried into it. A hand fell on his shoulder and a loud voice filled his ear, "Just a moment … "

It was a sentence never completed. Hahn swung around, flicking open the switchblade as he did, without looking – without thinking. He slashed the knife hard across the throat, slicing so thoroughly he thought he cut the man's head off.

The figure crumbled to the pavement while, in a futile gesture, reaching for his throat that was slit open and bleeding profusely. The blood-smeared knife dropped from Hahn's hand and clattered noisily on the pavement. Hahn stepped back. The man was face down, gurgling.

Hahn's eyes quickly searched around. Seeing no one, he hurried up the alley to a street.

Lost, he raced down one block and up another, becoming confused. He stopped under a street light to get his bearings. His lungs ached from gulping the cold night air, and he sweated, profusely. He heard running footsteps and panicked. A bell pealed; he lurched across the street.

He went through an arched sandstone entranceway and found himself on the grounds of a church. He entered. It was an ornate cathedral, softly lit, filled with statuary, the air permeated by the pungent smell of burning incense. Its silence frightened him.

He walked tentatively toward a set of doors at the back, but stopped at the sound of a door opening somewhere in the sanctuary. He looked to his right – at a short stairwell leading down. He quietly followed it to a small room with an altar and archway.

Hahn started to read a sign, but approaching footsteps hurried him through the archway into a dark, narrow passage lit by dim lights. He noticed deep indentations in the earthen walls; spaces to lay the dead, he thought. He realized what the sign said: catacombs.

Hahn stopped and examined his surroundings. He needed a place to hide, to regroup; to figure out what to do next. He continued to move along the passageway until he came to a well-lit chamber with a narrow set of stairs leading upward.

He ascended slowly, entering a small low-ceilinged room. He crossed and went through another doorway and found himself on the other side of the sanctuary. He stood trying to figure things out when a soft voice startled him: "Sir, the catacombs are closed."

Hahn turned to a young, lanky man in sandals and a chocolate-brown robe with a Greek cross – two bars of equal length and colored red – emblazoned on the right breast. A white rope was tied loosely around the waist. The young friar repeated himself and asked, "Have you come for confession?"

"What is this place?"

"You are in the Franciscan Monastery," the friar replied. "Your first time here?"

Hahn nodded and the friar motioned to a confessional box and said, "If you're interested, Father Sebastian is on duty tonight."

Hahn looked at the dark-wood door with a green light glowing over it. He set his suitcase inside a pew and entered. He knelt. A small door separating priest from confessor slid open.

It was near the end of a quiet day in the monastery. Few had come for confession. Father Sebastian was a little surprised to hear someone enter his confessional. He asked to hear the sins, but Hahn was a Lutheran. He had stopped attending church when he joined the Hitler Youth. He knelt in silence, unsure what to say. The priest urged, "Go ahead, please."

"Father, it has been so long since I have been to confession … "

Father Sebastian interrupted, "But you have returned and that is what matters."

Hahn detected a familiar accent in the priest's voice. "Father, I am in trouble and I need your help and your protection."

The priest answered carefully, not sure what to expect. "Yes?"

"The authorities are searching for me, but I am an innocent man."

The words startled the priest. "Are you seeking sanctuary, here at the monastery?"

The idea had not occurred to Hahn, but it made sense. "Yes, Father."

"Why do the authorities want you?"

Hahn was silent for a moment. "I witnessed a man's death." Father Sebastian listened quietly as Hahn spoke. "They suspect me because the criminal fled."

"You cannot explain this to the police? You do not think they will understand?"

"No, Father."

"Do you not have family or friends you can turn to?"

"I know no one here. I have only just arrived for the first time."

Father Sebastian pondered the situation. No one ever had come to his confessional seeking asylum, but his duty was not to judge, only to minister. He said through the dark screen to the confessor, "Have you any sins you wish to confess?"

Hahn thought about the untruths he just told the priest. "Lying and slothfulness," Hahn said. Father Sebastian blessed him, told him to go to the pews and seek God's grace by reciting the Lord's Prayer ten times and the Hail Mary five times.

"When you are done," Father Sebastian whispered, "I will come for you."

Hahn knelt in the pew, clasped his hands together and stared at a large canopied altar. He listened as the confessional door creaked and hurried footsteps echoed through the church. Hahn worried whether he made a wrong decision, but where could he go? He knew no one; his contact was gone. He needed time to regroup; to figure out his next move.

A hand lightly squeezed his shoulder. He jerked his head around to see a young man in a chocolate brown robe, short brown hair and a beard. Concern etched across the man's face. "I'm Father Sebastian, please come with me."

Hahn followed the priest through the church to double dark-leather covered doors that led into a small hall. They walked through the hall, climbed a stairwell; went down another hall then through another door that brought them to an entrance hall. Against a wall, glass cases contained artifacts from the Holy Land in Jerusalem.

A black, iron spiked ball attached by chain to a short club caught Hahn's eye. A placard described the medieval weapon as used during the Crusades.

"This is the friary," Father Sebastian said, softly. "Please wait here until I speak to Father Anthony, my superior."

Father Sebastian ascended a few stairs to a landing, followed a long hallway then up a flight of stairs to the second floor. He found Father Anthony playing cards with three brothers. Father Sebastian leaned over and whispered into his ear.

"Father Anthony, may I have a moment please?"

Father Anthony, a cherub of a man with short, thinning gray hair, gave a playful smile and nodded. Of the thirty-three brothers and seven priests, he was one of only two Americans living in the friary. The others were from Europe and Latin America.

The priest took another card and finished playing his hand. He rose, excusing himself with a sigh, and gestured Father Sebastian to follow him. In the hall he jokingly complained, "The Poles are getting better at rummy. I'm going to have to find another game."

He noticed Father Sebastian's expression. "Is there anything wrong?"

"I don't know, Father. I have a young man who is seeking sanctuary."

Father Anthony raised a concerned eyebrow. "Sanctuary? This is a problem. We have no authority to offer him sanctuary here."

"Not in the friary, I know," Father Sebastian said. "I have had a few moments to think on this and I thought perhaps we could hire him as the gardener."

"The gardener?"

"Yes. Our last man quit months ago. The brothers have done a wonderful job, but Father Fabian planned to hire a gardener in the spring."

"I see." Father Anthony listened as Father Sebastian explained.

"He can live in the garden house. It has a small living quarters, but should be adequate," the young priest said.

"I see," Father Anthony repeated. He liked and trusted Father Sebastian since he arrived at the monastery two years ago, but he was not sure of the soundness of the young priest's plans. "This man is in trouble with the law, I presume?"

Father Sebastian nodded.

"How serious is the trouble?"

"I'm not sure."

"You advised him about going to the authorities?"

"Yes, Father, but he says he needs time to work things out before doing that. For some reason I don't doubt his sincerity."

Father Anthony was understanding – the church had an obligation to provide sanctuary – but skeptical about the motive of the man seeking it. "Okay, Father, do as you believe best. Tell no one else the reason behind his being hired."

"Yes, Father."

"And you will continue to encourage him to go to the authorities?"

"Yes, Father."

"Have one of the brothers bring a meal to the garden house. Now, if there's nothing else, I'm going back to my rummy game."

"Nothing else. Thank you, Father."

Father Sebastian returned to the entrance hall to find the young man sitting on one of the benches, looking nervous and impatient. Startled by the sound of footfalls, Hahn was relieved to see the priest.

Father Sebastian gripped a skeleton key as he led Hahn out of the friary and into the cold night. They followed a long mosaic-tiled portico to the monastery's vast and mostly tree-covered grounds.

A crushed-stone path winding down a steep embankment past little grottoes brought them to a creaky, wrought iron gate. Father Sebastian opened it to an endless garden illuminated by the light posts along the path.

The back of the friary overlooked the garden from atop the slope they had descended, the walls rose like a fortress, where strands of light peeked from behind blackout curtains. Following a serpentine path through the gardens, Father Sebastian oriented Hahn to the monastery routines.

"We rise at five each morning for prayer and meditation – this, of course, is not required of you. Breakfast is followed by chores. The brothers make candles, bread and shoes. We have a mid-day meal and return to our chores. We pray and meditate at five in the afternoon."

They came to a small cabin. Father Sebastian used the skeleton key to open the door. He switched on the light, exposing a modest room with garden tools, a sink and a work table at one end; at the other, a bed, night stand, stuffed chair, footstool and an iron coal stove. A door led to a small bathroom with toilet and shower stall.

Father Sebastian looked at Hahn. "It is not possible for you to stay in the friary, but I can offer sanctuary providing you hire on as the monastery's gardener."

Hahn was confused. "I don't understand."

"You are safe here."

"I want no one to know I'm here."

"No one will know," Father Sebastian assured him. "Only Father Anthony and I know you have requested sanctuary. As far as everyone else is concerned you have been hired on as our new gardener."

"What happened to the last one?"

"He went to a Maryland nursery," Father Sebastian explained. "We don't pay very well, but room and meals are free."

Hahn walked over to the bed, sat down and removed his fedora. He looked at the priest. "Thank you, Father. You are very kind."

Father Sebastian nodded with satisfaction. "Good," he said, in that familiar accent Hahn recognized. The priest went to the coal stove, opened the iron door and peered inside. "This will provide heat. Coal bin is on the side of the house. I'll return with bedding. Are you hungry?"

Hahn nodded.

"I'll have soup and bread brought to you." The priest paused as he started to leave. "I'm sorry, but what is your name?"

Hahn had now begun to relax. He smiled. "Henry. Henry Martin."

Early the next day, following morning prayers and meditation, Father Sebastian entered the dining hall. Jan, a young Czechoslovakian brother he mentored, approached holding a copy of the *Washington Post.*

"Father Sebastian, have you seen the morning paper?" Brother Jan held it up to show a bold headline – SPY NEST RAIDED. "It happened a few blocks from us. Can you imagine? A few blocks."

Father Sebastian took the newspaper and started to scan it when he noticed Father Fabian approaching. He handed the paper back to Brother Jan and stopped the priest.

"Father Fabian, may I have a word, please?"

An Australian, Father Fabian had a knack for organization and handled personnel matters and overseeing the monastery's maintenance. He kept things as he often liked to say, "Tuned like a fine piano."

"Yes, Father," Father Fabian said.

"With Father Anthony's permission, I've hired a gardener," Father Sebastian said.

"Yes, I've been told," Father Fabian said. "He's right for the job, is he?"

Father Sebastian hesitated. "Yes. He doesn't have too much experience, but he appears bright and looks healthy."

"All right, then," Father Fabian said. "I'll stop by a bit later and get him started."

"Thank you, Father."

"By the by, what did you think about that murder down by the shops last night."

The news startled Father Sebastian. "What murder?"

"Why, it was in the paper you were just reading," Father Fabian said. "Some bugger knifed a store clerk in an alley. Makes you wonder if the streets are safe anymore."

Father Sebastian's mind raced as he nodded absently. "Thank you, Father," he said. He went back to Brother Jan, who was sitting down to eat, and asked for the newspaper. He found the story below the fold and read it.

Was there a connection, he thought, *between the murder and the stranger's arrival?*

In the garden house, Hahn foraged for breakfast. He found a half-empty tin with a red, white and blue label that read, American Ace Coffee. The coffee percolated in a tin pot on the iron stove when a young friar appeared with eggs and toast.

Hahn had finished his meal when Father Sebastian arrived with a quick rap on the door before entering. He carried the newspaper in his hands. He solemnly handed it to Hahn. "News that I thought you might want to read."

Hahn felt the priest's unease as he looked at the item Father Sebastian pointed to, but his eyes diverted to the banner headline; his heart pounded. As he read the murder story he tried not to show emotion.

"Is there anything else you want to tell me?" the priest said, his accent even more distinct and to Hahn clearly German.

Hahn pondered for a moment about whether to reveal his identity, but he did not want to take a chance on the priest not being a sympathetic patriot. "No, Father."

"I'll let you think about that because your story doesn't entirely make sense when I read the newspaper," the priest said. "If you need forgiveness, ask for it. Please do not wait until it is too late for you."

They stared at each other in the morning's stillness. Father Sebastian spoke. "Very well then," he said. "Father Fabian should be here soon to get you started on chores." He turned and left the garden house.

Hahn anxiously read the story about the book shop raid. Two saboteurs were in custody at Washington's Naval Yard, FBI Director J. Edgar Hoover announced. The men faced military tribunals and possibly execution.

With no means by which to contact his superior in Germany, Hahn was alone. He wasn't worried about the captured agents divulging him. The man who collected him at the island knew nothing about him and the one at the book shop didn't know when exactly to expect him.

His more immediate worry was Father Sebastian. Though priests were bound by church law to keep confessions confidential – they can't report to the authorities – the good Father was disturbed by the newspaper article and suspected his involvement.

This was problematic, Hahn thought, because he needed to remain at the monastery until the espionage story died down. He needed the sanctuary it provided. He needed to decide how to proceed next.

He would just have to watch Father Sebastian.

Hahn read the murder story again and realized to his surprise he killed the store clerk. It was dark and he was frantic; he never did look at the man's face. It bothered him that despite his training he had panicked.

The paper said the police found $49.95 next to the corpse.

The man died for a five-cent chocolate bar.

Hahn shrugged off the remorse he felt as he reached into his coat pocket. He sought to remove the worn photograph of his parents, but his hand clutched something else, too, and he removed it from his pocket and stared at the Hershey bar.

He shivered at the sudden, disturbing thought: Had he not stopped at the drug store, he would have been at the book store when it was raided.

Weeks passed. The spy story faded from the newspapers, eclipsed by American military advances in Europe and the Pacific. Father Fabian kept Hahn busy with daily chores and tending the monastery's fallow gardens.

Hahn became comfortable with the old Australian who taught him about flowers and shrubs and preparing for spring plantings. Hahn also grew to like the monastery, its Moorish architecture and its placid environment.

As the weeks passed into months, the Lutheran-raised Hahn began attending mass in the mornings before setting off for the gardens. He questioned his purpose for being there and sat in the pews seeking answers, but never receiving them.

Occasionally, though, he heard things that would make him think, as during the Apostle's Creed: *From thence he shall come to judge the quick and the dead.* But he never lingered long in contemplation.

Hard labor demanded by Father Fabian kept him in shape. He felt as healthy and vigorous as he did at the Hitler Youth camp.

Hahn had grown to feel secure behind the monastery walls. He refused to venture beyond them and grew more resistant to the idea when the papers reported one of the saboteurs had been hanged at the Naval Yard. The other was sentenced to life imprisonment.

Spring arrived with news of Germany's collapse, as the Americans, British and Russians closed in on the country.

A heavy feeling of depression weighed on him. He left his breakfast unfinished to sweep the north walkway of the Rosary Portico, just off the monastery's clay-tiled arched entranceway, the same archway he passed through the night he arrived.

As he swept, he recalled General Rhonen's instructions: *"You decide how to undermine the enemy. You won't fail. You are well trained."*

Hahn was lost in thought when startled by a tall man in a suit who stood under the arch, watching him. The man smiled. "Sorry, I was just looking around."

Hahn nodded and the man said, "You don't mind if I look around, do you?" Hahn shook his head and gestured with a nod toward the church. The man stared at him and shrugged. "It's okay. I've seen enough."

He walked to a dark-blue sedan across the street, climbed in and drove off.

A few weeks later, Father Sebastian approached him as he hoed the garden. "A couple of brothers say they keep seeing a tall man coming to the entranceway, but never entering."

Hahn stopped tilling and looked at Father Sebastian. "Yes, I've seen the man, too. He told me he was just looking around."

Father Sebastian nodded, kicking clumps of dirt with his worn leather sandal. He hadn't broached the subject of the sanctuary the church granted to Hahn since the young man's arrival. The tall stranger's appearances renewed his concern.

"I wonder, Henry, whether he has anything to do with why you are here."

"No, Father," Hahn said, curtly. "I don't think he does."

Father Sebastian watched Hahn dig the hoe into the earth, wondering whether to push the issue. "Very well, then," the priest said, and went off to serve afternoon confession, frustrated by Hahn's unwillingness to communicate.

In the garden one April morning, Hahn heard the church bells tolling. As he stood from his plantings, Brother Jan came hurrying toward him, distraught.

"What's wrong?" Hahn asked.

The young Czech friar choked back emotion. "The president is dead."

The news stunned Hahn. He lost his chance to assassinate Roosevelt. He had failed a part of his mission. He inquired, "Was he killed?"

"No," Brother Jan said. "The radio said he died at his home. Father Sebastian wanted me to tell you we are having a prayer vigil later, if you want to attend."

While Roosevelt's death surprised Hahn, Germany's surrender and Hitler's death brought deep grieving. He retired early one evening and cried uncontrollably. The Germany of his youth was forever gone. He was without a homeland.

All that was left were memories of his parents; of Hamburg; and of her. She and Munich haunted his mind again and figured into the sum of his losses.

How, he thought, *was he going to make it?*

He was alone to fight for a cause he was starting to question – more than ever.

For days he remained despondent, though kept up his usual appearance of contentedness around Father Sebastian and the other friars. But things started to change the following Saturday afternoon in the large hall next to the church gift shop.

There Hahn found Father Anthony and Father Sebastian examining the breads and cakes sold to the parishioners and tourists on Sundays. Sales were off. They wondered whether people were tiring of the same selections.

As he listened to the priests discuss new ideas, Hahn realized he could use his chocolate making skills. His knew his father's recipes. He told them he could make chocolates, explaining he once worked in a chocolate factory.

Father Anthony approved. "Can we do it inexpensively? Like everything we sell here, the proceeds go to maintaining the Holy Land shrines in Jerusalem."

"Yes, Father." Hahn nodded, eagerly; the prospect reinvigorated his perspective on life.

This pleased Father Sebastian, but he remained cautious, never sure of Hahn's motives, although he found the young man's daily mass attendance a hopeful sign.

"Very well, then," Father Sebastian said. "Provide me a list of your needs. We'll set you up in the kitchen this week."

When Hahn gave him the list, the priest shook his head in disbelief at what he read: bulk chocolate and large quantities of butter, milk, sugar and caramel.

"Henry, where can I find these five-pound blocks of chocolate you list here?"

Hahn suggested a candy factory, which the priest considered.

"I have a friend at Our Lady of Victory near Hershey, Pennsylvania, where they make the chocolate bars," Father Sebastian said. "I'll talk to him."

Hahn reconfigured the friary kitchen, much to Father Fabian's consternation, getting the brothers to set up long, Formica-topped tables and collecting large pots for melting the chocolate and mixing the candy ingredients.

A few days later, Father Sebastian approached Hahn in the garden and informed him the ingredient list was completed. He immediately went to work in the kitchen; the aromas brought exciting memories of working in his father's chocolate factory in Hamburg.

Hahn's enthusiasm surprised Father Sebastian. Hahn enlisted Brother Jan as his helper and they made the first batch of candy with star-shaped metal baking molds. The production's warm, sweet aromas tempted the friars as they walked to vespers.

After dinner one evening, Brother Jan set out two plates of milk chocolate stars for taste testing. Father Anthony reached the plates first, eagerly popping one of the warm candy stars in his mouth. His eyes brightened as he chewed.

"Delightful!" he declared. The candy qualified for sale after Sunday masses.

Neither a Franciscan nor clergy, Hahn was not allowed to eat with the friars and hear their reviews of his chocolates. Father Anthony stopped him in the garden the following day, raving about his candy.

"I've never tasted chocolate like that. How do you make it so?"

Hahn chuckled. "It's a secret recipe."

"Certainly you can share it with us?"

"I'd rather not, Father," Hahn said.

"It's exceptional," the priest said. He tried slyly to get Hahn to reveal his recipe. "I detect a familiar flavor within the chocolate; a couple of brothers suggested it might be brandy."

Hahn only smiled in reply. One ingredient he hadn't put on the list, but had resourceful Father Fabian procure without telling him its intended use, was black currant-flavored liqueur, using just enough to lace the chocolate.

Later in the day, Hahn sat down to lunch in the garden house. Father Sebastian appeared in the doorway, pleasant and smiling. He informed Hahn he had been anointed chocolate maker for the monastery by Father Anthony.

"He's trying to find out your secret recipe," Father Sebastian said, as Hahn ate his meal of cold sausage, cheese and milk. "He's asking the brothers who buy the groceries what's on the list you gave them."

Hahn chuckled. "It's not on the list. Tell him his search will be futile, but not to worry, I will be happy to make the chocolate."

"Father Anthony knew you would," the priest said, then lowered his voice. "But I'm here on my own to ask that you prepare to leave."

Hahn stopped chewing his food and looked at the priest. "Why?"

"It's time. You've been indispensable to which we're eternally grateful, but I know why you're here – even if Father Anthony has forgotten – and the stranger is no longer appearing at the gate. So, it seems this is the time to leave."

The priest paused. "It would be best for you and us."

Hahn realized Father Sebastian was correct. The monastery had become home after more than six months and he needed to start assimilating. He certainly could not do this from his self-imposed cloister. The problem was where to go.

Father Sebastian was little surprised when Hahn agreed. "Father, I need to find work." The priest nodded. "I would never turn anyone out without assistance. The Hershey factory is hiring. You might want to go there since you have skills they need."

"How far is the factory?"

"Maybe a couple hours by train," Father Sebastian said. "The town is small, but the area is rich in German tradition."

Hahn glanced at the priest and wondered about the last comment. The town was ideal, if he could get a job. Father Sebastian, however, worried him. Had he figured out who he was? A priest was bound never to reveal a confession, but could Hahn take the risk with this priest?

Father Sebastian stood and offered his hand. Hahn grasped it. The priest was still unsure about Hahn's soul and said to him, "Henry, are you certain there is nothing else you want to say before we part?"

Hahn understood what the priest was asking, but nodded. "Yes, Father."

"Will you kneel and pray with me so I'm assured God will protect your soul?"

Hahn fell to his knees as Father Sebastian gently laid a hand on his head. Hahn closed his eyes to the touch as thoughts raced to the fiery deaths of his parents.

He listened to the soft voice, "May God be with you." He opened his eyes moments later to see Father Sebastian closing the garden house door behind him.

Chapter 9

Dover, Delaware

Purple and orange streaked the evening sky as the British Airways 747 touched down at Philadelphia International Airport. It was after midnight before Grey arrived at his apartment in Dover, the eight-hour flight from Berlin tired him.

Marta stirred his thoughts for most of the flight. When he entered the living room to see the telephone message light flashing, he hit the button hard, hoping to hear her voice.

"This is your favorite police chief. Call me as soon as you get in. We got an interesting development in our case. Your guy's a gal."

Exhausted and badly disappointed to bother with the cryptic message, Grey went to bed.

He called Christopher in the morning and the police chief spoke coolly.

"Hey, that skinhead we locked up?"

"Yeah?" Grey said.

"He's a she."

"Excuse me?"

The police chief chortled. "She's a very masculine young lady."

Grey was speechless for a moment. "When did you find this out?"

"Day after you left the country."

"*How* did you find it out?"

"Guard noticed when she used the toilet in her cell. At first he thought she was one of those hermaphrodites – you know a person with both male and female organs – "

"Yeah, I know what you're talking about," Grey interrupted. What'd they do with her?"

"They moved her into the county prison's women's wing."

"Do we have any leads as to who she is?"

"We may," Christopher said. "She was registered at a motel on Savanna Road at the time we arrested her. The owner called us about her unclaimed luggage."

"What'd you find?"

"A duffel bag with clothes, a newspaper, toiletries and a purse with an identification card you should find interesting."

"Why is that?"

"The German government issued it."

Grey could still hear the smugness in Christopher's voice as headed into the bathroom to shower, but the ringing phone stopped him. He put the receiver to his ear to hear Jack Davis, his supervisor. "How was your trip?"

"I may have picked up a lead over there," Grey said.

"Good." Davis' voice sounded strange. "Listen, we need to talk."

"I'm headed to Lewes, but how about this afternoon?"

Davis hesitated. "How about in an hour, Sam? We need to talk."

"Can you tell me what it's about?"

Another hesitation, then, "When you get here."

Grey informed Christopher he would meet him later, and left for Davis' office. He found the lanky lieutenant leaning back in his chair, coffee mug in hand, reading a report. He smiled as Grey entered.

"Sorry for sounding vague, but I didn't want to discuss this over the phone."

"What's wrong?"

"The CIA wants to talk to you."

"The Central Intelligence Agency?"

Davis nodded.

"About what?"

"Don't know other than they seemed to think we're interfering with them. Two agency officials are coming in shortly to talk to you."

"I don't understand," Grey said.

"Neither do I," Davis said. "What were you doing over in Europe?"

Grey told him about meeting Gerhard. Davis shrugged. "Maybe that's it."

Now Grey wondered what Davis might know. His Vietnam stint included several months of covert operations with National Security Agency officers.

"You mean maybe the CIA still has Gerhard on their payroll?"

Davis shook his head. "I wouldn't doubt it." He looked curiously at Grey. "I thought you were going to take a vacation over there?"

"I told you I was going to follow a couple of leads."

"Hell, it sounds like that's all you did. No wonder Woody's losing hope on ever seeing grandchildren."

Grey laughed. "He hasn't given up just yet. What should I tell these guys?"

Davis trusted Grey's instincts. "I'll leave it up to you, Sam, just keep me posted."

When the CIA men arrived, they appeared as Grey expected – business suit, clean-cut, bureaucratic, and professional with an edge. Davis leaned back and listened as they sat around his desk.

Marcus Vance, light-haired and in his fifties, spoke while Robert Toll, a large man with a deep voice, occasionally expounded on a point Vance made.

"I'll get right to it," Vance said, his tone friendly, but terse. "We had a complaint about you from one of our overseas associates."

"What kind of complaint?" Grey asked.

"Well ... " Vance paused for a moment. "You misrepresented yourself in Switzerland."

"Misrepresented myself? To whom?"

"Mr. Gerhard."

"I thought the old Nazi was off your payroll?"

Vance smiled wanly and glanced at Toll.

"He's a longtime associate who has been very helpful to us."

"And to this country," Toll said.

"He has no reason to complain," Grey said. "I identified myself correctly."

Vance nodded reassuringly. "Perhaps it's a misunderstanding, I'm sure."

"You're not in any trouble," Toll said.

Grey looked at Davis who sat quietly watching the exchange before turning to Toll and Vance. "I'm relieved," he said. "Imagine my concern."

Vance ignored the sarcasm. "Can you tell us why you met with him?"

"Not really."

Vance turned to Davis who ordered, "Go ahead, Sam."

Grey shrugged. "A murder case."

"A Delaware murder took you to Switzerland and Berlin? What kind of case is this?"

Grey turned to Davis. His superior's facial expression and slight head shake conveyed he need not offer any more information.

"I'd rather not say until I've finished my investigation. But what about General Gerhard – What role does he play for the United States government?"

Vance spoke curtly. "We don't discuss agency business."

"I see, but you can come in here and demand to speak about this agency's business."

Toll grumbled, "We all have our jobs to do."

"Tell you what," Grey said. "Tell me what Gerhard does or did for the CIA and I'll tell you about my investigation."

"We don't discuss agency business," Vance repeated.

Grey smiled. "Well, I hope I didn't upset the CIA or the general too much."

"Please don't meet with him again," Vance said.

"Why?"

Vance ignored the question and handed Grey his card. "If you have any further questions for him, please contact me."

Vance and Toll stood. Vance extended his hand to Grey. "Corporal, good luck with your investigation."

As the men started for the door, Grey stopped them with a question. "I'm glad we cleared things up. By the way, tell Bill Smith I said 'hi,' will you?"

Vance stopped and looked at the state trooper. "I'm sorry?"

"Bill Smith, you know."

Vance smiled wanly. "I can't help you on that one, corporal. Have a good day."

When they were gone, Davis said to Grey, "Who the hell is Bill Smith?"

"I'm not sure; some expatriate I met on the train to Berlin."

"What about him?"

"A hunch," Grey said. "I was trying to figure out how they knew I was in Berlin."

"Maybe the old general told 'em."

"I don't know how he would have known," Grey said. "I never told him."

Davis looked concerned as he shook his head and leaned back. "How did this case get to old Nazis and the CIA?"

Grey shrugged. "There's always a Nazi hanging around."

"You're worrying me on this one, Sam."

Grey chuckled. "I'll be fine, stop worrying."

Davis didn't like the cocky response. Intrigues troubled him; something his experience in Vietnam had taught him too well. He snapped. "Just watch your hunches, okay?"

On the drive down Route 1 to Lewes, Grey thought about the latest development in the case. It bothered him. It wasn't as much a development as a wrinkle. He doubted the woman in the county jail killed Hoest, yet there had to be some connection.

At the station, Christopher greeted him with sarcasm about his hasty trip to Germany.

"You should have called," the police chief said. "I could have joined you."

Grey ignored the teasing. "Can I see the purse?"

Christopher stopped laughing, slid open a desk drawer and removed a worn, black leather purse. Grey examined it, finding three-hundred dollars in traveler's cheques, ten German marks, matches, a half-empty pack of Marlboro cigarettes, a bank card and the identification card.

The card held her picture. He examined the name: Erica Artz. She was listed as a resident of Munich, age: thirty-five.

Grey looked at Christopher. "Is she still not talking?"

"Hasn't said a word, not even to the public defender, who's trying to get her released."

"That's not going to happen."

"And the public defender's getting nasty, called the prosecutor a fascist the other day."

"Really?" Grey said, suppressing a smile.

"Told the local paper the way he was treating the skinhead smacked of Nazi justice."

"Does Miss Artz know we know her identity?"

"Yeah, but she's not going to talk," Christopher said.

"Well, I'm going to talk to her anyway."

A matron escorted Erica Artz into a windowless room with peach-colored, concrete-block walls and a waxy, green-tiled floor and sat her at a metal table before leaving to stand outside the door. Grey looked at Artz.

"Erica, what brought you here from Germany?"

She didn't respond. He tried his limited German. *"Sie wohnen in Munich, nicht wahr?"*

Artz stared at the scratched table top.

Grey watched her sit mute and motionless.

"You know, you're going to serve a long prison sentence, possibly face execution, for a murder you and I know you didn't commit. Did you know they hang people in this state?"

Artz sat staring. Grey finally stood. "Okay. I'll be back, but your time's running out."

At the courthouse, Grey visited the county prosecutor, Dave Cooksey, a small, doughy man who spoke with a southern-like drawl and liked crew cuts and cowboy boots. He listened patiently to Grey's report on what he learned in Germany.

"Well, Sam, that's fine and good, but it boils down to just your hunch. I have a suspect sit'n in jail await'n trial. That's all I'm worr'n about now."

"Come on, her worst offense is breaking and entering. How can you say she's a suspect?"

Cooksey held up a finger. "The evidence – "

"Is little and circumstantial. Hell, Dave, her hands didn't show a trace of powder burns. I wonder if she's ever fired a gun."

The prosecutor smiled knowingly. "This investigation is still ongoing so you have some time – not much, mind you, but some. If you find evidence of another suspect then I'm ready to listen, but I have to tell you, I think it's unlikely."

Grey encountered similar resistance that afternoon at the University of Delaware campus, when he sought a deadline extension on submission of his thesis proposal. He wanted to write on a different topic, which Jennings greeted skeptically.

"I don't think you can prove it."

"But that's the historian's challenge, isn't it?" Grey said. "I think I can."

"Then Mr. Grey, I want to see primary sources, especially if you are going to argue some in command in the German navy knew unequivocally the Allies had broken their code."

"I didn't say command, I said 'ranking officers.'"

"Nothing less than primary sources on your central point; quite honestly, I don't think it's possible. By late forty-four the Atlantic and Mediterranean were slaughtering pens for the Germans."

Grey nodded and picked up his book bag.

"Show me a ship, Mr. Grey, even the Walter boat, which I also doubt was used."

"Why?"

"The British built Walter boats from captured plans after the war and the damn things blew up on them," Jennings said. "Show me a U-boat that went undetected by Enigma's code breakers, if you want me to recommend your thesis proposal to the committee."

Under the towering, four-mile long twin bridges linking Maryland's east and west shores, the Chesapeake Bay sparkled on a brilliant, windswept morning. As Grey sped over the span, he mulled over the conversation he had the day before with the prosecutor.

Cooksey and Christopher sounded more interested in a conviction, regardless of who was guilty. He worried his investigation would be halted, if the prosecutor sought to indict Erica.

When Grey left Cooksey, he returned to headquarters and called Interpol with a request to check Erica's home. Munich Inspector Helga Schmidt contacted him later and promised she would have information for him within a few days.

Grey reached the bridge's crest, high above the waters. From there he had a panoramic view of the large cargo ships steaming toward Baltimore. He was headed west to Washington, D.C., where he wanted to do archival research to find an answer to a question pounding in his head: What happened in 1945 to make the spy disappear for 55 years?

Academics taught him research should start with newspapers – *the first drafts of history.*

Upon arriving in the city he went to the Library of Congress and asked for Washington-based newspapers dating from January through March of 1945. A librarian directed him down a long hallway to a large reading room, where Grey sat before a microfiche, reading headlines.

He started with the *Washington Star.* The front page for the first week in January carried war headlines, but nothing unusual at home. But in the second week, Grey found a headline that made him catch his breath – GERMAN SABOTEURS ARRESTED IN CITY. He read the one column story with its scant details. He photocopied the page.

He went through more front pages, scanned the inside pages, but the newspaper had only a couple of follow-ups. The story seemed to die.

At another file cabinet Grey removed a film roll of *Washington Post* editions for the first weeks in January of that year. He threaded the microfiche. The January 11, 1945 edition had the headline, SPY NEST RAIDED.

The story also lacked detail about the spies. An FBI agent named Steve Brooks is quoted identifying them as Germans, but no other personal information such as name and age. The story faded in later editions. Odd,

Grey thought. Why didn't the papers have an interest in spies toiling in the seat of the national government? That's a story they would pursue relentlessly.

He spent several hours culling months of front pages before spotting a brief mention on the lower left-hand corner of a *Post* front page reporting on one spy's execution and the other's life sentence. Grey scanned more pages until a clerk announced the library was closing.

Grey slid behind the wheel of his car with copies of the front pages and drove to a cheap motel on New York Avenue. He called Jack Davis to report his progress and told him he would visit the FBI in the morning to check their archives.

"You still feel pretty good about this hunch of yours?" Davis asked.

"I can pick up this guy's trail."

Davis paused as he considered how long he could spare Grey. "Okay, you got two days."

Grey entered the concrete and glass building along Pennsylvania Avenue that was named for J. Edgar Hoover, the agency's first director. A security officer directed him to the archive but a researcher could find little about the spy case.

"The papers say the FBI investigated," he insisted. "Why wouldn't you have records?"

The researcher shrugged. "We have no records."

"How then would I go about finding this agent who is quoted in the article?"

"If he's still alive, personnel might have something on him."

The researcher directed Grey to the office. A clerk there searched records for ten minutes before informing him: "Mr. Brooks' employment with the bureau terminated in June of 1945."

"Any address or phone number on him?"

"No sir."

Outside, he stood staring down Pennsylvania Avenue at the Capitol's gleaming white dome. He was worried that he had reached a dead end. As he diverted his gaze to the crowds hurrying along the sidewalk, he saw a woman speaking into a cell phone.

What the hell, Grey thought. *I'll check the phone book.*

He crossed the street to the Old Post Office, a neo-Gothic gray stone structure converted to restaurants and shops. At a bistro, he asked the hostess for a phone book. She directed him to the telephone booth by the bar. The morning was late. The wait staff were quietly preparing for the lunch crowd.

Grey pulled the phone book from a shelf underneath the phone. Under Brooks, he found seven listings for "Steve," one "Steven," two "Stephen," and four with initial "S." He decided to first call those listed as "Steve" and "S," then "Steven" and "Stephen."

An answering machine picked up on the first three calls he made. Grey decided to return to his motel and make the remaining calls there. He ripped out the page and took it with him.

As he walked to the parking garage he sensed someone shadowing him. He stopped at a shop window and tried to detect anyone out the corner of his eye – nothing.

At the hotel room, amid empty boxes of Chinese take-out and a can of iced tea, Grey sat dialing the phone and asking, when someone answered, whether Steve Brooks had once worked for the FBI. It was a frustrating task. Two of them had died the previous year; one was a college student; one was a smart-ass kid; and for three others their wives answered.

As it began to seem futile he dialed an "S" listing that brought a raspy sounding voice.

"Mr. Steven Brooks?"

"No, this is Saul."

Grey apologized and started to hang up when the voice on the other end said, "Well, hold on now; are you're looking for my brother? His number's unlisted. Identify yourself and maybe I could help you."

Grey tried to calmly explain himself. "This man I'm looking for worked for the FBI back in the forties, helped arrest some German spies."

"You called the right place," Saul said.

With the correct number, Grey dialed, his hands shaking in anticipation. The phone rang three times before a tired, raspy sounding voice answered.

"Mr. Brooks?"

"Yeah, who's calling?"

Grey introduced himself and mentioned Saul. A pause followed on the other end of the line. "Delaware?" The voice groused. "What in the hell you want with me?"

"As an FBI agent, didn't you arrest two German spies in 1945?"

A long silence followed. "Why do you want to know?"

"I'd like to talk to you about a case I'm working on."

"What's it about?"

"I think I'm looking for a spy who has been living here since that year."

Grey listened to a long silence and was about to say something when the man, sounding saddened, recited his address and said, "I'll be here."

Steve Brooks lived in a three-story federal-style row house half a block behind the U.S. Supreme Court on A Street. Grey hurried up the black, wrought-iron stairs and knocked on the front door. An elderly man – tall and lean, with short, scraggly white hair – invited him inside.

In a small, well-furnished, high-ceilinged living room, Steve Brooks sank into a leather wing-back chair by the fireplace and offered Grey a sofa seat.

"There were three," Brooks said, as Grey seated himself.

"I'm sorry?"

"Three spies, not two, and I can prove it," Brooks said. "Granted, it's all circumstantial, but it's been a hunch that has stuck with me all these years."

Grey smiled. "A hunch?"

"I'm sure my brother made light of my hunches, but as an investigator you know what I mean, don't you?"

"Oh yeah, I do." He handed the old agent copies of the newspaper pages, which Brooks studied carefully with a pair of reading glasses he removed from his shirt pocket.

"Can you tell me why there is no record of this case at the FBI?"

"You might find a record of this in the military archives," Brooks said. "But as far as the FBI is concerned, this never happened."

"I don't understand."

"Cover-up."

"But it's there on the front page of major newspapers."

Brooks nodded and repeated himself. "Cover-up."

"What are you saying?"

"J. Edgar said it never happened and so it never happened."

Grey expressed confusion. Brooks peered over his glasses and said, "As you and I know, of course, it did happen."

"Why did Hoover expunge the record?"

"Oh, plenty of reasons – ego, bureaucratic face-saving – but primarily because the third spy got away."

"How do you know a third spy got away?"

Brooks handed him one of the front pages and his finger tapped at a story on the lower, left-hand corner. "A store clerk was murdered less than three blocks from the book shop about the same time of the raid. Police never found a suspect, called it robbery. I never believed it."

"Why not?"

"The clerk was killed in an alley, two blocks from his store. According to the other clerk on duty that evening, he ran after a customer who had left without getting his change. There was forty-nine dollars and ninety-five cents near the clerk's body. Tell me, if this was a robbery, why would they leave all that money?"

Grey listened as Brooks said, "Not in 1945, not in 2000, would a robber leave money – not even forty-nine dollars and ninety-five cents. That's one reason why I think the missing spy killed the clerk."

"That's a big hunch."

"The spies Germany sent during the war came with cash in large denominations because their operations were expensive. That clerk had change from a fifty dollar bill. The poor bastard died over a nickel."

"A nickel? What did a nickel buy back then?"

"Chewing gum, soda, candy, that sort of thing, but there's more on the murder." Brooks leaned forward. "The weapon was a switchblade. It was used, from my training and experience, professionally."

"How?"

"The clerk's throat was slit, cleanly."

"And a robber, who may or may not have intended to kill, may have left multiple stab wounds," Grey said.

"Correct," Brooks said, calming down and settling back in his chair. "You know, Mr. Grey, what most frustrated me about this case, even more than the bureau's refusal to listen to me, was I had the guy, I know I did."

"The third spy?"

Brooks nodded. "I'm a native of Washington, lived here all my life; went to law school at Georgetown. Know lots of people around town, which is how I learned two months after our raid on the book shop about the gardener the monastery hired around the same time as the raid."

"What monastery?"

"You don't know the city, do you?"

Grey shook his head. Brooks described the monastery's location and history and his long-held suspicion that the spy had taken refuge there.

"How are you so sure it was him?"

Brooks paused to choose his words carefully.

"When we interrogated the first German spy, the guy who owned the book shop, he told us after some rather harsh persuasion that he was waiting for an agent. He didn't know his name or even his mission, only that he was expected."

"How could you be sure he was telling the truth?"

"Men are honest when a hot radiator is toasting their testicles," Brooks said, and then his face darkened, an expression that suggested regret. He paused. "Anyway, I learn from one of the brothers at the monastery that the new gardener never leaves; keeps to himself. So I start making occasional visits, hoping to meet the guy."

"Did you?"

"Once. He was sweeping a portico one morning and I think I startled him because he had this wide-eyed look when he saw me. I apologized, but he didn't reply, just looked at me."

"Why didn't you talk to the gardener's superiors about him?"

"I tried, but when someone seeks sanctuary in the Catholic Church they are as protected as if they were in an embassy. The priests wouldn't even tell me his name, though a brother told me his first name was Henry."

"What happened to him?"

"I lost him, which is one reason I quit the bureau. I was assigned another case and by the time I visited the monastery again the gardener was gone. A brother said he just disappeared one night and told no one where he was going."

"Didn't other agents help?"

"The bureau refused to believe a third spy was out there." Brooks became angry. "They didn't want to consider my hunch. The time I put into trying to find the guy was my own."

"You were one of the lead agents investigating, is that correct?"

Brooks nodded.

"Why wouldn't your superiors back you up?"

"You have to understand what was going on. War in Europe was winding down. People sensed victory after some hard years and the last thing J. Edgar wanted was the publicity about spies on the loose. Hell, when they executed the shopkeeper the press barely noticed."

"Wasn't that a big chance for Hoover to take?"

"I thought so, but I guess in his mind Germany's defeat rendered harmless the spies who were left running around the country."

"Spies? You mean there are more?"

"Absolutely!" Brooks became defensive. "Fifth columnists. In fact, the second spy, the one who got life, he was a member of the German-American Bund. I don't believe a spy could have made it into this country without help from American sympathizers."

"This second spy, what happened to him? Is he still living?"

"His name was Folker, no, Volker? That's it, Volker," Brooks recalled. "He died in the penitentiary in Pennsylvania sometime in the '70s."

"Did he know anything about the third spy?"

Brooks shook his head. "He never let on, if he did. He had brought the third spy in from somewhere on the Chesapeake. That's what the book dealer confessed. Volker always denied it, and, like I said, the bureau didn't want to believe there was a third spy."

"Why?"

"The Navy told them it was not possible for a U-boat to cross the Atlantic by that stage in the war without them knowing about it. That convinced the bureau."

"But not you," Grey said.

"No," Brooks said, bristling. "The Navy did a terrific job, but it wasn't perfect."

Grey sat silently, considering Brooks' information when he remembered the question that began nagging him while reading the news clippings.

"What espionage activities were these spies engaged in and how did you catch them? The newspapers don't mention any specific charges."

Brooks' mouth opened slightly as surprise enveloped his expression. "Why, contact with the enemy." He started to stutter. "They had made contact and provided information the military tribunal had determined jeopardized the security of the country."

"How did you catch them?"

Brooks looked confused. He stammered. "The, uh, Turkish embassy tipped us," he said. "One of their people was using the diplomatic pouch to get the information to Germany through Switzerland."

Brooks interrupted himself and rose from his chair. "I've not been a good host. You're the first person in years to listen and take me seriously about this. How about tea – English Breakfast or Earl Grey?"

"Earl Grey, please," Grey said, distracted by a sense Brooks was hiding something or at the least trying to avoid saying something.

"Good!" Brooks' angled frame headed into the dining room. "Come into the kitchen and tell me how your case may be connected with mine."

Grey followed him into a bright kitchen with a breakfast nook overlooking a small yard and narrow alley. Brooks invited him to sit as they waited for the water to boil. Grey explained his case to the old agent, who listened intently, interrupting once to ask a question:

"Did you find any fingerprints?"

"On shell casings and an interior door knob to the front door, but the prints on the casings don't match those on the door knob," Grey said.

He described his case until the teapot whistled. Brooks rose. "Pour your water while I go upstairs. I want to get something that may help your investigation."

Grey poured steaming water over the teabags Brooks dropped in cups of fine china. He was steeping his when the man returned and set a large, worn manila envelope on the table and told Grey to open it.

Inside was a plastic bag containing a faded white card – a fingerprint file – with the date, January 1945, written on the bottom.

"Those are latent prints taken from the handle of the knife used to kill the clerk," Brooks said. "You may have this under one condition."

Grey looked at Brooks. "You must let me know the outcome of your case. I've wondered about that spy for fifty-five years. I'm tired of wondering."

"Certainly, but something's troubling me."

The old agent nodded; his expression dour.

"What are you *not* telling me about those two spies?"

Brooks sat in stony silence. He knew how interrogations worked. The young man sipping tea had the experience to know when someone was not truthful. Maybe, the old agent thought, he wanted the corporal to ask the question he longed to answer for many years.

"The bookshop owner wasn't executed," Brooks said, his body shaking. "He had a heart attack during an interrogation that got out of hand."

They dragged Emil Baum out of his shop that evening and flew him to rural Maryland, where the FBI maintained a farmhouse for training and interrogation. Baum was taken into a room with boarded up windows. He was stripped naked and sat in a chair.

The room was bare except for a small writing table, a bare-bulb ceiling light and an old, hissing steam radiator. Brooks could see Baum was frightened, but the book dealer managed to keep his answers short, non-committal, to avoid betraying himself or the Bund.

Brooks was just an observer, there to collect whatever intelligence he could from Baum as Reese and Forbes, the two agents expert in interrogation, began their work. Brooks did not know much about the procedures the agents applied. He didn't understand the need to strip the man naked.

"Make the subject feel as vulnerable as possible," Reese told him during a break. "We need as much information from him as fast as we can to capture whoever else is involved."

Brooks nodded. He had many successful interviews without stripping suspects naked, but this was wartime and he understood it required different tactics, no matter how unorthodox.

After two hours under the light, Baum disclosed Volker's name and role, which prompted Brooks to alert the bureau to immediately find the factory worker. It wasn't difficult. Agents from Baltimore went to his home that night and arrested him as he and his wife prepared for bed.

Volker went without a fight. He had kept his indifferent, cool demeanor, which he would maintain throughout the military tribunal and his life in prison. His wife looked questioningly at him just before the agents took him. "I'm goin' fishin'," he said, without affectation.

Baum relented after several more hours of a harsh interrogation that alternately involved shouting, beating and refusing water to quench his parched mouth. He revealed the third spy, but he was unable to say anymore because he did not know anymore.

The two agents didn't believe him and subjected him to more punishing treatment. It was near dawn, when the phone rang. Forbes went to answer it and returned a few minutes later.

"The Director wants us to get everything we can out of him," he told Reese.

Reese, a linebacker for Ohio State in his college days, was a big, burly man; strong as a horse. Forbes had a similar build. The men continued their interrogation; Forbes would speak softly to Baum while Reese shouted and struck the book dealer with his fists.

Hours of questioning left them with no information about the third spy. Reese's voice was hoarse; he was sweaty and tired. They had been at it for nearly 20 hours. Forbes started asking questions in his soft voice again when Reese suddenly melted down in frustration. He pulled the book dealer off the chair with violent force.

"Get up, Emil!"

The FBI agent lifted the naked Baum and set him on the steaming, hissing radiator. The book dealer shrieked and howled as Reese held him there for a few seconds before pulling him off and forcing him to stand. The exhausted Baum couldn't. His legs collapsed as searing pain inflamed his groin, testicles, upper back of his legs and the low part of his buttocks.

Forbes looked at his partner, surprised, but not shocked, by his action.

"Where is this spy?" Reese barked.

Baum crumpled at the agent's feet, his cheek against the cold floor. Whimpering, he kept repeating, "I don't know," in German. For Baum, who FBI agents had to carry out of his shop kicking and arguing, his ordeal began as a nightmare – men in dark suits, grim faces; throwing him into a car, then a plane; dragging him into a house; talking at him; yelling at him; striking him; demanding information. Now it was horrifying.

Forbes was now standing over him, speaking softly. "Emil, tell us where the spy is and we'll take care of your pain."

Now delirious, Baum kept repeating, "Ich weiß nicht, bitte. Ich weiß nicht."

"Help me pick him up," Reese said to Forbes. As they hauled Baum on his feet the book dealer's body suddenly convulsed. Pain pounded in his chest. His eyes bulged as he gasped for air. His lips turned blue. He was in the throes of a heart attack.

The agents, not sure what was wrong, sat him in the chair, which he promptly fell off and writhed on the floor before his body stiffened and finally succumbed.

Reese and Forbes called in Brooks and a doctor from the nearby town of La Plata who pronounced Baum dead.

The agents argued over whether a third spy even existed; Reese and Forbes doubted it or Baum would have confessed. Brooks believed there was, why else would he have mentioned him? The book dealer had been truthful. He didn't know anything other than he was expecting him.

Brooks finished his story and stared forlornly at the floor.

"Why was it reported he was executed?" Grey asked.

"Cover-up," Brooks said, quietly. "The man was never going to be executed. They had evidence for a life sentence, not a death sentence."

"Have you thought about at least correcting the record?"

"Sure, sure I have," Brooks said, his tone sad. "But at this point why bother? It was war and amid all the horrors, particularly in that war, it was just a simple tragedy. For whom does it benefit to 'correct' the record?"

Back at his hotel in the evening Grey called Davis and briefed him. Davis listened and gave Grey a name – Tom Morgan. "He's an investigator in the Justice Department's Office of Special Cases. They hunt old Nazis living over here."

"What's that got to do with my case?"

"Call him," Davis replied, rattling off a number. "He's waiting to hear from you."

"Why, Jack? I don't understand."

"This Gerhard you met in Switzerland worries me with his ties to the CIA. Morgan may have some interesting information for you."

"How do you know Morgan?"

"Vietnam."

Grey arranged to meet Morgan the following morning in his Pennsylvania Avenue office, just across the street from the FBI building. Morgan was a short, stocky man with gray hair and a serious, but friendly demeanor.

"Is there anyone Jack Davis doesn't know?" Grey slid into a worn leather arm chair in Morgan's office, a small room cluttered with filing cabinets, teetering piles of files, document filled boxes, old cassette tapes and CDs.

"Jack's a good man," Morgan said, standing at his desk and tapping a pen on the blotter. "Tried for years to get him to Washington, but says Delaware's his home."

"He says you have some information for me?" Grey said.

Morgan nodded and reached for a thick accordion file. He ran his fingers rapidly through it before pulling out an old black-and-white photograph and handing it to Grey. In the photo was a guillotine set in a medieval-looking courtyard and a young man in a black SS officer's uniform, smiling. Grey recognized him. It was Gerhard.

"That the man you met in Switzerland?" Morgan asked.

Grey nodded as he stared at the picture.

"That's at SS headquarters in Munich about 1944. Gerhard had seven men and women executed that way."

"Jews?"

Morgan shook his head. "German students whose only crime was staging protests against Hitler and the war – as you can see, Gerhard enjoyed his work."

"Apparently he was good at it. The CIA has him on payroll."

Morgan stood and handed Grey the accordion file. "That's why Jack wanted us to talk. My office investigates war criminals who manage to reach this country and assume a new life, but we cast wide nets and in the process come up with information about other Nazis."

Morgan paused. "The CIA still watches after Gerhard, but they officially dropped him after the Berlin Wall fell in '89, leaving him to his own devices."

"Which means?"

"Which means he's dangerous," Morgan said, a grim tone creeping into his voice. "I don't like to tell fellow law enforcement officers how to do their jobs, but the way you went about approaching Gerhard could have got you killed."

Grey let out a nervous laugh. "Is this why Jack sent me here, to get lectured?"

"Actually, no, that was for free," Morgan said. "Jack wanted me to show you the file so you could make your own conclusions."

Grey was perplexed. "About what?"

"About continuing to pursue a case he thinks is becoming too dangerous."

Grey started laughing. "He's starting to sound like my mother."

"Corporal, if our government had not decided Gerhard was useful to them after the war they would have prosecuted him, and likely executed him, as a war criminal in Nuremberg. He has spent a life in murder, espionage, assassinations – "

"He's ninety and likes to eat borscht in the afternoon, how dangerous can he be?"

Morgan spoke firmly. "The beheadings made him infamous in Munich, but there's been no interest in trying him for the atrocity."

"What are you telling me? He's well connected?"

"Neither the U.S. nor the Germans nor the Swiss seem interested. Tell you anything?"

Morgan took a sheet of paper off his desk and handed it to Grey. It was a legal document with twelve names listed on the bottom.

"Last year families of those students petitioned the U.S. to either intercede on their behalf or turn him over to the Germans for prosecution, but it's never going to happen."

"Why?"

"Two reasons. One: the CIA considers him too valuable an asset. Two: so much time has passed there are no documents or witnesses to his crime, at least none that have been found."

As Grey studied the petition, a name grabbed his attention.

"What's wrong?" Morgan asked, noticing Grey's change of expression.

Grey shook his head and held up the paper. "Any chance I can get a copy of this?"

"Sure," Morgan said. "You can have copies of anything in the file."

Grey was not interested in Gerhard's sordid past. "Anything you can tell me about what he's like today?"

"Ruthless opportunist," Morgan said, returning to his chair. "He double-dealt during the Serbian ethnic-cleansing – first with Milosevic; then the U.S. – and some human rights group in Europe contends he's using African children for slave labor and soldiering."

Grey's thoughts turned to Marta as he joked, "Didn't anyone love this guy as a kid?"

Morgan looked at him seriously. "You're kidding, right?"

"Well, it does make you wonder."

"He came from a prominent Berlin family, that's all I know. Want to hear more?"

"Sure."

"He mediates arms deals with terrorists fighting the Israelis; he funds South American mercenaries – for what we are uncertain – he's been military consultant for some of the worst African despots; and he has his own soldier of fortune army. There's even more."

"I've heard enough."

Morgan leaned back in his chair and nodded. "The government hired Gerhard because he supposedly ran an effective counter-insurgency just before the war ended, but – "

"Supposedly? I thought his "werewolves" reigned terror down."

"Yeah, I'm sure Gerhard wants everyone to believe that, and initially he convinced U.S. forces of it when he surrendered to them in 1945, but historical records show there were only a few small pockets of insurgents around Germany – nothing more."

"Why then didn't the U.S. try him for war crimes?"

"Because he was an expert in intelligence, knew were all the bodies – alive and dead – were in Eastern Europe. And he was effective in counter-espionage in Europe during the Cold War, but he's really been more problems than he's worth."

Morgan shook his head. "They should've hung the son-of-a-bitch at Nuremberg."

Grey had returned to headquarters in Dover, disturbed by what he learned from his visit with Morgan. He had more than he wanted to think about, but at the moment he focused on the latent fingerprints Brooks gave him.

Before he could get started, a phone call from Herman Franks, nephew of Oskar Franks, interrupted him.

"I wanted to check on the progress of your case, for my uncle, of course."

"Not much I can really tell you right now," Grey said. "How is your uncle?"

"He's fine, just concerned about being under suspicion."

"He's not and never has been."

Grey listened to a long pause before Franks said, "Well, you're questioning him – "

"Was routine, as I told him – nothing more, I assure you."

Franks let out an awkward laugh. "That's what I told him."

Something in Franks' tone intrigued Grey enough to keep the conversation going. He remembered Oskar Franks introducing his nephew as a history professor.

"Where do you teach, Herman?"

"At a little liberal arts school about an hour north of Cape May."

"What's the name?"

"Atlantic College, why?"

"Just curious; I'm studying for my doctorate in history."

"It's a noble field, though you'll never become rich."

Grey finished the conversation, curious as to whether another motive existed for the call.

In the forensic lab, Grey had Brooks' prints compared with prints from the Luger's shell casings and the door knob to Hoest's house.

A technician peered into a microscope and found each had an arch in the fingers' pattern of ridges; the pattern was common among fingerprints. The lab tech said, "These old prints are a bit fuzzy, but they appear very roughly to match those on the shell casings."

"No match on the door knob?"

The technician shook his head. "Ridge pattern's entirely different."

"How certain are you about the match?" Grey asked.

The technician sighed and shrugged. "I'd say maybe fifty percent." He handed back the old fingerprint file. "By the way, how old is this print?"

"About fifty-five years."

The technician whistled. "Hell, don't think I've heard of anyone identifying prints so old, at least I've never done it."

"Fifty percent is the best you can do, though, huh?"

"Yeah, sorry; if the print was clearer I could be more certain."

Grey went to call Brooks to let him know. Although the lab tech's lack of absolute certainty bothered him, the evidence should keep the prosecutor at bay until he completed investigating the case.

Moreover, Grey believed he knew where to pick up the trail – at the monastery. He felt confident, but as he walked to his office questions he had kept in the back of his mind started nagging him again.

What, he asked himself, has this spy been doing all this time? Why would he kill the U-boat captain? Something else occurred to him: the prints on the door knob didn't match anyone involved in the case. Whose were they?

Chapter 10

Hershey, Pennsylvania
July, 1945

Men in starched-white uniforms and white caps listened to the din of clanking machinery while watching iron vats arrayed across an immense factory floor. Piston-like arms pumped hard in each vat, creating waves out of the thick, warm liquid chocolate.

Hahn wore his uniform and cap as he followed a foreman onto the hot, noisy floor of the Longitude Room, where his job was to dump heavy buckets of liquid chocolate into the bathtub-shaped containers that were set on wheels for rolling around the factory.

After a few weeks on the job, Hahn had impressed the foreman with his quiet, determined work ethic; punching the clock on time, always finishing the required eight hours, never arguing, never questioning his superiors.

"You're a good soldier, Martin," Mike, the old foreman, said with a hard slap on the back. "You're not bad for a greenie."

"Greenie?"

The lanky foreman with his slight paunch and wiry smile winked at him and said, "That's what we call a new man on the floor."

Warm smells of roasting cocoa beans permeated the factory. Hahn felt comfortable, and at home. The region's landscape reminded him of Germany, as did the customs and foods of the Pennsylvania Dutch, a confusing term until he learned the 19th century misnomer came from the locals asking German immigrants their origin and hearing in thick accents: "*Deutschland*."

After slipping a few times at the monastery, Hahn felt comfortable enough to use his real name. The authorities weren't searching for him, he had no family, and who would learn his true identity in a German-speaking region filled with people with German names?

As he arrived in Hershey by train, he could see from his window what looked like a castle atop a forested hill. It reminded him of Heidelberg as he inquired about the imposing green-tiled, tan brick building overlooking the town. "Hotel Hershey," the conductor said.

He rented a three-room flat in neighboring Hummelstown, catching the streetcar to work or the bus to Harrisburg, ten miles away. War in Europe was over. Germany defeated. America's Roosevelt dead. Hahn wondered if his mission had ended. Was there an objective anymore?

Such thoughts occupied him on the train. Rohnen warned his mission could last a lifetime – *assimilate into society; wait for the moment.* What did it matter now? Hitler and the Reich were gone. Rhonen and his ideas, far away in time and space, diminished in Hahn's estimation, but the Nazis' cultural bond tugged, though much weakly, on Hahn's absolute fealty.

Weeks passed. Hahn's worries about his mission were overcome by his focus on being an American, which his mother, with her Chicago upbringing, made easy. She had taught him about the United States – how people here thought, talked, looked at things, which often was foreign to the German perspective.

Shortly after starting at the chocolate factory his superior told him he needed his Social Security number. "Gov'ment requires it," Mike said. Hahn inquired about getting one and was told he needed a copy of his birth certificate.

"How do I get a copy?" he asked the secretary in the personnel office.

"At the state Health Department, in Harrisburg," she said.

"Why there?"

"Every birth in Pennsylvania is filed with the state."

"But I was born in Chicago."

"Then that's where you go."

Hahn switched two weekday shifts for weekends then caught the train to Illinois, where a copy of his birth certificate waited at the Health Department's Chicago office. On the trip out, he realized America's immensity and the power its government had, giving every one of its citizens a number by which to identify them. He loved this country.

On the return train, passing endless farm fields and huge humming cities, Hahn began to seriously doubt Germany ever had a chance at defeating this country.

He would look at Hoest's Luger and wonder: should he return to Washington to wait for President Truman? The man went for strolls off the White House grounds nearly every morning, an easy assassination target.

He thought it through. He would approach the president, and when Truman came close enough, he would fire the weapon and shout: *"Heil Hitler – ein volk, ein land, ein fuhrer!"* The idea depressed him. He dismissed it. He wanted to live.

When America dropped two atomic bombs on Japan in late summer, showing the world the awesome power it now possessed, Hahn decided to end his pointless mission. Newsreels of one bomb's devastating effects shocked him as he sat in a fan-cooled Harrisburg theater.

Watching scenes of flattened, rubble-strewn Hiroshima, Hahn trembled as he realized the bomb's enormity. It had taken a thousand allied bombers and thousands of bombs to do the same destruction to Hamburg.

He returned to his flat late that humid September afternoon and decided to concentrate on settling down, on becoming an American. Work at the chocolate factory paid well, but he wanted more. He wanted, like his father, to start his own chocolate candy company.

He marked his mission's end by buying a gallon of Red Arrow grease at the local filling station. He sat at his kitchen table, disassembling the gun and packing it and the bullets into the grease. He sealed the can air-tight and stored it in his closet, thinking he may need it one day.

Hahn had most of the twenty-five thousand dollars given him for the mission that he kept inside his mattress. He decided to take a year putting small amounts every few weeks into a bank account. He didn't want attention drawn to large deposits.

He would use the account as collateral for a loan to start a company. He remembered his father's chocolate candy recipes and started making batches of candies in his apartment kitchen, packaging them in small boxes he sold at local fairs, carnivals and church bazaars, offering free samples. His father taught him the importance business plans play in securing capital. He had to show the bank his product was marketable.

"What's the name of your candy?"

Hahn was seated at a table with his samples, watching crowds wander Hummelstown's autumn fair. He turned to the sweet-sounding voice. She was blond, with almond-shaped blue-eyes and pouting lips painted red. He stared, savoring her beauty. She repeated her question.

"What's the name of your candy?"

"*Es tut mir leid, fraeulein* ..." He caught himself and in English, "I'm sorry miss, what?"

She affected a tone of frustration. "What's the name of your candy?"

Hahn judged her about his age. He glanced at the curving figure underneath her sweater and smiled. Between his job at the factory and his business venture, he had no time to socialize and this young woman made him yearn.

He hadn't considered a name, but maybe it was time. "Martin's. Martin's Chocolates."

She smiled as she delicately nibbled a sample. "Oh my, I like that. Where's your store?"

Hahn raised his nearly six-foot slender frame off the chair and said, "I don't have one, at least not yet. I make these in my kitchen."

"Well," she said, opening her pocketbook and picking two quarters from her tiny change purse. "I'll buy a box, but where can I go, if I want more?"

Hahn looked at the woman, not sure of her intentions. She smiled as she held her box of chocolates, waiting for a reply. He took a pencil from his pocket. "Why don't I get your address; I can drop by with more candy."

"I live in Harrisburg, but you can meet me at Pomeroy's anytime."

"Pomeroy's?"

She gave him the location of the large department store on Market Street near the square in Harrisburg and said, "I work the cosmetic counter and I quit at six."

"I'll try," he said, flustered.

He went home having sold all but a single box of chocolates and thinking about the girl until he realized he had not asked her name, but she hadn't offered it. Late the next day he took the bus into Harrisburg and entered Pomeroy's.

He approached the cosmetic counter and spotted the girl showing a customer new shades of lipstick. She noticed him with a smile. Her blue blouse and gray skirt accented her blond hair and brought out the color in her eyes.

She finished with the customer and approached Hahn smiling. "Why, is there anything I can help you with, sir?"

Hahn blushed. She giggled excitedly.

"I didn't get your name," he said, sheepishly.

"It's Susan," she said, softly. "And you're Martin?"

He reacted in alarm; how did she know his name? She laughingly reassured him, "That's the name of your chocolates, right?"

Hahn laughed at himself. He smiled at Susan, finding her more beautiful.

"I get off shortly," she said. "Would you like to go down to the drug store for a soda?"

Hahn happily accepted. They chatted a few minutes until he noticed a six-pointed Star of David dangling from the gold chain around her neck.

"You're Jewish?"

"Yes," she said, not hearing his contemptuous tone; not seeing anger in his eyes.

"But, you are beautiful," he said.

Susan heard the tone now, could see the eyes with their expression of betrayal. She was confused and stepped back.

"What's wrong?" she said.

Hahn could say no more. He shook his head and walked away, leaving Susan calling after him: "Martin? What's wrong? Martin? Martin?"

Passion faded into angry disappointment and he dismissed her, but he questioned whether it was wrong to like a Jew as lovely as her. She didn't look Jewish. He put Susan out of his mind, deciding instead to focus on building a business. That was foremost to his life.

As the months slipped away, Hahn was finding it harder to keep up with demand for his chocolates; working day shift at the factory and night shift in his kitchen, making his candies. It soon became too much. He advertised in the evening paper for a helper.

The first applicant was a woman about his age. Her brown flowing hair framed burning hazel eyes. She stood, slightly plump, in tight skirt and blouse. He showed her the kitchen and explained the work.

"Have you any experience making candy?"

"I can bake," she said, sitting in a chair, crossing her legs. She removed a pack of smokes from her purse, offering him one. He declined. He watched her light the cigarette and exhale. He found in her an intriguing attitude, an almost male coarseness that masked sensuousness.

"I forgot to ask your name."

"Eileen," she said, taking a puff and quickly exhaling. "Eileen Long. Look, mister, I can do the job, it's not a problem and I learn fast. What are my hours?"

"Well, I would need to supervise your work so from five o'clock in the evening to ten, but that's to start, once I am satisfied with your abilities, you could start earlier."

"Pay?"

"As I said in the ad, seventy-five cents an hour."

Eileen looked at Hahn like she was trying to guess his suit size. "You live alone?"

Hahn nodded. "Is that important?"

"My father isn't going to let me take a job in a single man's apartment. If you want to hire me, I'm telling him you're married. And you *do* want to hire me."

Hahn tried to suppress a smile. She seemed unlike any girl he knew, yet … she reminded him of someone he did know, once, and what now seemed so very long ago.

"How old are you?" he asked.

"Twenty one."

"Where were you employed previously?"

"The war factory in Harrisburg"

"Why did you leave?"

"The war ended so they sent us away with a pat on the ass."

Hahn asked her to start the next evening. She crushed out her cigarette. "I finish work at ten o'clock, no later. Streetcars stop running at ten-thirty."

He helped her with her coat. She smiled as she went out the door and descended the two flights of stairs. He looked forward to her return.

Eileen quickly mastered Hahn's candy recipes and within weeks had his confidence. She arrived at his apartment by mid-afternoon, getting several batches made before he arrived.

Hahn enjoyed her company. They grew closer and their working relationship appeared ready to expand into a more social arrangement, but he was reticent, frustrating Eileen.

She worked over a hot stove and kitchen table, but she started wearing buttoned blouses, tight skirts and high heels, none of which went unnoticed. Hahn, trying hard to resist his desires, stole glances at her shapely behind and the seams running up the back of her nylons.

Eileen felt his gaze. It excited and frustrated her because she was not sure how to break through his regimented social discipline. She grew up in a hardscrabble steel worker's home – was twelve when her mother succumbed to an unbearable depression and ended her life with a broken shard from the state hospital's bathroom mirror.

Left alone in the throes of womanhood, Eileen received no empathy or sympathy from her father and brothers, and she never expected any. She learned to do for herself.

In Hahn's apartment, taking a break, she wondered why her employer had yet to make a pass. It would be welcomed. She crossed her shapely legs, put a cigarette to her lips and inhaled, feeling her tight-fitting blouse stretch. A button popped off.

Eileen went into the bathroom and looked at herself in the mirror. She unbuttoned the top of her blouse and smiled proudly at the deep cleavage. She laughed to herself and thought, "This should certainly get a rise out of Mr. Hahn."

Hahn found Eileen that evening sensuously stirring a bowl of chocolate. Her unbuttoned blouse exposed plump breasts in a tight-fitting, white-laced bra. Her eyes appeared to burn with fire as she went to him. She raised her arms and laid them on Hahn's shoulders. He slid his arms around her waist, no longer wanting to resist, and pulled her tightly against him.

She pressed her lips against his and felt the bulge in his pants. The kiss was moist and warm. She wrapped her arms tightly around his neck. They kissed deeper and longer, melting together on the floor; their bodies in motion, heating into liquefaction.

They lay in bed a few hours later, sharing a cigarette as he caressed her smooth figure. Darkness had fallen and they felt content with each other. They spoke little and listened to the sound of a lonely train whistle in the distance.

"Well," said Hahn, "this was certainly a productive night."

They laughed and kissed. Hahn crushed out the cigarette and they spent another hour in heated passion, leaving them exhausted and pleased.

Later, walking her to the streetcar stop, he said, "I should fire you. I don't know how we can work together."

They listened to the low rumble of the approaching street car. Eileen smiled. "You won't and we will," she said. They embraced as the car stopped, clanging its bell. They stole a last kiss before Eileen hopped onto the rolling streetcar with a squeal. Watching her go, Hahn wondered whether he made a mistake.

Eileen became ever more indispensable to him, designing the company logo by scripting *Martin's Chocolates* in delicate brown letters, elegantly angled on cream-colored box tops. They had become partners emotionally and professionally.

She hired a second employee, an older woman retired from the factory, and they arrived mornings. Sales grew much faster than anticipated. Even Hahn was surprised at the chocolates' popularity. Five-and-dimes, little grocers, and drug store fountains were now placing orders.

She ran production. He came home evenings to find the day's batches in boxes ready for distribution. He would fill two large bags with the cream-colored boxes and ride the streetcar to Harrisburg to deliver the orders.

Hahn returned from deliveries in time to spend an hour or two with Eileen, often in the bedroom. After a passionate romp one evening, she confronted him. "You need to talk more."

"What do you mean?"

"You speak so little about yourself I feel I hardly know you."

"I tell you I love you."

"That's not enough." She sat up and reached for her cigarette case on the night stand. "I love being your lover but I want more."

Her tone frightened him. He had not thought as deeply about her as she about him. She sat naked, knees pulled up to her breasts, the cigarette's burning tip glowing in the darkness.

"You provide so much that you don't give a man time to think," he said.

"Really? You certainly think about sex enough."

"That's not fair."

"You're selfish; admit it and we'll go on from there. I can take it, if you'd just admit it."

He moved his hand to gently press her legs down then took her in his arms. "I've never had a relationship as close as you. Give me a little time. Please."

Eileen crushed her cigarette out and reached up and caressed Hahn's face, feeling his rugged, high cheek bones. She tried not to cry as she ran her fingers through his hair, but her eyes welled and she sobbed softly. "I love being with you."

He kissed her gently and they lay in each other's arms until it was time for her to catch the streetcar. Seeing her off, Hahn weighed his feelings – what was love? He wasn't sure – but what life did he dare share? The one he was concealing or the one he was pretending?

It was Saturday, a few days later. At Eileen's urging, he went to her home for dinner with her family. They lived in half of a fair-size clapboard duplex in a suburb of Harrisburg, just three blocks off a streetcar line.

Eileen waited for him on the porch. When she spotted him at the corner down the street, she hurried along a tree-lined sidewalk to greet him. Since they had become lovers, her clothing had become less provocative. She approached him in a pleated skirt, which swayed at the knees, and a loose-fitting sweater underneath her top coat.

They embraced and walked to the house, her arm through his. Eileen admired Hahn's tie, sport jacket and woolen trousers. "This is nice." She smoothed the lapel. "It must be new."

Hahn smiled, appreciatively. "To impress the bankers."

"What about me?"

He laughed. "Yes, you and your family."

"My father will be, I'm sure, but I don't know about my brothers."

"How did you explain to your father you are seeing your married employer?"

"What?"

"You said he wouldn't let you work in a bachelor's apartment."

"Sweetheart, I wanted to know if you were married, but didn't want to make it obvious."

"You can be deceptive, can't you?"

They laughed as they climbed the porch steps and entered the house, a warm, inviting place on a cold March afternoon, filled with dinner's aromas – a pot roast and potatoes. Hahn moved almost reluctantly while Eileen smiled brightly as they stepped into the living room.

Her father, a husky man with a tight crew cut, sat in an over-stuffed chair reading the newspaper. A young man with the same build but taller was slouched on the couch, flipping through an issue of *Life*. Someone unseen banged around in the kitchen.

Eileen made introductions. Her father rose and extended his hand. "Bobby." Her brother moved slower, standing at the couch, forcing Hahn to step forward and shake his hand. Another young man came from the kitchen.

"The lug you shook hands with is Bill, but everyone calls him 'Bull,' and standing in the doorway is Tommy. Everyone calls him 'Scout.' We're missing Robby, he's the oldest."

Hahn felt nervous and nodded at the young men. "What do the second names mean?"

The brothers stayed silent, but Eileen spoke. "Bull got his name because he's stubborn and has a tendency to act before thinking and Scout likes to cook and does the feeding around here when I'm not home."

"What about Robby?"

"I don't know, we never gave him a nickname," Eileen said.

Her father nodded his head. "No, he don't have one. Can I get ya a beer?"

Hahn declined. Everyone settled into the living room. Bobby said, "Robby's working second shift. Sorry you missed him."

To Hahn's relief, Bobby dominated the conversation. One of the two boys, both of whom Hahn estimated to be in their early twenties, interjected comments on occasion. Bobby rattled on about everything and sprinkled his monologue with questions about Hahn.

"Eileen says you're from Chicago – where at?"

"The south side."

"South side, huh? Know any gangsters?"

"Dad!" Eileen admonished as she got up from her seat next to Hahn.

"What the hell," Bobby said. "Mobsters run that town."

Eileen shook her head and started out of the living room. "Oh, I'm going to check on dinner, and Martin, you don't have to answer that."

Bobby turned to railing against the Russians and Truman's handling of Stalin.

"Ya know what I think." Bobby pointed at Hahn. "I think, and I know this may not sound right, but goddamn it you can't trust communists. We should've helped the Krauts defeat them."

The comment intrigued Hahn. "Why do you think that?"

"Look, I know Hitler and them Nazis were bad, but I don't think they were as bad as the goddamn communists," Bobby said. "Honestly, I never saw Germany as our real enemy."

"Did you fight in the war?"

"Too old," he said. "My boy, Robby did – served the Navy in the Pacific. Now the Japs, those goddamn bastards, they attacked us. The Krauts didn't."

Hahn started to question him when Eileen announced dinner. At the table, Bobby asked Hahn about his business. "I seen your candies for sale; you steal Milton Hershey's recipes?"

American humor was sometimes lost on Hahn. He defended his candy as fine chocolates a bit more expensive than what Milton Hershey made for the masses. "I'm soon going for a bank loan so I can open a shop and hire another employee."

"Bank, huh? Don't let 'em Jew ya," Bobby said.

"I'm sorry?"

"Watch they don't make you pay more interest than you should."

Hahn nodded. "You don't like Jews, Mr. Long?"

"Dad doesn't like a lot of people," said Scout, who, unlike his brother, Bull, was slight and quiet spoken.

Bobby waved a dismissive hand. "Hell, those people don't bother me."

Hahn looked at Eileen. She appeared disinterested in the table conversation.

Bull said, "Hey, Martin, how much they paying at the chocolate factory?"

"You ain't quitting the steel plant," his father ordered.

"If I can get more pay somewhere else, why not?"

"You got a job for life and a good pension," Bobby said. "Why risk that?"

"Martin's getting ready to risk it, going into business for himself."

"Yeah, well he's smarter than you. And he's college educated."

"But I'm not."

Bobby looked surprised, almost disbelieving. "No? Hell, ya sound like it."

Eileen looked at Hahn, anticipating new information about him. He realized he had put himself in the position of having to discuss his background, something he avoided with Eileen, giving her only sketchy information when she asked him questions.

"Well," he said, hesitantly. "I read considerably."

"You're one of those self-educated kind, are you?" Bobby said.

Hahn shrugged, slicing the meat on his plate. "I guess you could say that."

He turned the conversation to the Longs, to which Eileen's brothers delighted in telling embarrassing anecdotes about their sister growing up.

"I'm going to put coffee on," she said, calling over her shoulder, "Save room for dessert."

When they went for a walk in the cold evening, Eileen said to Hahn, "For a moment there at dinner I thought you were about to reveal something of yourself."

"What?"

"I haven't seen you read anything but a newspaper since I met you."

"But I've read considerably," he said. "Since we met I haven't had time to read that much because I've been busy with the business."

She looped her arm through his and kissed him gently. She knew he wasn't forthcoming, but decided to let it go, for now.

As they walked under elm trees lining the sidewalk, the enormous branches creating a cavern effect, Eileen expressed dismay over some of her father's remarks at the table. "I don't think like him. My brothers do, except for Scout. He thinks for himself."

Hahn listened and decided he could never tell her how much he shared her father's views.

A year after his country's defeat and his failure to assassinate President Roosevelt, Hahn was a successful entrepreneur; earning a small profit, enough for him to qualify for a bank loan from the East End Trust Company in Harrisburg.

He realized one day how far away his German life was from him. It was like the end of a chapter in a book or perhaps the end of a book. He was building another life and found much of what the party had taught him, and what he believed as a young Nazi, challenged.

So he initially found his friendship with Moss Bergman unsettling. They met when Hahn entered Bergman's cluttered grocery on a sales call. They took an immediate liking to each other, finding a connection and easy rapport. But the relationship disturbed him. It was contrary to what the Hitler Youth had taught him.

He realized Susan and Bergman were the first Jews he had met in his life. By the time he came of age most of Germany's Jews were gone – shipped out like cattle on east-bound trains to so-called labor camps that were actually death camps like Treblinka and Auschwitz.

When Hahn realized Bergman was Jewish – he noticed the man's black yarmulke on that first sales call – he ingratiated himself, fearful, as he was taught, of a Jew rejecting his product or trying to cheat him.

"Mr. Hahn, please say no more." Bergman was small and thin, with a shock of gray hair and a round face. "I'm happy to place an order and honored to sell the candy."

"Oh?" Hahn looked surprised.

"Yes." Bergman shrugged his shoulders. "It's very good chocolate and I've been meaning to call for an order. I've had several customers looking for it."

"Thank you, Mr. Bergman."

Bergman smiled. "Everyone calls me Moss. Tell you what: If the chocolate sells fasts, I'll double my next order. If that sells, I'll double the next order after that. Okay?"

Hahn nodded happily as he took notice of the store's merchandise with Hebrew labels.

"I like to help people who do business with me, especially new businessmen like yourself," Bergman said. He stood behind the check-out counter and started ringing up a customer's order. "That's how good things start, you know?"

The grocer's enthusiasm was infectious. Hahn said, "How can I help you?"

"Why, you already have," Bergman said, punching cash register keys. "You came here and offered to sell me a product my customers like. That's helping me."

When Hahn returned two weeks later, the shopkeeper showed him the shelf. Only a few boxes of his chocolate had sold. "I thought it would go faster than it has," Bergman said.

Hahn's mind echoed with Nazi warnings. He stammered, "You're not going to order any more, are you? You want your money back?"

The shopkeeper was taken aback, but he shook his head. "I like to give products a chance to catch on. I'm sure the rest will sell, it just takes time."

Hahn relaxed, feeling foolish and remorseful. He apologized.

"I've been running my grocery twenty-five years, Mr. Hahn – "

"Martin, please."

"I came to America thirty-four years ago and I've done well for myself, but I still miss my Germany, regardless of what has gone on over there."

"Germany is a beautiful country."

"It is a wonderful country, but I'm afraid people like me are not wanted there, and I don't want to go somewhere where I'm not wanted, even if it is my home."

Hahn promised the grocer another order the following day and headed out the door. The shopkeeper cheerily called to him. "Martin, if you don't mind?"

"Yes?"

"Consider making some kosher chocolate. It would please my Jewish customers."

With the loan, Hahn rented a large old house in a Harrisburg neighborhood. It was once a bakery with an enormous kitchen ideal for candy making and living quarters upstairs. He quit the Hershey factory and hired a third employee.

Hahn and Eileen married. Martin's Chocolates prospered as a family-run company. She supervised two employees in production. Hahn hired Bull to deliver the candy, and he handled sales and accounting.

He eventually bought the house. With eight rooms including kitchen and bathroom, the upstairs made a comfortable home for Hahn and Eileen. The first floor and basement was more than adequate for the business.

They had a happy marriage, though Hahn maintained his deception, telling Eileen his parents died when he was eighteen, leaving him no family and to finish adolescence in a state boarding school.

She accepted his explanations because the men in her life never spoke about themselves; and she put aside the sense her husband wasn't entirely truthful – another male trait as far as she was concerned.

The Hahns settled into a predictable, but comfortable life. Hahn on occasion would find amusement in what he was doing. It was far removed from the life he had expected and Rhonen had intended for him.

He was reminded of *that* life whenever he went to the basement and spotted on the shelf amid paper supplies the old Red Arrow can of grease that entombed Hoest's Luger.

"Why do we still have this can of grease around?" Eileen was down in the basement one day to collect a couple of boxes when, for some reason, the can caught her attention. She stared at it and remembered when she first saw it – in Hahn's apartment closet.

Hahn was in his office going over sales figures. He looked at Eileen.

"I'm sorry, what?"

"That can of grease in the basement. You've had it for years. What's in it?"

Hahn shrugged. "Grease." Eileen rolled her eyes. "I know that, but why do you keep it?"

Agitated at her questioning, Hahn snapped. "I don't know. Maybe one day we'll need to apply some lubricant to the car. Is it bothering you?"

"Oh, Martin, I was just curious. Why are you getting all upset over a can of grease?"

Hahn slumped back in his chair and sighed. "I'm sorry."

Eileen went to him and slipped into his lap, putting her arms around his neck and gently kissing him. "Okay. I think you've been working too hard."

"You think so?"

"Yes, I do," Eileen said, her warm lips pressing his. "And I think we should make love tonight to get your mind off work."

"You're kind and generous, wanting to make love for my benefit."

She giggled. "It's the only way I'm going to get pregnant."

Their love making, though always passionate, was never fruitful. It was possible, her physician informed her after an inconclusive examination, she might never conceive.

Years went by and when they sadly accepted they would stay childless, Eileen became pregnant, just shy of forty. She gave birth to a healthy boy, but the delivery was traumatic and the doctors had to perform a complete hysterectomy. Kurt would be her only child.

Hahn doted as a father and for Kurt's first few years of life, they were happy. Martin's Chocolates remained small and profitable, providing them more than enough income. He was content, successful beyond expectations, grateful.

America, he concluded one day, had freed his thinking so much he questioned his past, something he would never have done – dared not done – under the Nazis. The indoctrination no longer chained his conscience.

As Kurt neared the age of nine, Eileen began seeing symptoms of the depression that plagued her mother. His reclusive behavior worried her. Hahn listened to her concerns, but was busy with the company and told her to stop over-reacting.

"My mother was manic-depressive," she reminded him.

Hahn looked at her coolly. "What are you saying?"

"They say depression can be genetic," she said. "I think he needs a doctor."

Hahn argued nothing was wrong with Kurt, but then Hahn had grown up in a Germany where the government considered the mentally ill genetically inferior and removed them from society, murdering tens of thousands through a euthanasia program.

Eileen reluctantly let it go, but watched her son until a few months later when Kurt told her he sometimes blacked out for short periods and that he heard voices in his head.

The doctor diagnosed bipolar depression, treatable with medication. He told Eileen and Hahn that being supportive was just as important as the drugs. "Even with treatments, he could still have an episode, triggered by any number of reasons; say a stressful event of some sort."

Hahn's unwillingness to accept his imperfect son brought Eileen dismay. He turned his focus on his company, becoming an acquaintance, rather than a father, to Kurt.

Father and son shared a bonding that was limited to the front of the television, tuned to what Hahn watched, and with an almost obsessive compulsion – documentaries on the Second World War, with their grainy, black-and-white, and some color, footage of Nazi Germany.

Kurt never understood the gulf between him and his father, though he tried desperately to win his approval.

Dana leaned back, her elbows resting on the towel, and surveyed the near desolate beach and sparkling green waters of the Atlantic. She basked in a wonderful, breezy and cloudless day as The Clash's *Train in Vain* drifted from Kurt's radio.

They celebrated college graduation with a short vacation to Ocean City, Maryland, where they found a cheap two-bedroom apartment. Close since middle school, Dana was among Kurt's few friends, making him all the more special to her. They behaved towards each other more like siblings. They even looked the part – both dirty blonds with slender figures.

Kurt trusted Dana implicitly, always seeking her advice. Dana, in a fleeting moment, had once considered intimacy, but she could see he never thought of her romantically.

She looked at him sitting on the blanket, a loose fitting tank-top hung off sun-browned shoulders, his back to the ocean. He stared at a cylindrical-shaped tower rising amid the dunes, flat roofed with vertical window slits. It was one of a number she had noticed as they drove along Ocean Highway into Delaware.

"What is it?"

Kurt turned with that absorbed look he got whenever he drifted off in thought. "Huh?"

She pointed at the structure, its concrete having browned with age. Kurt shrugged. "It's an observation tower from World War II." She smiled, thinking to herself; World War II, one of Kurt's favorite hobbies.

"What did they watch for?"

"German U-boats," he said.

"What's a U-boat?"

Kurt smiled. "*Unterseeboot*; It's a submarine."

"And why did they watch for them?"

"They sunk merchant ships off the eastern seaboard."

Dana teased. "Is that why we're here today, so you could dabble in your pornography?"

Kurt looked at her stretched out on the towel in a one-piece bathing suit wearing yellow, funky-shaped sunglasses. With a half-hearted laugh he defended his choice of beach.

"I thought this would be a nice change from the crowds in OC."

"Sure," she said. "I've often wondered why World War II fascinates you."

Kurt leaned back on the blanket. "Maybe it connects me to my father," he said. "I mean, it's the one damn thing I *can* talk to him about – the war. He finds it just as interesting as I do."

"Was your father in the war?"

"I'm not sure."

Dana sat up. "You're not sure? Did you ever ask him?"

Kurt shook his head. "I asked my mother. She said he got a deferral because he lost his parents just before draft age."

"Why didn't you ask your father?"

"I don't know."

He shrugged, wanting to change the topic, and turned to face the ocean.

Dana listened. For as long as she knew Kurt, she had understood his ambiguous feelings toward his father, his struggle to establish a meaningful relationship with him. She wondered if he understood it.

"How's your dad doing these days?"

"Fine, I guess."

He stared at a line of waves coming in, arcing beautifully as they crashed along the shore, and a favorite memory returned from his second year of junior high.

He had joined the school's soccer team, delighting his father, an avid player in *his* youth. The sport started to create a bond between them. Kurt would return home from practice and over dinner his father would listen and laugh at his son's experiences.

Kurt was a capable player, but not exceptional and he passed the season on the bench. The coach had interest only in stars and winning – not athletics and sportsmanship. Hahn lost interest in the relationship, disappointed once more in his imperfect son.

Kurt never again pursued sports and never knew why his father drifted away, but always held onto the memory of that season.

He watched as another line of waves crashed and thought: *I love that old bastard.*

Chapter II

Washington, D.C.

The rubber-tipped windshield wipers squealed loudly as they swept away the sprinkling remains of a furious downpour. After a few days of routine work at state police headquarters in Dover, Sam Grey was eager to return to his pursuit.

While in Delaware, he conducted, with trepidation, a personal investigation into Marta's background. To his relief he found nothing suspicious, but questions remained.

Washington's hot asphalt streets steamed from the rain as Grey navigated his car through tree-lined neighborhoods. He tried ignoring a sense of betrayal he had felt since that day in Tom Morgan's Justice Department office, when he found her name on the petition seeking Gerhard's prosecution.

He believed he behaved foolishly with her, like a teenager in love. But he also was deeply disappointed as he struggled over how he could care for her so much after just one night. Was he trying to recapture what he thought he lost with Sana? He needed to talk to Marta.

Grey found the monastery in an old, quiet neighborhood. Sunlight poked through clouds, opening patches of blue. Fresh-smelling grass and flowers lingered in the air as he walked under a sand-colored Moorish archway and onto the monastery's floral grounds.

He stepped inside the church; a welcoming cold blast of air conditioning hit his body. He wandered around the sanctuary until he arrived at the gift shop. It was empty except for a young Franciscan in a brown robe sitting behind the counter reading a book.

Grey introduced himself and asked for the head of the monastery. The brother hurried off in his chocolate brown robe. He returned a few minutes later and said, "Father John will see you, please wait here."

Grey busied himself with postcards when the smiling middle-aged Father John, in brown robe and sandals, appeared. In a gentle voice, he directed Grey to follow him through a labyrinth of halls and stairwells until they entered the friary.

"I must say I can't imagine what you are investigating here," the priest said. "You're from Delaware, you say?"

"Yes, Father."

To Father John, eternally concerned about the Catholic Church's image, the presence of a police officer worried him. He would never permit scandal, not in a monastery designed solely to support the Holy Land.

"What brings you to us?"

"Well, it's rather complicated, so I'd like to sit down and talk to you about it."

They arrived at a large room with tall windows casting sunlight across a long table. They sat at one end, their voices echoing among the sparse furnishings. Father John sat with his hands folded before him.

Grey tried to take the measure of the man before explaining what he wanted, but he was unsure how to appeal to the priest. Father John smiled self-consciously. "Please, go ahead now."

"Father, how long have you been at the monastery?"

"Twenty-three years, why?"

"A murder suspect may have worked here long ago as a gardener."

"A gardener? We have no gardener here. When did this person work here?"

"About fifty-five years ago."

The priest gasped and leaned forward. "Fifty-five years? Are you joking, sir?"

"No," Grey said, shaking his head. "This is not a joke."

"I'm sorry, but I'm going to have to ask to see some identification."

Grey removed his wallet and his badge, and gave them to the priest. Father John studied them closely and handed them back.

"It's not that I didn't take your word, it's just that I find your search quite impossible."

"So do I, Father, but is it possible to search your records on this gardener?"

"For what year?"

"Nineteen forty-five, perhaps the first few months – "

Father John shook his head. "We don't have employee records back that far, I'm sorry, and we don't always have a gardener."

"Do you have any records of any kind?"

The priest shook his head and rose from his chair. "You see, we employ few because the brothers here run the monastery and tend the gardens. I'm sorry, but I can't help you."

Grey tried one more time. "He may have sought sanctuary from the monastery. Are there perhaps other priests or brothers who may have been around then?"

"I'm sorry," Father John said, becoming impatient. "I can't help you."

The priest escorted him back to the gift shop and bid him goodbye before returning to the friary. Grey lingered, reluctant to leave. Father John's response to his inquiry left him suspicious. The priest had been too quick to dismiss him.

A group of elderly couples entered the shop, led by a young Hispanic woman. Gathering them together, she announced, "Please follow me. We will go through this door and into the hall for our tour of the catacombs."

Grey looked over at the young brother behind the counter. "What kind of tour is that?"

"An excellent one," the brother said. "Under the church are replicas of the catacombs of ancient Rome. You may follow along with that group; the tour takes about fifteen minutes."

Curious, Grey wandered into the hall to join the seniors. Among them a talkative little man in a blue seersucker and baseball cap stood by his silent little wife, who just nodded and occasionally replied, "Yes, dear."

The little man chattered on for several minutes until an old, slightly stooped Franciscan entered, introducing himself as their guide. He related a brief history of the monastery in a soft, commanding voice. "I am Father Sebastian, now please follow me."

The tour moved through the church and into narrow dark passageways of earthen walls and chambers where Father Sebastian explained the purpose of the catacombs. The man in the blue seersucker asked the priest how long he had been at the monastery.

"I've been here for nearly sixty years," Father Sebastian said.

The words grabbed Grey. The little man repeated aloud, "Sixty years? My, that's more than half a century; quite a long time at any one place, isn't it?"

"Yes." The priest spoke in a tone of bored indifference. "Now let us move on."

At the end of the tour, Grey approached him.

"Father, I was wondering if you could help me."

"Yes?"

"I'm looking for a gardener named Henry. He worked here in 1945."

The priest's eyes widened; his lower lip quivered.

"You do know him, don't you? He sought sanctuary here."

A long moment of penitent silence passed before Father Sebastian said, "Who are you?"

Grey showed his identification. The priest stared at the trooper's badge.

"Do you know him, Father?"

"Yes." Father Sebastian handed back the badge. "Yes, I did know him."

"Can you tell me about him?"

Father Sebastian sighed. "Why don't we take a walk along the portico?"

Through the church, scented by burning incense and candles, he led Grey outside to an arched walkway, flanked by sandstone columns. It extended around a large, flowery garden.

They walked slowly, the portico's pillars casting long shadows in late afternoon. Rose and honeysuckle fragrances pinched the air. Over the years, Father Sebastian often wondered whether he would one day have to answer for the past.

"Tell me, why you are interested in our old gardener?" he said to Grey.

"There's been a murder and he's a suspect."

"A murder?" Father Sebastian sounded concerned. "Where?"

"At a beach town in Delaware."

The priest stopped. He long ago atoned for not alerting the authorities to the man he knew as Henry by forgoing every opportunity to live in the Holy Land, his life's dream, yet he knew he would one day have to answer for his sin of omission.

Grey studied his face. The priest appeared to be deciding something.

Father Sebastian sighed. "I must, as a priest, abide by the confessional so there isn't much I can say, but your assumption about why he was here is not incorrect."

"Do you know where he went when he left here?"

"I don't know, but it's possible he went to Pennsylvania."

"And why do you think that?"

"That is where I suggested he go."

The answer astonished Grey. "Father, did you know he was a German spy?"

"You're asking me to divulge a confession – "

"No, I'm asking whether you knew he was a spy, not whether he told you he was."

Father Sebastian sat silently. Grey said, angrily, "Could it be, Father, the confession you are protecting is your own?"

The priest looked sharply at him, but Grey pressed. "Where did he go in Pennsylvania?"

The priest moved to a bench to sit. The question angered him because it was correct.

"Yes, I knew who the man was – he was a boy actually. But I also knew who I was."

"I don't understand."

"I was and I am a German," Father Sebastian said. "This is neither a confession nor even an excuse, but Henry Martin left me torn between my love for the Fatherland and love for God. I did what I believed was right as a German and as a priest."

"Then why did you send him away?"

"I felt there would be trouble here if he stayed."

"Trouble for whom?"

A door slammed shut, distracting Grey. He glanced up at Father John hurrying toward them along the portico from the church. He was about to reproach Grey, but Father Sebastian waved him off. "It's okay, Father."

The priest looked compassionately at Father Sebastian. "Yes?"

"Yes, Father."

Father John glared at Grey and went back into the church.

Grey continued. "So where did you send him?"

"The town where they make the chocolate, Hershey."

"Why there?"

"He had a skill for making candy, but whether he went there I never knew."

"Making candy? I thought he was the gardener."

"He was, but he also made chocolate candy, something he offered to do for our Sunday bake sales. We were looking for ways to increase our revenues."

The information left Grey in wondering disbelief. What kind of spy was this guy?

"Father, I'm having a hard time following you. Why would an enemy spy sit around the monastery in wartime and make chocolate? It doesn't make sense."

Father Sebastian nodded, knowingly. "I can only assume since the war was over by then he changed his priorities in life. He was very good at not revealing much about himself."

"How did you know he was a German agent?"

"Simple deduction; his arrival coincided with the capture of other spies and the reaction he had to the murder."

Grey said, "You mean the store clerk who was murdered the night of the raid?"

"Yes," the priest said, quietly. "He was unmoved by it when I confronted him."

"Was he aware you had figured out his identity?"

"He may have been suspicious, but not certain. I never told him I was German, although I'm sure he suspected because my accent was heavier then."

"What about his accent?"

"He had none; he sounded like an American."

"Did anyone else here know his identity?"

"It was rumored after an FBI agent came around and suggested Henry was a spy."

Grey thanked the priest and began to leave. Father Sebastian stopped him.

"Just so you know, I never believed in Hitler, just in Germany. And Henry never struck me as just a German."

Grey smiled wanly. The priest provoked in him mixed feelings of pity and contempt.

"I try to live my life according to the Scriptures," Father Sebastian said. "As it says in Micah, "What does the Lord require of you? To do justice, love mercy and walk humbly with your God."

Grey shook his head. "Just so you know, Father, Henry's suspected of killing an old U-boat commander – a German."

Evening fell as Grey steered his car onto busy New York Avenue, northbound, out of Washington. His destination was Hershey, about two hours by highway, but he wanted to get some rest and decided to drive an hour and spend the night in Baltimore.

He noticed a white Chrysler sedan two blocks from the monastery and kept an occasional eye on it. The sense he had of someone following him was back. He was unsure about the sedan, but watched it nonetheless.

He traveled north on the Baltimore-Washington Parkway. The sedan, its windows tinted and missing a front license plate, stayed well behind him, but always in view. When he reached Baltimore, Grey pulled into the hotel garage, a block from Oriole Park at Camden Yards.

Hopping out of his car, he hurried to catch the sedan's license plate, but the car was too far up the street. Inside his room, he called Jack Davis, telling him where he was headed.

"You got another hunch, Sam?"

Davis was preoccupied with security for the next day's campaign visit at the state Capitol by Connecticut U.S. Senator Joseph Lieberman, the vice presidential candidate.

"It's the best lead I've got going right now," Grey said.

"But it's fifty-five years old."

"If you're German and you like chocolate, where else would you go?"

"Explain that to me later," Davis said. "I've got a meeting in a few minutes on this event tomorrow. Keep me posted."

"One more thing: I think I'm being followed."

"With who you're hanging around these days, I don't doubt it. Look, I can't spare anyone right now, not with this Lieberman event."

"I don't need any help," Grey said. "I'm just keeping you informed."

"You're starting to worry me."

"Uh, you're not going to send me back to Tom Morgan for another lecture, are you?"

"Watch yourself," Davis admonished.

Grey hung up and dialed the front desk for the location of an Internet café. A concierge directed him to Thames Street in Fells Point, an old, cobblestoned, now trendy, section of the city. He left the hotel and hailed a taxi.

The cab pulled away from the curb and Grey asked the driver to keep an eye out for a white sedan. The driver nodded as he scanned his rear- and side-view mirrors. Outside Ruth's Café, the cabby said to Grey, "No luck, pal; didn't see anything."

Grey bought a coffee and checked his e-mail. He left the café and started toward the bars and restaurants he spotted on the ride into Fells Point. He was hungry and wanted a drink. As he walked, he stopped to check menus in the windows. People crowded the sidewalks on their way to an evening of dinner and bar hopping.

At the third menu, he spotted his shadow's reflection in the restaurant window. The man was tall, perhaps blond. Grey wanted to see whether he was being followed. He stopped to look at two more menus – the man still there, stalking him from across the street.

Grey started to walk, turned suddenly and confronted him, but the man disappeared. The trooper stopped. A horn's blare from a speeding sports car made him jump back. He crossed the street and entered a loud bar, the last location of his shadow, but found no sign of him. Outside, he went up the street in search of him.

"How the hell did I miss him?" Grey muttered.

He retraced his steps and wondered whether someone really was following him. *Maybe I'm working this too hard*, he thought. He decided to get dinner at the hotel and walked toward Thames and Broadway to hail a cab.

He passed the noisy Cat's Eye Pub, but failed to notice a blond man seated at a window table, watching him.

The smiling candy bar greeted everyone driving on the concrete highway: "Welcome to Hershey, the sweetest place on earth." The sign beckoned from a grass rise beyond which farm fields stretched to distant forest-covered hills.

He exited onto HersheyPark Drive. As he drove, he caught sight of a tree-covered hill topped with a large castle-like building. The distant structure and its setting reminded him of another place, but he was unable to remember what exactly.

Grey had been on the road nearly two hours, watching for the white sedan in his rearview mirror, but the vehicle never appeared. Before leaving Baltimore, he called the corporate offices of the Hershey Company to explain his impending visit.

A young woman waited for him when he entered the modern structure. It sat one hill over from the castle-like structure, overlooking the chocolate factory and amusement park.

A pinch-faced woman greeted him. "Jody Bitterman, human resources."

He followed her down a hallway, inquiring about the castle with its Mediterranean-style architecture and green-tiled roof.

"The Hotel Hershey," she said. "Modeled after a Spanish hotel Milton Hershey visited."

"When was it built?"

"The 1930s."

In her office Bitterman pointed to a chair as she sat at her desk. "I scrambled this morning after you called, but a search of our employee records was inconclusive."

"Oh?" Grey shifted in his chair.

"We have no employee named Henry Martin."

Considering the spy might have changed his name, Grey inquired about employees who worked at the factory in 1945.

"Our records don't go back that far unless an employee was still here, but we have no one employed today who's been here since the forties," Bitterman said. "I'm sorry, but you may want to try the union hall in town."

She directed him to the office of Chocolate Workers Local 464, a low-rise brick building a few blocks from the factory. There, a heavy-set guy in an open-collar shirt identified himself as the local's secretary and shook his head when Grey asked about Henry Martin.

"Can't help you," he said, after looking through files.

Grey could hear someone in the next room, tapping on a computer keyboard. "How long have you worked here?"

"About thirty-two years."

"You've never heard the name Henry Martin before?"

The man thought. Whoever was tapping on the keyboard had stopped. "I heard the name before, but don't recall hearing of or meeting any Henry Martin."

"You said you've heard the name before?"

"Martin's a common kind of name; there's Martin's Honda over in Palmyra and Martin's Potato Chips, I think they're down in York."

"Hey, Gene?" A female voice called from the next room.

"Yeah, Linda?"

"Excuse me for eavesdropping, but don't forget Martin's Chocolates."

Grey's pulse quickened.

"Martin's Chocolates?" Gene said. "Where're they?"

"Oh, for God's sake," she said. "Harrisburg! You know – Martin's Chocolates."

"Well, if you say so, honey."

A middle-aged woman in a green Eagles football jersey and jeans appeared with a mock-look of reproach. "Sweetheart, you know."

She looked at Grey. "He's a little slow sometimes."

"Do you have an address?"

"It's in the phone book, Gene," she said. "Can you manage that?"

He produced a thick yellow book, found the address, and wrote it down. Grey looked at the telephone directory eagerly.

"Do you mind if I take a look at this?" he said, flipping the pages to the listing for Martin. He scanned the names but found not even an H. Martin. He tried to shrug off his discouragement as he left the union hall.

Outside, he studied the slip of paper with the address for Martin's Chocolates. It's a long shot, he thought, but what other leads did he have?

He drove up the street, turned left and stopped almost immediately at the red light on the corner of Cocoa and Chocolate avenues. He was on a rise, facing north. Through the windshield he could see the Hotel Hershey in the distance.

Heidelberg. Grey realized the hotel and hilltop distinctly reminded him of the imposing *schloss.* Was it a stretch, he thought, to believe this would be a comfortable place for a German who likes making chocolate? He felt more confident about finding his suspect.

Grey stopped at a restaurant for a sandwich and coffee. Afterward, he called Jack Davis to tell him about the latest development. Davis sounded somber.

"I wish you'd use your cell phone. Where are you?"

"Outside Harrisburg, I think I may have a lead – "

"Put that on hold and come on back."

"Let me just check this lead," Grey said, impatiently. "If nothing pans out – "

"Sam, your father passed away last night," Davis said. "I'm sorry to give you the news this way, but whatever you got up there can wait, okay?"

The news dumbfounded him. For the last few years, since his father's eightieth birthday, Grey had tried to prepare for the eventuality; with his father gone, he had no more family except distant relatives living in Managua whom he did not know.

"Are you okay?" Davis asked.

"Yeah, yeah, I'm fine; what happened?"

"Hospital said it was a severe heart attack."

"I'm heading back now."

Grey walked to his car. He suddenly felt light, as if angels had fluttered to his side and were carrying him. On the long homeward drive, he relived happy memories. He laughed and cried, and he regretted having last spoken to his father nearly a week ago.

In his grieving, he failed to notice the white sedan behind him as he crossed the state line into Delaware. The sedan followed him until the outskirts of Dover, where it took the exit to the Dover Downs race track.

On a balmy afternoon three days later, Grey rode out on Davis' boat to spread his father's ashes over the waters of Delaware Bay. As the wind hit his face, Grey found his grief shallow because of a deep love he and his father shared; it would keep them together, even in death.

The sound of glass bottles pulled from a bed of ice interrupted his thoughts. He turned to see Davis closing a cooler lid while holding two beers.

"How 'bout a brew?" Davis handed him a bottle.

The boat rocked gently on the waves. Grey unscrewed the sweating bottle's cap and took a long swig. It was cold and foamy and slid down his throat.

"Woody was a good soldier," Davis said.

"Yeah, he was all right."

Grey took another swig. A memory of a high school track meet flashed; 17-year-old Sam Grey, running, stumbling then falling; his father appears almost instantly, he had rushed from the stands; he's lifting him, telling him how proud he is, and helping him to the finish line.

Davis smiled. "In a little while we'll head in. The wife insists you come to dinner."

"Sure, that'll be great."

"I want you to take some more days off; go somewhere, get your mind off things."

"I'll be fine," Grey said. "I'm going back to Harrisburg tomorrow."

"Sure you want to do that?"

"I'm close on this one."

"How about I send someone along?"

Grey started laughing. "Come on, Jack, just because I lost a father doesn't mean I need a mother. I'll be fine."

"You've been working this pretty hard."

Grey shrugged. Davis said, "How close are you?"

"Close."

"Did you ever figure out if you were being followed?"

Grey shrugged again and looked across the bay. A freighter painted red, white and green steamed up the shipping lane toward Philadelphia. He wasn't going to tell him about his shadow in Baltimore. He learned that to avoid supervisor interference you limit information. Davis was a trusted friend, but he was still a supervisor, and Davis understood this.

"Just be careful up there," he said.

Grey returned home after a pleasant evening of lasagna and red wine to find a message on his answering machine from Inspector Helga Schmidt of the Munich police. She had information concerning Erica Artz.

Grey eagerly waited the four hours, when it was nine o'clock in the morning German time. He called Schmidt, who answered on the first ring.

She was a serious-sounding woman who wasted no time in telling him the news.

"Fraulein Artz is related to your dead U-boat captain; she's his daughter."

"How'd you find this out?"

"I interviewed her mother; the young lady has a police record. Petty stuff, mostly; being in the wrong place with the wrong people."

Schmidt told him Erica Artz's story.

Before leaving for America thirty two years ago Hoest had a brief affair with a young woman less than half his age. Gerlinda found she was pregnant shortly after he departed the country, but Hoest never knew.

"Why didn't she tell him?" Grey asked.

"She wasn't entirely clear."

Gerlinda enjoyed single motherhood, but later married a man her age. Erica was two. Her stepfather never cared for her; considered her a bastard, and when Erica was in her late teens she wanted to find her real father. Gerlinda had no idea how to find him.

"Is this horrible childhood the reason Erica has these weird tattoos?"

"Tattoos?" Schmidt said.

"She had a swastika on her arm, among other things."

"According to our records, Erica was involved with a lot of crazy groups and at one time a neo-Nazi bunch in Munich."

"How did she find Hoest?"

The Munich newspaper ran the Associated Press story about Hoest in America, which Gerlinda read. She started planning for her daughter to meet her father, but Erica disappeared before she could tell her.

"Why?"

"Gerlinda had torn the article out of the paper and hid it in her dresser. She thinks Erica found it, figured out who he was and went to visit him."

Schmidt gave him Gerlinda's telephone number and address, but warned him the mother and daughter appeared to have a strained relationship, based on her conversation with Gerlinda.

"I don't think there's much love. She accused her daughter of stealing money from her."

Grey heeded the advice, but believed he knew how to approach Erica.

Grey sat by his telephone, holding the petition, trying to decide what to say. Everything Marta told him about herself in Berlin was true, according to his background check.

What she omitted was her relationship, which was still unclear to him, with the German families whose sons and daughters Gerhard executed. Why hadn't she told him? What gain was there for her to be deceptive?

He dialed and listened to the ring at the other end of the line; heard the "click" when she picked up. "Hello?"

Grey's pulse quickened. "Marta?"

"Sam? Is that you?"

"Yes, how are you?"

"I'm wonderful now, hearing your voice. Is everything okay?"

Grey was taken aback. "Yes. Why?"

"You stopped e-mailing a couple of days ago and haven't answered mine."

"I've been away the last few days."

He told himself to confront her.

"Busy with your investigation?"

"Yes," he said. "I want to talk to you about it."

"Sam?"

"Yes?"

"I have some exciting news."

"Oh?"

"Next week I will be in Philadelphia to attend a human rights symposium and I thought we could meet. Philadelphia is not far from you, yes?"

Grey listened to her tone and inflection trying to discern whether she actually cared for him. Listening to her voice made him long for her. He decided not to confront her, not yet; not over the phone. They would meet. He wanted to look in her eyes when he asked her.

"It's not far at all," Grey said. "I can't wait to see you."

"I want to see you so much," Marta said. "Now, what did you want to talk about?"

"It doesn't matter," he said. "I've forgotten."

Grey entered the warden's office at Sussex County prison. Police Chief Christopher sat waiting with Beth Cohen, the public defender. He asked about Erica.

"Has she spoken to anyone yet?"

The warden, a beefy-looking man with gray stubble for hair, shook his head; his heavy jowls moved with his mouth. "Not one word."

Grey looked around. "Where's our prosecutor, Mr. Cooksey?"

"Dave's on his way, he's running late," Christopher said.

Grey explained what he learned about Erica.

Christopher expressed doubt. "It doesn't make her less a suspect in the murder."

"Nonsense," Cohen argued. "Why would she make up such a story, and why would she kill her father who she finally met for the first time?"

"Oh, hell," Christopher laughed. "I can think of a dozen reasons."

Cohen, short, dark-haired and always ready for a fight, snorted. "That's the same kind of attitude she found at home. It's no wonder she's angry at the world."

Grey interceded. "I need to know what she knows about Hoest's murder – and no, Chris, as you well know, I'm not convinced she killed him."

Christopher shrugged and folded his arms. Cohen sensed an ally in Grey and said, "Okay, Sam, what do you need from us?"

Grey smiled. "I'd like you in the interview room in case she decides to take advantage of the state's free legal services. Chris? How about you and Dave in the next room listening on the intercom?"

They left the warden's office and went down a painted cinderblock hall to the interview room. Opening the tan-colored metal door, Grey and Cohen found a sullen-looking Erica at the metal table. A prison matron stood behind her, but left as Cohen took a seat next to Erica. Grey sat across from them.

The prison's blue jumpsuit hung off her lanky figure. She sat motionless, hands clasped tightly together on the cold table top. Cohen told her Grey had important information.

He watched for Erica's reaction. "We've spoken to your mother in Munich and we know Eric Hoest was your father."

Erica's eyes flickered; her expression softened. She stared at the table as Grey continued. "Why didn't you tell us he was your father? It would have certainly cleared up a few things and may have kept you out of jail."

She did not respond.

"I know it's very hard for you, having lost a father you just found."

Erica snapped her head up and glared. She spoke in husky tones. "You don't know how I feel. How could you or anybody know that?"

Grey sat quietly before speaking. "I just lost my father a few days ago, but unlike you, he and I had a close relationship. I miss him terribly. I can only imagine how hard it must be to love someone who you only knew briefly."

Erica moved uncomfortably in her chair.

"Look, from what I've learned about your father, he doesn't sound like a man who would want his daughter to take the blame for a murder she didn't commit."

Erica turned to Cohen. "I want a cigarette, please?"

"I'm sorry, but they don't allow smoking in the prison."

"Give her a cigarette and don't worry about it," Grey said, impatiently.

Cohen opened her purse and removed a pack of Marlboro Lights and a lighter and gave them to Erica. Cohen and Grey watched her light a cigarette and exhale. Grey noticed her hand shaking.

"He looked at me," she said, her accent heavy.

"Who looked at you?" Grey said.

She paused in the lingering cigarette smoke. "The man who killed my father."

"What did he look like?"

She shrugged. Her manner told Grey she was familiar with police interrogations. "I don't know. He was a young guy."

Grey sat in disbelief, wondering whether she was telling the truth, or had he missed a clue because he was too caught up in trying to find an old spy.

"A young guy shot your father?"

"Yes, it is true."

"How young?"

"I don't know; my age, perhaps a little older."

Cohen asked her, "Why do you think he didn't shoot you?"

Erica shook her head. "I don't know, maybe he noticed my tattoo." She tugged back the sleeve covering her bony left arm to expose the black swastika.

"What happened after he looked at you?" Grey said.

"He left the house," Erica said. "It happened quickly."

This new development confused Grey and he needed a moment to consider it. He told Erica to relax before leaving to go into the next room, where Christopher stood with Cooksey, who had arrived minutes earlier. They had been listening on the intercom.

"Looks like you're chasing the wrong man," Christopher said.

Grey ignored him and looked at Cooksey. "Dave, what do you think?"

Cooksey appeared unimpressed. "I wanna hear more. If her story's credible, well, along with the fingerprint analysis you sent me, we may drop some of the charges."

"Some?"

"Sam, we still have her on breaking-and-entering, and now fleeing the scene of a crime, and not reporting a crime," the prosecutor said.

Grey rolled his eyes in frustration and returned to Cohen and Erica.

As he paced, Cohen advised Erica she did not have to continue. Erica watched Grey and shook her head. "No, I will talk to him."

The matron brought a pot of coffee and three Styrofoam cups. Grey poured for everyone.

"Let's start from the beginning," he said. "How did you find out Eric was your father."

"Let me ask you a question, please?" she said.

"Fine, go ahead."

"Your father, he is really dead, yes?"

"Yes, he died of a heart attack and it has not been easy for me."

"Why?"

Grey's voice became dry. "I wasn't there and never had a chance to say good-bye."

Erica nodded and reached for another cigarette. Grey cleared his throat. "Okay, now, tell me about you."

Her childhood became lonely when her mother married a demanding engineer who made it clear he had no interest in her as a stepdaughter. Gerlinda focused most of her time and energy on her husband and their two children, leaving a widening gulf between Erica and the family.

Erica grew up an outsider, which often left her despondent. Her adolescence was aimless as she came to understand she was not loved because she had no father.

Gerlinda saw her choice: husband or daughter. She chose her husband and insisted Erica accept the decision. Erica struggled to obey her mother, but by her early teens she was rebelling, searching for acceptance.

"It was sex, drugs and rock 'n roll," she told Grey. "It still is."

"And neo-Nazis?" Grey said.

Erica rubbed the arm bearing the swastika and said, sheepishly, "I dropped those guys a few years ago. They were too violent."

"How did you find your father?"

"My mother showed me the article in the newspaper."

"I had the impression you and your mother didn't get along?"

"Yes, for a long time we didn't, but in the last year we have been working to know each other again. Perhaps she has some guilt, I don't know."

"Why didn't your mother come with you to meet your father?"

"Her husband would not permit it. She gave me plane fare and money along with a letter and an old photograph of her and my father, which I gave to him."

She held the letter and photograph the entire time on the bus she rode from Philadelphia to Lewes. She checked into a motel. She was tired, but eager to see her father. She put away her black boots, black jeans and white T-shirt and dressed in a long-sleeved yellow blouse, skirt and sandals. It was late afternoon when she stood on his porch and rang the doorbell.

Erica recognized him immediately and started to shake. Tears streamed down her cheeks, upsetting Hoest who stood in the doorway confused. "May I help you?"

"My name is Erica Hoest." She handed him the letter from her mother.

Hoest held the envelope carefully, stunned by the woman's remark. He removed a pair of wire-rimmed glasses from his shirt pocket and examined the old, color photograph and the letter. He gasped and looked closely at Erica.

"Come inside, please."

Erica stood in the living room under Hoest's inspection. He could see familiar features around her eyes, her chin, her nose. She was tall, like him. He started to cry and said in a tone mixed with anger and happiness, "Why did she not tell me?"

Erica, eyes red and teary, shook her head. "I don't know; are you happy I'm here? I've wanted to meet you for so long."

Hoest held her and spoke softly. "Yes, Erica, of course, of course; how old are you?"

"Thirty two."

"Well, I want to spend the next thirty two years finding out what I missed."

They laughed and cried until Hoest thought to offer dinner. In the kitchen, she helped him prepare fresh Atlantic halibut, broiled jumbo shrimp, small red potatoes and salad with an oil and vinegar dressing. He uncorked a bottle of Chardonnay and they spent the next few hours talking.

"I cared for your mother very much, but our relationship wasn't strong enough, I felt, for marriage. Your mother felt that way, too," Hoest said. "It's unforgivable, though, for her to have never told me about you."

Erica loved the lanky seaman, his weather-beaten face smiling at her. She was proud of him, proud to be his daughter; ecstatic over how he accepted and loved her. He listened with all the compassion she always needed as she told him of her troubled life.

"Later, I want to show you my tattoos." She smiled, but worried about what his reaction would be to the swastika.

"Tattoos? Why does a beautiful young woman need tattoos?"

"Oh, everyone gets tattoos these days."

"They do?" Hoest stood and started to clear the table. "I haven't noticed."

Erica laughed as he winked at her.

She excused herself and went to the bathroom. She removed her blouse and looked in the mirror. The tattoos scorched most of her gaunt torso. They marked pain, anguish and foolishness. She stared at herself a long time, unable to decide whether to show him, fearing rejection.

She didn't hear the doorbell ring, didn't hear the short conversation; but she heard the two shots. They were loud and clear. Still in her bra, she opened the door. Her father lay sprawled on the floor, blood soaking his shirt; a young man stood over him, holding a newspaper clipping.

He glanced at her in panic, the clipping dropped from his hand to the floor. He fled. Erica fell to her knees; calling to her father through her tears, but she could see he was lifeless.

"I grabbed my blouse and hurried out," she told Grey.

"Why didn't you call the police?"

"I was afraid no one would believe me, that I would be blamed; and I was angry at him for dying, for ending my hopes."

Erica returned two days later wanting something of her father's as a remembrance. She broke in through the basement window and wandered through rooms in search of the keepsake she felt she desperately needed.

"I was upstairs when you and the other policeman came to the house. I hid in a closet."

"Is there anything else about the shooter you can remember?" Grey asked.

Erica considered the question. "He may have had brown hair; I'm not really sure."

"What about the gun, did you see the gun?"

Erica looked emotionally drained. "No, I'm sorry."

Cohen said, "I think that's enough for today."

Grey agreed. The matron arrived to escort her to her cell. Erica inquired, "What is going to happen to me now?"

"We're going to get you out of here," Cohen said.

Erica turned to Grey. "I'll talk to the prosecutor," he said.

Christopher remained skeptical, but Cooksey agreed to drop all charges as long as Erica agreed to stand as a material witness once the murderer was caught.

"One more thing," Cooksey said to Grey. "We're releasing her into your custody."

"My custody? Why?"

"You're handling the case, you seem to be on the murderer's trail," the prosecutor said. "I can't imagine anyone more capable."

Grey grudgingly agreed. Cohen volunteered to let Erica stay with her.

"You sure you want to, Beth?"

"Sure, it's not often a Jew gets to entertain a neo-Nazi in her home." Cohen had sympathy for Erica. "The only person she really hates now is herself and the man who killed her father."

Grey accompanied the women to Cohen's home the next day. The public defender sent him off with a reassurance Erica would be fine. He headed to Harrisburg, hoping to find Henry Martin, and hoping Martin had answers to Hoest's murder.

He alone felt confident. Even Davis, after hearing Erica's story, doubted he would find the man. "How are you still so sure?"

Grey offered his slim clue: After failing to find Martin listed in the Harrisburg-Hershey metropolitan area directory, he re-checked calls to Hoest's house in the two weeks prior to the murder and found one from a diner in Harrisburg.

"Sounds like a long shot, Sam."

"It's the best one I have."

"Even if you find this guy, how are you sure he's connected to the murder?"

Grey smiled. "Let's call it a hunch."

Chapter 12

Harrisburg, Pennsylvania

Three days before Hoest's murder

Martin Hahn glanced at the headline before turning the front page. Politics never much interested him, but this caught his attention, only momentarily, and he turned the page back to read: "Lieberman first Jewish candidate on a national ticket."

He flipped the page for something more interesting. He found it several pages inside the newspaper. "U-boat Captain" – the words made him pause to study the article. His hands shook as he looked at the accompanying photograph and the name in the caption – Eric Hoest.

Is it possible? He examined the unsmiling man whose aged features slightly resembled those of the Hoest he had known.

Like gentle beach surf picking up rhythm from an approaching storm, the past lapped at his memory just before a wave came crashing down, and there was the young U-boat captain in his white cap with a big, toothy grin stretching across his bearded face.

"Can't you talk to me without spouting a line from the Hitler Youth manual?"

He was sure this was the man who befriended him on the long voyage into uncertainty; to his relief he found no mention of the secret mission. From the description of him and his quotes, Hoest sounded like the same compassionate man Hahn had come to know.

"Good luck, Hahn. You'll do fine."

Hahn needed to talk to him. Hoest was a link to his German past severed from him when he landed on American shores. A past he had dared not share with his wife. A past he had spent years subverting to avoid revealing himself.

A past he could no longer suppress as memories of Munich came back to haunt.

"We are marching! Hitler Jugend!"

Through smoldering rubble of a Munich neighborhood destroyed by allied bombs, Hahn chased a member of the student resistance movement.

He had identified the suspect for the three Gestapo men who were now, with two local policemen, in urgent pursuit.

Hahn was nineteen, faster than the men. He raced ahead, sprinting across the endless mounds of brick and splintered-lumber debris; running through charred, roofless remains of bomb-gutted shops and apartment houses.

He was catching up to the student; just yards away – then, an echo from the crack of rifle fire. The figure fell forward, forcibly, as if shoved by an unseen hand.

Hahn stopped, breathing hard. He approached the student who lay writhing in pain with a pant leg soaked in blood. The young woman's eyes pleaded with him, but Hahn, in his black HJ uniform, stared back impassively.

The Gestapo men and police, one with a rifle slung over his shoulder, were upon her, out of breath, enraged.

"*Schwein*!" They screamed as they viciously, almost manically, kicked her.

Hahn watched their booted feet strike her back, her buttocks. He grew angry – at her, at himself – as she cried and begged until they stopped and dragged her off.

The next morning Gerhard summoned Hahn, commending him for his counter-espionage work. The general, in his black SS uniform, put on his billed cap; a shinning death head insignia fastened in the center, and beckoned Hahn to follow.

They walked casually through Gestapo headquarters to the courtyard, where a guillotine stood atop a three-foot high platform. Soldiers marched the young woman out, her hands bound, her face expressing a mixture of fear and defiance.

Stillness clung to the air. All was quiet except for the crunching of boots marching across gravel. The soldiers stopped before the guillotine.

Gerhard stood next to the apparatus and gave the order. "Proceed."

The executioner shoved her to her knees and forcibly bent her over as he placed her thin young neck under the apparatus's glinting blade. Sunlight flashed off the slanted metal as it fell hard, loud – a dull thud, the head apart from the body, plopping into a blood-splattered bucket.

Hahn showed no emotion, but turmoil raged in his heart and mind. The scene repeated with six other students until blood dripped like paint off the guillotine blade. He felt Gerhard's hand squeeze his shoulder, guiding him back to his office.

"We are marching! Hitler Jugend!"

"Hahn! Komst du heir, bitte." HJ Leader Schickle – brown shirt and tie, tan breeches, well-polished black jackboots – stood in his office doorway. He has a slight build and serious expression. Hahn, already at attention, walked into the office. Schickle ordered him to sit.

"Hahn, we're at war and in war we make sacrifices," Schickle recited. "I regret to inform you that, according to a report from Hamburg, your parents are dead."

The Hitler Youth required – taught until it become rote – that the individual think of the group first; always the group, not the individual; the group was more important. Any weakness hurt the group – outward expressions of emotion were not tolerated.

Hahn looked at the *oberfuhrer* blankly and nodded.

"They along with other loyal and courageous citizens died in the bombing raid," Schickle said, crisply, perfunctorily. "Therefore the party will provide for you. *Heil Hitler.*"

Fire trucks screamed past the house, jarring him back from his memories. He dropped the newspaper to peer through lace curtains. The sirens faded and a car door slammed shut. His blue eyes shifted to see Kurt coming toward the house.

Kurt worried him. He suffered emotional problems Hahn never accepted, leaving Eileen or school counselors or doctors to handle. He worsened in his mid-teens, when Eileen turned ill and died of breast cancer. Only the medication calmed Kurt's anger.

Eileen's illness at first left Hahn unable to cope. He could not bear to consider losing her and focused his attention on the candy company, which by then had become a local institution.

His employees – four candy makers, two delivery drivers, two sales people, bookkeeper, and receptionist – urged him to take time off, but Hahn found excuses to avoid frequent hospital visits. He would hardly speak about Eileen's illness to his son while Kurt spent every day where Hahn could not – at his mother's bedside.

Hahn questioned whether Kurt had contributed to her death. He had been born late in her life and was a difficult delivery. After burying Eileen, Hahn realized he and Kurt never had much to say to each other about anything.

He tried to reach his son by involving him in the company, figuring it was a way to bring them closer together. He had expressed hope Kurt would assume control of the operations when he retired, but Kurt had no interest in carrying on a business that consumed his father.

Hahn grew frustrated and lost interest trying; never learning what interested Kurt. Their relationship developed into moments of awkward silence between an idle chatter of two people resigned to each other.

Hahn heard the door open and keys jangle. Kurt came into the living room as Hahn was getting back into his chair. He was lean, kept his blond hair unkempt. He had his father's sharp jaw line, but his mother's dark eyes and small nose. At thirty-four, he had few friends, dated infrequently, spoke quietly.

He greeted his father with a soft, "Hi." He wore a suit, his tie askew. He was a computer analyst with the state. He had decided to visit his father on the way home.

"Got anything to drink?" He headed toward the kitchen.

Hahn followed, his hand gripping the newspaper. He watched Kurt search the refrigerator and remove a bottle of beer, twist off the cap, and sip.

"Would you like to stay for dinner?"

"Uh, I don't know," Kurt said. He spied the newspaper headline. "A Jew, huh?"

Hahn shook his head and shrugged. "He's a politician."

"He's a Jew," Kurt said, taking another sip.

To hear his son utter the word in such disdain disturbed Hahn, more so because he could hear himself sixty years ago. He also could hear his father, admonishing him.

"I don't care that your teacher believes these things, Martin, I have not raised you to hate people, not even Jews."

Young Hahn was thirteen, soldierly in manner and appearance, wearing a brown and gray school uniform with his red and black swastika armband. He glared at his father, suspiciously. "I could report you for that."

"Martin!" Hahn turned to his mother in the doorway of their Hamburg home. She angrily reproached him. "You never speak to your father that way, never!"

Young Hahn protested. "But it's true. My HJ leader warned us that's how enemies to the Fatherland speak, my HJ leader told us."

The anger drained from his mother's expression and she smiled at him and said, "Yes, but your father's a good German." She glared at her husband admonishingly. "Klaus, must you be so harsh? He's only repeating what he's taught."

Klaus Hahn seethed over his American wife's rebuke. He quickly left the room to end the discussion, fearing his son would indeed report him to the Gestapo.

Hahn looked at his mother. "It is true what they say about the Jews, isn't it?"

Mary Hahn, born of German-American parents and raised in Chicago, smiled warmly at her son. She considered herself German first, and unlike her husband, she believed in Hitler and Nazism's racial views. She put her arm around her son. "Yes, dear, yes."

Kurt's mother certainly never expressed such sentiments. Hahn himself had over the years realized how misguided his anti-Semitic views were, partly because of Eileen, largely because he discovered what the Nazis taught him was not true as he came to know Jews.

Moss Bergman perhaps helped him the most, though inadvertently, one spring morning in 1949. Now a successful businessman, Hahn wanted to show this man appreciation and friendship by inviting him to the country club other Chamber of Commerce members urged him to join.

Bergman wore his yarmulke and Hahn was oblivious to the stares they were getting as they waited for the maitre d' to seat them. The club's manager approached him and whispered into his ear something he had not heard since his days in Germany's Third Reich.

"I'm sorry sir," the man said. "It's club rules."

Hahn turned to his friend, embarrassed. Bergman knowingly nodded and took the young man by the arm, escorting him outside. They climbed into Hahn's new blue Dodge convertible, and Bergman smiled. "At least I got to see what I'm missing."

"What do you mean?"

"I was surprised you brought me here. Didn't you know Jews are not allowed?"

"But how is that possible?" Hahn said, angrily. "This is America."

"Sure," Bergman said.

The 51-year-old memory faded. Hahn studied his son. He doubted Kurt hated Jews, but wondered why he expressed such dislike. Was it related to his battle with depression?

As a teenager Kurt would infuriate Hahn on this issue.

When the family sat down – at Eileen's urging – to watch *Holocaust,* the first television drama about the Nazi's genocide against the Jews, Kurt commented inappropriately at scenes of naked women and children being herded to their death in gas chambers.

His giggles provoked a ferocious rage in Hahn, quieting his son and startling Eileen. She sensed a moment in him. Was he about to share something of himself? Nearly, but Hahn caught himself, fearful of his family's reaction after what they spent the last few nights watching.

Even as death closed in on her the last morning as he sat by her bedside, a place he finally reached only because he knew she would soon be gone, Hahn could not bring himself to tell her.

He once considered telling Kurt – shortly after his son graduated college – but decided it would be pointless. What did it matter anyway, the war was history.

Hahn admonished his son. "Are you off your medication again?"

Kurt looked at the floor and uttered a barely audible whisper. "No."

"Let's not have such talk then."

Kurt sipped his beer and went to the living room.

"So, how's your friend, Dana?" Hahn asked, following him.

"She's living in Philadelphia," Kurt said, plopping into a chair.

"Oh? No longer working for the state?"

Kurt shook his head. "Quit two months ago to work on the Gore campaign."

Dana's father was an attorney active in Pennsylvania's Democratic Party. When she told him about her interest in going to work somewhere in Washington D.C., he urged her to join Al Gore's presidential campaign.

"It's a smart step to make the right contacts," her father told her. He helped her land a job as an assistant state coordinator.

"Would you like to stay for dinner?"

"I've got things to do tonight."

Hahn bristled. "When was the last time we had a meal together?"

Kurt sat, staring at the wall, not wanting to answer the question.

"It's been weeks. I feel like I don't know you anymore."

Kurt took a sip of beer. "Did you ever?"

"What the hell does that mean?"

Kurt set the bottle on the end table and stood. "I have to go; maybe we can have dinner later this week." He started for the door. Hahn followed, demanding an answer. "I asked you a question."

Kurt turned and spoke calmly. "You never cared to know who I am or to know who mom was or to share who you are. That's how it's been so I'm not sure there's any need to change."

"I'm your father whether you like it or not."

"I've got to go."

"No. Wait."

Kurt detected desperation and wondered whether his father was lonely in his old age. He didn't know Hahn had been lonely most of his life. "I'm sorry," his father said. "Can we try later this week to have dinner together?"

Kurt let go of the door knob. He felt sympathetic toward his father and hopeful, though just slightly, about their relationship. "Tomorrow night?"

Hahn smiled. "Come over around six."

The next morning Hahn sat at the counter of the East Shore Diner. He had been having breakfast there since Eileen's death. He read again the article on Hoest, which he had carefully cut out of the newspaper.

Toast and eggs set before him an hour earlier went unfinished. He sipped coffee and tried to decide whether to contact the old U-boat commander. He feared doing it. Hoest might want to turn him in or worse, thought Hahn, might not remember him.

"Marty, you keep looking at that phone. If you've gotta make a call, dear, make a call." Vivian was a young, talkative, waitress with bleached-blond hair and an attitude to match. She always waited on Hahn.

"Do you need some change for the phone, dear?" She gave him a pink lipstick smile.

Hahn handed her a dollar. With long, pink-painted finger nails, she scooped four quarters from the cash register drawer and dropped them in his hand. He climbed off the stool, went over to the phone by the restrooms and dialed information. He jotted Hoest's number on a napkin, but couldn't get himself to make the call. He went back and sat down.

"That was a short conversation?" Vivian said.

"I only called information to get my friend's number," Hahn said.

"So why aren't you calling him, honey?"

Hahn shrugged sheepishly. "It's been so long – "

"Oh, call him, or is it her?"

Hahn smiled and shook his head. "It's not a woman."

"Well, I've got to get a gentleman at the end of the counter some coffee, but I think you should call him." She wandered off in her white uniform.

Hahn stared at the number on the napkin for a long time. He didn't know what to expect. Over the next quarter hour he glanced furtively toward the phone several more times.

Vivian noticed. She picked up the napkin by his plate and noting the number was a long-distance call grabbed a calling card out of her purse and went to the phone.

Hahn protested, but remained at his seat. "What are you doing?"

"Marty, relax." She dialed the numbers on the calling card and napkin. "Just come over here and say 'hello.'"

Hahn walked over reluctantly. As Vivian handed him the receiver he could hear a male voice saying, "Hello? Hello?"

He put the receiver to his ear and heard the voice again. "Hello?"

Nervously, Hahn said into the mouth piece, "Eric Hoest?"

"Yes?"

Hahn paused.

"Yes? Hello?"

"This is Hahn. Martin Hahn."

Vivian smiled and walked away. The voice on the line paused. "Yes?"

"I just read the article about you in the newspaper."

"Yes?"

"I'm not sure, but I believe I was your last mission to America."

A pause, then a gasp; the voice sounded excited. "*Mein Gott! Hahn*? Is it true?"

"Yes," Hahn said, feeling relieved.

"It's been so long."

They exchanged a few more pleasantries before Hahn urged a meeting.

"I'm leaving in a few minutes for my annual visit to Longwood Gardens," Hoest said. "It's not too far from you, is it?"

The mention of Longwood Gardens in Kennett Square, Pennsylvania, surprised Hahn; His monastery gardening experience never left him and he visited Longwood each year in late summer. It was a few miles from Delaware's state line.

The two men agreed to meet there early in the afternoon.

Hahn returned home excited, but anxious. He sat at the kitchen table and read the article once more before going down to his basement workshop.

He found the dust-covered gallon can of Red Arrow grease, its age denoted by a few rust spots here and there. He had not opened the can since he had sealed it fifty-four years ago, never expecting to reopen it, but keeping it for reasons he never questioned.

A screw driver pried opened the air-tight lid. Hahn thrust his hand into the thick amber gel and removed the Luger and bullets from their hermetic tomb, setting them carefully on the workbench. He grabbed some rags and cleaned the weapon.

As he worked, he remembered when and why Hoest gave him the gun – on the U-boat, shortly before the landing; the commander was looking out for him – *"In case you need it."*

When Hahn finished, he loaded the bullets and brought the Luger upstairs, setting it on the kitchen table next to the newspaper story on Hoest. He debated whether to return it now or later, but decided to wait. He first wanted to see how their meeting went.

He drove two hours through rural Pennsylvania, past corn fields and Amish men in black hats and white shirts toiling behind horse-driven plows. At the vast estate he walked hurriedly to the designated meeting place – the stone Chimes Tower. It was a favorite spot where he enjoyed listening to the quarter-hour peals.

Ahead of him on the path he noticed a man standing alone, admiring the waterfalls and lush vegetation near the tower. Hahn watched him, sensing something familiar.

As he neared, the man turned and smiled. He looked curiously at Hahn.

"Hello," the man said.

Hahn now recognized him. The beard was gone, the face was weather-beaten and craggy, but he had the same big, toothy smile. The strangeness struck him; after fifty-five years he would meet the U-boat commander in a garden.

Hoest stepped back and shook his head in disbelief. He gripped Hahn's arm and looked at him closely. His blond hair was gray, but his taut skin had a healthy glow and the face still had a hint of the boy from 1945.

"What ever happened to you?" Hoest said.

"I took your advice and found a woman."

Hoest laughed, not sure what Hahn meant. They walked over to a wooden bench in a relatively secluded spot near the tower and talked for awhile about the past and what each of them had done since the war.

"Were you captured or did you surrender to the Americans?" Hoest asked.

Hahn sat silently.

"No surrender, no capture," he said, quietly. "I just assimilated."

"I don't understand."

Hahn sighed. "Technically, I guess, I still work for the Third Reich."

Hoest sat dumbfounded. It was incomprehensible. "Has the war not ended for you?"

"Of course," Hahn said, offended by the tone of the question.

"Why do you continue on?"

"I didn't know what else to do."

"All these years, how have you done it?"

"I've kept it secret." He shuddered at the void this left in his life and relationships. A wave of emotion crashed down and he sobbed with immense relief; now he could finally tell someone. "You are the first to know, the absolute first."

"Not even your family?"

"No, I was fearful about trusting them."

Hahn's situation and emotional state alarmed Hoest. The man spent more than fifty years leading a double life. He urged Hahn to go to the authorities.

"And be tried as a war criminal?"

"The war is over now; you need to stop hiding, if nothing else, for your sanity."

"I'm seventy-five. I don't need to worry about my sanity anymore."

Hoest tried to convince Hahn to turn himself in. "At least do it for your family; shouldn't your son know who you are?"

Their conversation could continue no further. Hahn worried Hoest might report him and Hoest worried about Hahn's emotional state. He invited Hahn to visit him in Delaware. Perhaps over time, Hoest thought, he could convince his old charge.

They parted. Hoest promised to call, offering to accompany Hahn to the authorities once he made the decision. Hahn was reluctant, but he told Hoest he would consider it.

On his way home Hahn thought how strange it felt after all this years of having jealously guarded his past to have finally revealed himself. Suddenly his scares of being found out swiftly came back to haunt him. It was the mid-1960s and a small group of American Nazi Party members, led by World War II veteran George Lincoln Rockwell, was conducting a rally on the courthouse steps.

Hahn, unaware of the rally, was downtown running an errand at the time when he came upon the sight of men wearing swastika arm bands, waving a large red and black swastika flag, and protestors jeering at them. His curiosity pulled him into the melee.

As he stood at the edge of the rally, one of the brown-shirted storm troopers standing next to Rockwell, who was shouting "white power," pointed at the tall, blond-haired, blue-eyed Hahn, and yelled: "You! You are one of us! Defend your race. Join us here!"

Some of the protestors looked at Hahn, now fear-stricken. He turned quickly and hurried away, scared and angry that such a silly, pathetic group could be allowed to have a rally. For the next few days, Hahn worried, needlessly, but the incident stayed with him.

As his vehicle rolled past Amish farmland, he decided surrender was impossible because it would mean losing all that he had built over the years.

It would mean losing Kurt.

He wondered whether Hoest would report him now, but shook off his fear, believing the U-boat commander more compassionate. Still, he considered what Hoest might do if he did not surrender.

Hahn checked his watch. It was five-twenty and he had nearly an hour's drive ahead of him. He hoped Kurt would wait.

He arrived home to find Kurt in the kitchen, sitting at the table, his hand resting on the Luger, his disheveled blond hair hiding his face. His son was reading the clipping and did not move to acknowledge his father until he finished.

Kurt turned his head slowly, a puzzled expression on his face, and looked at Hahn.

"What's this all about?"

For a split moment Hahn searched for a story, a lie, anything to conceal his true identity, but he felt very tired and beaten; the drain on his emotions opened earlier in the day and now he couldn't put a stopper in it. In a hoarse, nervous voice, he said, "It's about my past."

Kurt felt a sudden surge of excitement, sensing he was about to learn something about his father whose approval he sought so unsuccessfully over the years. All his life he wondered about this reticent man; his father's history began with his business and the courtship of his wife.

As his mother had, Kurt always sensed his father hiding something, not just from them, but from the world. He realized long ago his father's reclusive nature had become *his* reclusive nature; a comfortable, but unhappy existence.

Now, eagerly, Kurt wanted to know. "Can you tell me, please?"

Hahn, ashen-faced and nervous, moved a chair with a shaky hand and sat next to his son and told him about the mission; about the man he killed; about Germany; about his youth; about his parent's fiery death.

He shared everything except for his betrayal of the seven students. He was too ashamed to tell his son.

Kurt listened with intense interest, at times pride, as his father's life unfolded before him over the next few hours. When Hahn finished, his son said, "Mom never knew any of this?"

Hahn shook his head.

"Why tell me now?"

"I wanted you to know, in case I'm arrested."

"For what?"

"I met Hoest today." he nodded at the Luger. "That belongs to him. He believes I should surrender, but it's not possible."

"Why?"

"I'm a war criminal; what do you think they'd do with me?"

Kurt shook his head and said softly, "I don't know."

"I don't want to lose you, not now."

For the first time, Kurt sensed his father's love for him. "You won't."

Hahn leaned forward and firmly, but gently squeezed his son's shoulder. "I'm worried."

"About what?"

"Hoest. I don't believe he will tell the authorities, but I'm not sure."

"Is there anything I can do?"

Hahn shook his head. "This is my problem."

He looked around and said, "I promised you dinner so let me get started."

"No, it's okay. I'm not hungry and it's getting late."

"Are you leaving?"

"Let's have dinner tomorrow, at my place."

Hahn smiled. He took the invitation as a start, he hoped, of a relationship he should have long had with his son.

"I've never been much of a father, but I want to change," he said.

Kurt had lost hope of ever having a meaningful relationship with his father years ago and he was unsure how to react. "It's been a strange life."

Hahn walked his son to the door. Kurt turned to him. "Thanks, dad, for telling me." Hahn mustered a nod. It was the first time his son had called him "dad" in years.

He forewent dinner and retired for the night, emotionally exhausted.

Sunlight filled the kitchen when he returned in the morning. He noticed the clipping and Luger missing from the table. He wondered whether he had stored them last night and forgotten, but as he started to search he realized his son must have taken the gun.

Hahn was puzzled.

He called Kurt's apartment and got no answer. He tried to reach him at his job, but he had not reported to work. He would spend days trying to track down his son, but without success.

Kurt had disappeared.

Chapter 13

Harrisburg, Pennsylvania

Grey thought the sign's Old English lettering – Martin's Chocolates – looked dated and out of place on the boxy red-brick building; and so did the building, situated along a tree-lined street in a quiet neighborhood of old Victorian homes.

Rich chocolate aromas greeted him as he entered the small, homey front office. A pudgy, gray-haired woman at the desk chatted on the phone and glanced at him with disinterest. He had not found 'Henry Martin' in the phone book and decided to visit the company, still unsure of the name of the man he sought or whether he owned the little chocolate factory.

After a few minutes the receptionist sighed into the receiver. "Honey, somebody's come in, call me tonight, will ya?"

As she hung up, Grey introduced himself and asked for Henry Martin. The woman gave him a dour look.

"Who're you looking for?"

"Henry Martin," Grey repeated.

"There's no one here by that name."

"Who owns the company?"

"Martin Hahn," the woman replied.

Hahn. That sounded familiar, Grey thought. He remembered Gerhard had suggested the name to him.

Grey asked for Hahn, but the woman shook her head.

"He's retired," she said.

"Retired? How old is he?"

"Oh, I don't know, in his seventies."

The age was about right, Grey thought.

"Do you know where I can reach him?"

"No, I don't. Have you tried his house?"

Grey shook his head. She grudgingly wrote down the address and directions to the house, just a few of blocks away. He asked the woman when Hahn retired. "About a year ago," she said. "His son had no interest so he turned the company over to his brother-in-law, Bill Long."

"Son?" Grey said. "How old is his son?"

The woman answered impatiently as the phone rang. "Ask Mr. Hahn, I don't know."

Grey hurried to his car and pulled from the curb with a glance in his side-view mirror that failed to catch the white sedan and a blond man sitting behind the wheel, watching him.

Grey's silent dinner companion on the train to Berlin had been shadowing him since the trooper departed the Swiss alpine village. Gunter felt the end to his special assignment was near and he looked forward to a fee more generous than the general usually paid.

After Grey's initial meeting with Gerhard in Adleboden, the old general decided to have him followed. It was, he believed, his best chance at finding Hahn.

Gerhard cursed Rhonen for the situation he found himself in; the damn fool and his secret mission, he railed at Paul. After decades of American protection from Jewish hunters and zealous prosecutors, a ghost haunted him, a ghost who could help those traitors' families in Munich.

His CIA patrons had become infuriatingly unhelpful. They couldn't – wouldn't was what he believed more likely – shield him from German prosecutors, if witnesses or evidence surfaced connecting him to war crimes. He would be on his own, they told him.

Laughable, Gerhard thought. He had organized coups and assassinations in Africa, South America, Europe and the Middle East; provided mercenaries for counter rebellions and weapons to terrorists from Angola to Pakistan; and he led an insurgency using boys from the Hitler Youth – his "werewolves" – that slowed the Allies' occupation of Germany.

Now he was going to be brought down by a former ungrateful HJ protégé?

Never!

That evening Gerhard called Bill Smith, his American friend. Smith was former CIA, an operative the agency recruited in the Cold War's last years to report what he heard about Soviet military hardware during business trips to East Bloc countries.

Lucrative opportunities opened for Smith in the arms markets. The agency trusted him for his discrete conduct and for keeping secrets. Smith met Gerhard in his CIA days; they found they could each profit off the other's business dealings.

Gerhard also alerted Gunter, one of his protégés from the Stasi, the defunct East German secret police. Gerhard appreciated the Stasi. It was similar to the Gestapo.

A devoted bird watcher and trained assassin, Gunter was quiet and methodical with little need for human company. He met the general when the Berlin wall fell in 1989. East Germany's government had collapsed and unified Germany had no need for men like Gunter.

Gerhard did.

Smith set out from his home in Innsbruck and Gunter from somewhere in Europe. They arrived at Gerhard's alpine villa near Adleboden late that night and listened to the old general's orders as he sat on a couch, sipping wine in a large living room with a wall-sized window.

"I want you to find out from this police officer where Hahn is," Gerhard ordered.

Gunter would not think to question the command, but Smith worried his friend was overreacting. "What makes you think he's alive? It's been half a century," Smith said.

Gerhard snapped at him. "I know he is! As I told you earlier, that Negro would not have traveled this far."

"He could be wrong," Smith said.

Gerhard shouted; his voice in high pitch. "And what if he's not, Bill?"

Finding Hahn was of the utmost importance. He was the sole surviving witness Germany needed to convict Gerhard for beheading the seven students who the general still referred to half a century later as "bastard traitors to the Fatherland."

Gerhard calmed down and spoke in a low voice, "I want you to find him and have Gunter deal with him."

Smith lit a cigarette and nodded reluctantly, wondering whether the general suffered from the sad illusion as many men of his station – that he would live forever. Smith glanced at Gunter, who stood waiting to act on the general's order, then at Gerhard.

"Well," Smith said, "how do we find this guy?"

"I will visit the American at his hotel in the morning and tell him some of what he wants to know," Gerhard said. "That should give you two the time to prepare and follow him."

"Follow him?" Smith said. "We could be following him all over the world."

"I don't think so," Gerhard said. "Hahn's in America."

Smith was skeptical. "What if he lives under a new name? We don't even know what he looks like."

"That's precisely why I want you to follow the policeman," Gerhard said.

Gunter and Smith did as ordered, following Grey to Heidelberg and onto the train Smith routinely rode. With no success in getting information from Grey, Smith decided Gunter should follow him alone. Gunter agreed readily. He preferred always to work alone.

As he followed Grey through the streets of Harrisburg he sensed he would soon return home to his prized solitude and cherished hobby – ornithology; birds had fascinated him since childhood, particularly hawks and falcons; birds of prey.

Grey found Hahn's house and drove past. He parked in the alley behind it and, as he stepped out of the car, the back door of the house swung open. A tall, lean gray-haired man, unaware he was being watched, ambled down the porch steps, and entered an old garage.

Grey felt nervous energy at the sight of the man. Was this Martin Hahn? He had been hunting him so intensely that he had formed his own idea of what Hahn would look like. The man who walked out of the house had the same Nordic appearance Grey had imagined.

An engine started as the garage door opened. Grey got back into the car as Hahn, driving an old BMW, backed out and drove down the alley. Grey concentrated on where his suspect was going. Hahn drove past the front of his house and passed a white sedan parked across the street. Grey did not look in his rear-view mirror to see the sedan swing out of its parking space and turn sharply to join their little caravan.

The old German drove into downtown Harrisburg and stopped outside a 1920s style dark-brick apartment house along a busy street. Gunter spotted a space at the end of the block and out of Grey's sight and quickly parked. Grey pulled to the curb across the street and switched off the engine. He watched Hahn move tentatively up the building's steps before entering.

Grey hopped out and entered the building as soon as the old glass-pane doors closed behind Hahn. He found him standing in a dimly lit lobby, waiting for the elevator.

"Mr. Hahn?"

Hahn raised his downcast face and his tired eyes and carefully scanned the young, husky black man in jacket and tie. Perspiration beaded on Grey's forehead.

"You are sweating," Hahn said, in a startled tone.

"Mr. Hahn?"

"Do I know you?"

Grey produced his badge. "I'd like to talk to you about Eric Hoest."

The dark-painted elevator doors creaked open slowly. Hahn moved quickly and stepped inside. Grey followed and stood by the panel of buttons. Hahn nodded. "Third floor."

Grey pushed the button and the doors closed. As the elevator car ascended, Grey studied the man. He looked remarkably healthy for his age, but his eyes unmasked exhaustion; his right hand shook nervously.

Neither man spoke until the elevator stopped and the doors opened. Hahn stepped out of the car and a strong sense of hopelessness overcame him. He was deeply worried that he hadn't seen his son since the night he revealed his true identity. He turned to Grey:

"I'm going to see my son. I've not heard from him in weeks and I'm concerned."

Grey listened.

"I come every day and knock, but there's no answer." Hahn sounded frustrated. "Why won't he answer?"

They walked down the hallway and stopped at the apartment door. Hahn knocked hard, but no answer. He tried the knob. It was locked. He looked desperate.

"Can you help me?" he said to Grey. "Can you help me find my son?"

"Do you have a key to his apartment?" Grey asked.

Hahn shook his head. Grey took him to the building manager's office. A skinny guy in an oily pompadour and jangling keys dangling from his pocket took them back upstairs and opened the apartment door.

Inside, sunlight filtered through narrow window-blind slats in the living room. The five-room apartment had signs someone had been there recently. Grey noticed them, but focused on Hahn instead, watching him search for something.

Grey followed him to a cluttered bedroom – an unmade bed, newspapers and magazines littering the floor, and a low hum emanating somewhere. He followed the sound to a desk with a flat-screen monitor. He went over to the computer and casually moved the mouse across the pad. The screen lit up a montage of Nazi symbols and Hitler images.

Grey stepped back, startled. He scrutinized the room – book shelves filled with histories of the Third Reich and biographies of its leaders. German

Stukas with swastikas on their wings dived from the ceiling while tiger tanks roamed the shelves.

Pinned to a bulletin board above the desk were faded magazine clippings about the Gulf War and pictures of American soldiers in the desert, juxtaposed against black-and-white photos of Hitler's *Afrika Korps* in the desert of Libya.

Tacked by these was a newspaper article about U.S. Senator Joseph Lieberman, the vice presidential candidate.

Grey turned to Hahn, who looked dispassionate. "This is your son's home?" Hahn nodded, and Grey said, "Do you know what all this is about?"

Hahn shook his head. "I'm afraid to know."

He left the room and Grey followed him to the living room, where the former member of the Hitler Youth sat on an old, worn sofa. "We need to talk, Mr. Hahn."

"Martin. Call me Martin."

"Are you looking for something in here?"

Hahn nodded.

"What?"

"A gun."

"A gun?" Grey asked. "A German Luger?"

Hahn nodded in surprise. Grey said, "The same type of gun used to kill Hoest."

The news startled Hahn. "Hoest is dead?"

"This surprises you?"

Hahn stammered. "I'd seen him just a few weeks ago – "

He stopped, remorseful. When Kurt disappeared and Hoest never called, he suspected what happened and felt powerless. "Maybe it doesn't surprise me."

Grey looked at him. He had expected the type of arrogant, die-hard fascist he had seen in old newsreel footage on the History Channel, their arms extended as they goose-stepped down a cobblestone street; not a sympathetic figure with a broken spirit.

"Martin, do you know who killed Hoest?"

Hahn sighed, his voice tired. "I – I believe it was my son."

"Why?"

Hahn shook his head. "I don't know."

"You said you met Hoest a few weeks ago?"

"About a month ago, yes, after the article on him appeared in the newspaper. We met at Longwood Gardens."

"Was that the first you had seen him since the war?"

Hahn nodded. "He wanted me to turn myself in, thought it was for the best. I didn't want Kurt to know about my past, but he learned of it anyway."

"How?"

"He found the newspaper story about Hoest; I cut it out and left it next to the Luger."

"What was his reaction?"

Hahn shrugged. "He stole my pistol and disappeared."

"Where did you get the Luger?"

"It was Hoest's. He gave it to me in '44. I was preparing to return it to him."

"Loaded?"

"I wanted to return it as it was given."

Grey looked at the man. Something about the story didn't make sense. He said to Hahn, "You left the newspaper article and gun out for your son to find."

Hahn whispered, "Yes."

"So he would kill Hoest?"

A look of panic seized Hahn's face as he shook his head, pleading. "No, no that's not it."

"What then?" Grey demanded.

Hahn surrendered his emotions. He told Grey how he had kept secret his identity from his son. "I wanted to tell him, but I was afraid to, and thought letting him find the story would be the best way to approach it."

It was a dysfunctional way to communicate, Grey thought, but a plausible explanation.

"Where do you think he may have gone?"

"I don't know."

"How about a friend?"

Hahn shook his head, sadly and stared at the floor. "He's really never had many friends." The old German looked at Grey. "Unfortunately, I don't think I ever really knew my son."

Grey leaned over and lifted the lid of the cardboard pizza box sitting on the coffee table and showed Hahn the half-eaten meal. "Still smells fresh. And in the bathroom a damp towel's hanging over the shower curtain rod. Someone was here, last night or early this morning."

Grey wanted to question Hahn about his half-century odyssey, but felt it more urgent to find Kurt, who now was a potential murder suspect.

Unsure where to start, he wandered around, ending up in the kitchen. On the counter he noticed two brown-colored prescription bottles with labels describing psychotropic drugs. They were empty.

Grey called for Hahn, who lifted himself off the sofa and entered the kitchen. Grey held up the bottles. "Your son suffers from mental illness?" Hahn studied the bottles. "He has fought depression most of his life." Hahn frowned. "I hope he hasn't stopped taking his medication."

"Has he stopped taking it before?"

Hahn nodded, his concern deepening. "Never purposely; he would run out and forget to refill his prescription. His mother would usually get his drugs refilled."

"What happens when he's off the medication?"

Only once did Kurt go longer than a few days without medication. He was in college at the time and went missing for a week. Police found him 60 miles from the school, at a roadside campsite. He was delusional and confused, living out of his car.

Grey's desire to locate Kurt now intensified. He returned to the bedroom and stood in the doorway and stared, hoping for a sign of Kurt's whereabouts. Suddenly, he noticed on the desk a worn paperback: "Encyclopedia of Assassinations."

He walked to the desk. The book sat on top of a copy of *The Philadelphia Inquirer.* Grey moved it to see a big front page story on Joe Lieberman. His heart pounded; his eyes darted from book to article. He called to Hahn. "Martin, your son, he's a fan of Senator Lieberman?"

"Who?"

"Lieberman. The vice presidential candidate."

"I don't know," Hahn said, hesitantly as he entered the room. "Why?"

Grey cursed himself for not considering it sooner.

"What's wrong?"

Grey stared at the newspaper article. "He fits the profile."

"I don't understand."

"He's young, a loner with emotional problems; it's possible he could kill again."

"What are you talking about?"

"Often the profiles of political assassins are loners with fixations. Your son may want to kill Senator Lieberman."

"I don't believe it." Hahn slowly sat on the bed.

Grey waved expansively around the room to note the computer screen saver with Hitler's image, the books on Nazi leaders, and the war photographs. "Something's going on here and it's leading me to this conclusion."

"How do you know?"

Grey held up the *Inquirer's* front page. "Today's paper, how did it get here?" He studied the article. "Lieberman's campaigning in Philadelphia at four-thirty today."

He glanced at his watch. The event would start in four hours. It would take at least half that long to reach Philadelphia, not counting the traffic. He called his superior in Delaware, but Davis was at a meeting. Grey thought frantically.

He needed to alert the Secret Service and Philadelphia police, but going through channels would take too much time. He relayed his concerns to Davis' assistant and told her to contact the Philadelphia authorities. He returned to the bedroom. Hahn sat on the bed, staring at the floor.

"You'll have to come with me, Martin."

Hahn nodded absently and slowly rose. Grey hurried him to the car.

Gunter watched the two men emerge hurriedly from the building and followed. While they had been inside, he checked to ensure he found his prey. He went to Hahn's car, tried the door and found it unlocked.

He sorted through the glove compartment and found the automobile's registration and insurance cards. He checked the names and smiled. His assignment *was* nearing the end.

Blue and white Gore/Lieberman signs floated over hundreds of cheery supporters on the plaza at the corner of Broad and Market. A congressman stood on a flag- and bunting-bedecked platform, speaking into a microphone, joking, waving to friends as he gave a warm-up speech.

Kurt observed it all as he wandered the crowd's perimeter. He had taken the train in from Harrisburg earlier and spent the last few hours on a bench in 30th Street Station, watching people hurry to their trains.

He wore a worn sports jacket. He touched the Luger in his pocket and wondered why he brought it – for security? Security from whom? He felt confused, had been for days. He rubbed his face with his hands and felt the gun against his rib cage. The dream kept playing over in his mind, though he couldn't remember anything immediately before or after.

"You are Martin's son?" Hoest welcomed him into the house. "Where is your father?"

Kurt stepped inside. Hoest beckoned him to the study, located between the living room and kitchen. Kurt followed, removing the Luger from his pocket and pointing it at Hoest's back. He said, softly, "He's not coming."

Hoest turned around and stopped. "Hey, what the hell is this?"

Kurt perspired, his body shook. "The war ... " he squeezed the trigger "... is over."

He woke in a motel off a highway outside Baltimore. His thoughts were fuzzy. Was it just a dream? He had been on his way to Delaware, feeling exhilarated after hearing his father finally reveal himself, wanting to help him. He had planned to return the Luger and ask Hoest not to report his father to the authorities.

Something happened along the way; everything seemed to crash. Kurt did not leave the motel for days. When he did, he left his car in the city and took a Greyhound bus home.

He ignored the knocks on his door, the telephone, the messages his employer left on his answering machine. He felt alone. He felt angry for feeling alone. He spent days often sitting in movie theaters, avoiding people; coming; going. He disabled his e-mail when his employer sent him e-mails.

More knocks. He ignored them; knew it was his father, but he was embarrassed to face him. He blocked things, tried to focus on one thing; one thing to think about, and one morning the phone rang. He let the answering machine pick it up. It was Dana.

"Hi, it's me. Haven't heard from you in awhile. Give me a call or just come to Philly. Joe Lieberman is here tomorrow for a rally and yours truly is escorting him. If you want, come to the event and I'll introduce you. Hope all's well. And *call* me."

Dana. She could straighten this out, but did he want to involve her? He spent the day weighing whether to call her. When he did, he got her answering machine. He did not leave a message. He decided he would meet her there, at the event.

The crowd grew. Police sirens wailed: Lieberman was coming. Kurt started toward the corner of the plaza where the candidate's car was expected. Then he heard his name called.

His father was across the street, getting out of a car with a black man. They came toward him. Kurt ran as his father called after him.

"Kurt!" Hahn shouted, as he watched his son flee through busy traffic.

Grey grabbed Hahn's arm and rushed him across the street. They started to run, but Hahn, physically unable to keep up, stopped and bent over, his hands on his knees, breathing heavily as he insisted Grey go on without him.

Torn over what to do, Grey looked first at Hahn then down the street to see Kurt pushing through the crowded sidewalk.

"Go!" Hahn barked, hoarsely, still breathing heavily.

Grey decided to trust his instinct and raced off.

Hahn watched him as his breathing became more regular. He stood and began to turn when he felt someone at his back, pushing him into an alleyway.

"*Herr Hahn*," a voice snarled. He tried to see his assailant who shoved him behind a trash dumpster next to a loading dock. He was spun around and pushed up against a brick wall. He looked into the face of an unfamiliar blond-haired man.

A gloved hand went over his mouth as he looked into the man's cold dark eyes. He felt the excruciating pain from a knife getting shoved into his upper abdomen. He gasped as he slid down the wall. The last thing he heard was a loud bang and the rattle of chains and a motor.

The opening of the loading dock's heavy metal door startled Gunter. He pulled the knife out, confident of death as he felt Hahn's body relax. He moved fast, wiping the bloody blade on Hahn's coat and returning it to his pocket. He hurried away from gruff voices of men grumbling about work.

As Gunter neared his car he found he had hurriedly parked in a bus zone. He stopped. A policeman was peering inside the vehicle. He approached slowly while, halfway down the block, noise from the Lieberman event grew louder.

The patrolman glanced at Gunter, irritated. "This your car, sir?" Gunter nodded. "This is a clearly marked bus zone," the patrolman said, writing in his ticket book. "I'll need to see your license and registration, please."

Gunter was outwardly calm while inside he was nervous, cursing himself for the blunder that now jeopardized his assignment. He feigned ignorance of the language. "*Es tut mir leid, ich spreche kein englisch.*"

The patrolman looked at him. "What?

"*Ich spreche kein englisch.*"

The patrolman shook his head. "You don't speak English?"

"*Nein.*"

Muttering, the patrolman removed his own driver's license from his wallet and showed it to Gunter. "Do you have one of these, identification?" he said.

Gunter expressed confusion before handing over an international driver's license with its false name and address, and rental car registration. As the patrolman examined the identification, the crowd roared as Lieberman appeared on stage.

"*Was ist los?*" Gunter asked, sensing the officer was about to let him go.

"Ah, okay buddy," the patrolman said, handing back the identification cards and waving him off. "Let's get the vehicle out of the bus zone."

Once out of the city and onto the highway headed to Philadelphia International Airport, Gunter relaxed. It had been a long assignment, spent mostly living out of the rental car, waiting for a break he thought might never come.

Now he would return home, into the nether reaches of Europe, into the obscurity from which Gerhard had pulled him, absolutely confident there would be no trace of his ever having been in the United States. He would go back to studying birds.

Fear consumed Kurt as he broke from a knot of pedestrians and shot a look back to see Grey sprinting toward him. He tripped as he pushed by a woman, pulled up and darted down a narrow alleyway. Someone yelled "Stop!" But he kept running.

Grey shouted again as a big paneled truck lumbered down the alley, leaving no room on either side of the narrow passage. He watched, impressed as Kurt dropped to the ground and lay flat as the vehicle rolled over him and stopped.

He looked underneath to see Kurt scramble away. Grey yelled and frantically waved the driver on. Gears groaned, and the truck lurched forward, the driver cursing. Grey sprinted to the end of the alley and stopped. Pressed up against a brick wall, he peered around the corner to see his suspect at a subway station entrance.

Kurt glanced back furtively and descended the subway stairs. Grey hurried after. When he reached the platform he slowly moved along the wall, darting his eyes in search of Kurt. He spotted him near the end, sitting on a bench alone.

Air rushed out of the tunnel followed by a rumble and sounds of metal squealing against metal as the train hurtled past the platform. Moments later the doors hissed open. Kurt boarded. Grey followed in the next car. He found a seat that allowed him to watch Kurt without being seen by him. Kurt took a seat with his back to Grey.

From station to station, Kurt seemed immobile. As the train emerged from darkness into the sunlight, Grey wondered where the young man was going. The train rumbled away from the downtown's skyscrapers and entered a neglected part of the city.

Whole neighborhoods stood in ruin and immense factory complexes, once vital parts of the nation's economic engine, were now hulking shells. The scenes reminded Grey of those old photographs depicting the devastation in Europe just after the Second World War.

Kurt remained motionless as the train entered an elevated station overlooking a desolate, crumbling industrial area. A handful of passengers were now left in the car and Grey decided to approach him. He drew his service pistol and went into the car. Kurt leapt up and swung around fast with the Luger. He wanted only to scare off the man, but his finger pulled the trigger.

No time to react, Grey fell back from the force of the bullet, stunned to hear the gunfire and feel the accompanying pain in his chest. The train doors opened and Kurt rushed out of the car. Grey fell unconscious.

Kurt dropped the Luger into his pocket and hurried away from the station and into a no man's land of block after block of empty, dilapidated buildings – old row homes and apartment houses; stores and factories; some with shattered windows; others with crumbling bricks.

He turned the corner of one block and ran into a street gang as surprised to see him as he them. Fifteen of them stood around a sports car. On the hood holding court was Nate, a seventeen-year-old drug lord who wore size-too-large pants well below his waist, exposing paisley boxers.

Nate came from a home with a single mother and seven siblings – none shared the same father; all were fatherless. Growing up on welfare with a struggling parent who hardly had time for her children taught him self reliance.

He ran drugs at nine, sold at eleven and killed at twelve. Joined a mobster tied to a South American cartel; within four years, out of the debris of his forgotten North Philly neighborhood, he reigned over an empire, defending it with an army of youth.

"What're you doin' here?" Nate hopped off the hood, swinging a muscle-bound arm in an easy, although to Kurt, intimidating gait. "Lookin' for score?" He looked at the coat-jacketed white boy as just another coke customer from the suburbs.

Kurt nervously fumbled as he pulled the Luger from his pocket and aimed it at the youth, his arm shaking. Nate stopped and Kurt moved across the street, keeping the gun on him.

"Hey, man!" Nate called, opening his arms wide. "Hey!"

One of the gang members pulled a gun and fired, missing Kurt, who returned fire before racing down the street with gang members in screaming, cursing pursuit.

Kurt ran into an abandoned factory complex. Mounds of rubble piled from brick walls that had collapsed after years of neglect made an unforgiving terrain. He stumbled over debris, listening as distant sirens, and the nearby echoes of the angry mob, came closer.

They were upon him, knocking him down, screaming, cursing and kicking. Kurt fumbled desperately for the Luger. A fourteen-year-old girl grabbed it, aimed it, and fired – two shots into his chest. Darkness slipped over him then light. He floated on the sea, away from shore where his father and Dana watched him with worried looks.

Kurt called to them, assuring them he was fine.

And he was as he drifted off to sleep.

Philadelphia Police Detective Vinny Salvatore, a leathery-faced chain-smoker, arrived at the scene in an unmarked car. He glanced at the splash of blood on the worn asphalt where Nate dropped dead from a bullet in the face.

"Where we at, Dickey?" Salvatore asked, kicking the ground with his scoffed shoe.

"Suspect's hiding out in the old engine factory across the street," Captain Richard Keller said. "We got the place surrounded."

"Anyone gone in yet?"

The heavy-set police captain shook his head. He nodded at the gang members across the street. "Not sure what to do about them. They're out for blood."

Salvatore sighed as he scratched the dry skin on the back of his neck. An hour earlier he had been at his desk in the Roundhouse when a call came in that a man had shot a passenger on the El, killed a drug dealer and was holed up in an abandoned factory.

He slid his hand out of his pant pocket and opened the crumbled red-and-white pack of Marlboros. He freed a cigarette with his forefinger, lit it and exhaled as he looked at Keller.

"How long's he been there?"

"I'd say at least an hour."

"Anyone heard from him?"

Keller shook his head. "Not a peep."

Salvatore sighed. "I guess I'll go in and try to talk him out."

"Sure you want to do that?"

"No, but I don't want to sit out here all night waiting for him, either."

"I'm sending two armed men in with you," Keller said.

With the burning cigarette dangling from his mouth, Salvatore shoved his hands in his pant pockets and crossed the street with the two officers. As he did he watched the gang walk away, seemingly no longer interested.

Keller called after Salvatore. "That's strange."

"Maybe," Salvatore said. "Maybe not."

They entered the complex and walked until they reached a courtyard. A large empty building stood before them. They peered around in the fading light of late summer.

Salvatore's voice echoed in the cavernous setting as he called to the shooter, urging him to surrender. They waited for a response, listening for movement, but heard nothing.

"Well," Salvatore said, examining the outside of the building. "Let's go in."

They wandered over piles of debris in the gloomy caverns. Salvatore called to the shooter to surrender. From atop one pile they started down, but the sight of a crumbled figure lying at the bottom stopped their descent. The detective could see it was lifeless. They climbed down.

"Thought we'd find him like this," Salvatore said. "Get the coroner in here."

As one of the officers radioed in, the detective looked at Kurt's battered body and said to no one in particular, "They got their blood."

Chapter 14

Philadelphia, Pennsylvania

The following evening

A perplexed Bill Long paced the fifth floor hallway at Hahnemann University Hospital, anxious to speak to his brother-in-law who was still recovering from surgery. Gunter had been uncharacteristically inefficient in his task to dispatch Hahn.

Gerhard's reliable assassin moved too quickly and failed to press the knife as deep as he thought; the blade missed Hahn's heart and vital organs. The speedy action by the loading dock workers in calling an ambulance helped to save Hahn's life as much as his strong health.

Long still tried to wrap his mind around what was told to him. It had been a long day. In the morning as he poured over purchase orders at Martin's Chocolates, his secretary appeared in the doorway, wearing a concerned expression.

"Bull, the F.B.I.'s here – something's happened to Mr. Hahn."

Long peered over his glasses. "Marty?"

Two agents appeared behind his secretary and introduced themselves. They questioned him briefly about his brother-in-law and then about his nephew before explaining Kurt's death and the knife attack on Hahn.

The news stunned him and he stammered. "What were they doing in Philly?"

His question went unanswered. The agent who appeared in charge spoke respectfully, but urgently. "We need you to come with us to identify the body and to answer some questions."

They brought him to Hahn's house, where Long was shocked to see a dozen agents busily searching as a short, stocky man from the U.S. Justice Department politely questioned him about his brother-in-law's past.

"He said he was from Chicago, that's all I know."

Long, confused and intimidated, started to become angry, demanding to know what was going on. Tom Morgan assured him he was in no trouble and told him Hahn was a former Nazi agent in hiding.

For a man whose attention span never reached much beyond his immediate needs, Long was in disbelief. He remained in that state as F.B.I.

agents drove him to Philadelphia, where he identified Kurt's body before going on to the hospital. They wanted him to inform Hahn of his son's death.

As he paced the hall he wondered about his brother-in-law, a quiet, reserved man who he always liked: *Marty, a Nazi agent? That seemed so unlike him. The kid, on the other hand, was a little crazy, but to have killed someone, I didn't think he had it in him.*

"Sir?"

Long stopped pacing and glanced up. A dark-skinned doctor with a stethoscope over his shoulder was standing at the nurse's station, addressing him in a slight Indian accent.

"Are you Mr. Hahn's relative?"

Long nodded and approached the doctor who spoke compassionately. "I understand you must inform him of his son's death. He's awake now and talking. He seems aware of something having happened."

"Can I see him?"

The doctor nodded and waved his arm toward the door, where a uniformed police officer stood. "Yes, certainly, he's expecting you."

Long entered the dimly lit room. Hahn lay in bed, pale, but alert. He smiled weakly as his brother-in-law leaned over him and whispered. "Marty, how do you feel?"

Hahn nodded and said one word. "Kurt?"

Long shook his head, at first unable to mouth the words. "He's gone, Marty. I'm sorry."

Tears welled in Hahn's eyes. His body shook. The only comfort Long was able to muster was to repeat softly, "Marty … Marty … Marty."

On another floor in the hospital, Grey lay in bed, weak from surgery and angry. He had mishandled the investigation.

Two people were dead.

The bullet slammed into his chest, but barely missed his left lung and exited just below the shoulder blade. He woke the morning after the shooting to find Jack Davis sitting in a chair watching him. Davis was unshaven, his shirt collar open and his tie undone.

He arrived a few hours after his trooper was brought to the hospital, worried and unsure what to expect. The surgeon assured him Grey would recover fully. The bullet caused no serious damage. Davis stayed the night for his friend.

Grey lay groggy and numb while Davis told him a little of what happened. "Just so you know, in one day you managed to piss off the Secret

Service; the FBI; the Philly police; transit cops; Pennsylvania's state police; and the U.S. Justice Department."

Grey managed a wan smile and said hoarsely, "What about the CIA?"

"Haven't heard, but give it day. Next time alert people when you're in their jurisdiction."

"Yeah, I'll try to remember."

Davis looked serious. "What was all this about?"

Grey's eyelids felt heavy and he shook his head, too tired to speak. He fell into a deep sleep, waking hours later, not so groggy, but feeling the dull pain left by the surgery. A nurse came into the room to give him pain medication followed by Davis.

"How're you feeling?"

Grey nodded and Davis said, "Up for talking?"

"A little, sure."

"What happened?"

Grey recounted meeting Hahn, learning about his son, and his suspicions about Kurt.

Davis told him Philadelphia police so far failed to find Kurt's killer, but had the Luger, which was used to kill him. Grey remarked on the irony of getting killed by the same gun Kurt used to kill Hoest, but Davis shook his head.

"Kurt didn't kill him."

"What?"

"His fingerprints don't match those found at the bungalow and the slugs they dug out of him and the one that went through you don't match the ones found in Hoest."

"What about – "

"The prints don't match Hahn's either, but here's something interesting: the ammunition in the Luger comes from the same 1940s German armaments factory as the bullets you found in Hoest."

Grey absorbed this information and asked about Hahn's assailant.

Davis handed him a photograph. "Recognize him?"

Studying the enlarged, grainy black-and-white photo of a blond-haired man, Grey said, "I think I've seen this guy before."

"Maybe you met him on a train in Europe?"

Grey looked more closely and noticed the face's hawk-like features. "Gunter?"

Davis nodded and told him a security camera aimed at the loading dock where workers found Hahn caught the image on video. "I think Gunter was the one following you the last few weeks – any idea as to his motive?"

"No, but I think General Gerhard's involved."

"Really? Why?"

Grey shrugged. "Just a hunch."

"My intelligence source says he's former East German Stasi; went to work for Gerhard after the wall came down."

Grey gave him a skeptical look. "What intelligence source?"

Davis smiled. "Tom Morgan at Justice."

Drowsiness started to overtake Grey as the pain medications kicked in. He tried to keep awake. "Is anyone going after Gerhard?" he mumbled, before drifting off to sleep.

"Not sure yet," Davis said, watching Grey's eyes close.

Davis waited to tell him what the federal authorities decided. Gerhard wasn't a suspect in Hahn's attack. Philadelphia police cited Gunter as the prime suspect, but had no evidence linking him to Gerhard. They gave little chance to apprehending Gunter who disappeared, a grainy video the only trace he even existed.

Alone two days later, laying in his hospital bed listening to the distant sounds of traffic six stories below, Grey wondered where to pick up the pieces of his investigation. The light of late afternoon cast long shadows from the window as he considered pursuing Gerhard.

Davis explained the Gerhard situation the day before, angering Grey.

"Why the hell don't they do some investigating? They'll find the links between Hahn's attack and Gerhard."

Grey's attitude now annoyed Davis. He spent two days defending his trooper's tactics to federal and Pennsylvania law enforcement officials while getting little sleep at the hospital as he worried over his wounded friend. His patience gone, he snapped.

"The city has neither the manpower nor the funds to launch an international manhunt for a knife attacker, and the feds don't want a goddamn investigation. They don't want any attention drawn to that damn Nazi general and his CIA connections, so let's just drop it."

"I don't want to drop it."

"Then let me remind you the state of Delaware also doesn't have the funds or manpower to send people overseas. We have trouble getting money to police our own jurisdiction."

Grey pleaded. "Jack, there has to be a connection between Hoest and Gerhard."

"How do you know?"

"It's a hunch."

"That's not good enough anymore."

"Why?"

"Your last hunch put you in here."

"How the hell can I complete this investigation if I can't pursue Gerhard?"

"You're not going to complete it. I'm re-assigning you."

Grey lay back quietly, surprised. He had never been pulled off a case before. The room fell silent as the two men let their anger subside. Davis prepared to leave and calmly suggested Grey take a much deserved vacation.

"You did your job, Sam, let it go and move on. Take the time. Finish your doctoral."

Davis' parting remark echoed in Grey's mind the following day. He realized he had the evidence to write a thesis, even a book, on his U-boat theory that the Germans knew the Allies had broken the *Kriegsmarine* codes.

His thoughts roamed to the memory of the conversation he had in the car with Hahn as they raced to Philadelphia a few days earlier.

"Why didn't you return to Germany?"

Hahn answered with a question. "What is the statute of limitation for murder?"

"There is none." Grey pressed his foot on the accelerator as he steered the car down the Pennsylvania Turnpike. "What's that have to do with you not returning to Germany?"

"I would have been tried as a war criminal, just as I will be in this country."

As a student, Grey understood a concise question guides a researcher in his quest to prove or disprove a theory. He decided upon this simple question: Why did Gerhard want Hahn killed? The answer should provide him a clue, if not an answer, as to who killed Hoest.

He started going over the elements of his case in his mind when the hospital room door swung open. A blond-haired woman wearing a dark suit and heels entered, peering at him from behind a large bouquet of white roses. Her warm, familiar smile made Grey sit up in bed.

"Marta!"

He was delighted to see her. She looked at him and tried unsuccessfully not to show concern. His chest was bandaged, wires and tubes connected to beeping electronic monitors protruded from his arms. He could see the worry in her eyes.

"I'm going to be okay," he assured her. "When did you get in town?"

"Yesterday afternoon." She set the roses on a small table and moved a chair to the bed. "You've been all over the news."

"I messed things up."

"I don't believe it."

"Trust me." He sounded despondent.

She gently touched his face as she leaned over to kiss him softly on the forehead. They looked into each other's eyes until Grey gently pulled her close for a soft kiss.

"We met a few weeks ago yet we behave as if we've known each other for many years," Marta said.

Since that day in Tom Morgan's office Grey had been unsure how to broach with her the issue of her signature on a petition seeking Gerhard's prosecution. He decided now was the time to confront her. Marta sat speechless as he told her what he knew.

"It's not about child slavery on chocolate plantations, is it?" he said.

Marta shook her head, upset. "No, that's not true – "

"Why couldn't you tell me the truth?"

"I was telling you the truth."

Grey spoke angrily. "Then what's your name doing on the petition?"

She looked into his eyes and spoke softly. "He killed my aunt, my mother's sister." She opened her purse and handed him an old sepia-tone photograph of a young woman who bore a strong resemblance to Marta. "This was taken when she was at university."

He studied the photograph and said, calmly, "Your aunt?"

"She was executed for helping lead a student protest against Hitler."

Grey pondered this and thought: would it help answer why Gerhard wants to kill Hahn?

"Have you ever heard of Martin Hahn?"

Marta shook her head. "Who is he?"

"Gerhard had someone try to kill him."

"Does this mean you will be arresting Gerhard?"

Grey shook his head. "The CIA doesn't want him touched."

Marta became indignant. "Why? He's a criminal."

"I don't like it anymore than you do."

She stood, her fists clenched. "What's wrong with Americans?" She taunted. "You never finish a job. You proclaim faith in democracy, but allow African and Middle Eastern dictators to go free, and now you're going to do the same for Gerhard."

Grey tried to comprehend her feelings. "Why are you so angry? Certainly you can't have feelings for your aunt – you never knew her."

Marta sighed and sat down in the chair, trying to keep herself composed. She covered her face with her hands and when she removed them, tears streamed down her cheeks.

"True, but for years I listened to my mother tell me over and over again how they killed my aunt, a loyal German, for protesting the war. And I watched her spend years seeking justice, and getting none. I promised her before she died I'd make her cause my cause."

When she finished she trembled. Grey reached for her hand, pulled her close and put his arm around her. They held each other for a long time until a nurse came in to announce visiting hours were over.

Marta gave him a hopeful expression. "Tomorrow?"

He smiled. "I'll be here."

After she left, Grey felt exhausted and closed his eyes to sleep. Tomorrow, he decided as he drifted off, he would visit the person he believed had the answer to his question – Hahn.

As he finished breakfast the next morning, the nurse entered to collect his tray and inform him he had a visitor waiting. Tom Morgan of the Justice Department stood in the doorway with a slight smile on his face and one of his thick accordion files tucked under his arm.

He approached the bed and held out his hand. "Looks like you're doing well, corporal."

"Sam, please." Grey shook his hand. "I didn't expect to see you."

Morgan went straight to the matter at hand. The search he had conducted of Hahn's house uncovered little except for a small pack of documents. He removed a yellowed envelope from the accordion file and handed it to Grey, who opened it carefully.

He unfolded two pages of documents written in German, dated 1944, embossed with an eagle and swastika and bearing Gerhard's signature. Grey looked curiously at Morgan who told him it was evidence German prosecutors can use to convict Gerhard for crimes against humanity – Gerhard's signed orders authorizing the seven students' executions.

"It was in a lock box with stocks and bonds stored on a shelf in Hahn's closet."

Grey lay back with anticipating thoughts. Was his question getting an answer? He said to Morgan, "Why do you think Hahn had these?"

Morgan's face darkened. "It appears he was involved in the executions."

"Are these authentic?"

"Absolutely," Morgan said. "The Nazis were sticklers about keeping records on all their deeds."

The trooper nodded. "Does Hahn know you have these?"

"Not yet." Morgan had interrogated Hahn, but held off telling him who was suspected of being behind his attack, considering the CIA's position on Gerhard.

"With this evidence, though, I think the agency will have to cut him loose," Morgan said. "However, I'm not sure how these help your murder investigation."

"What's going to happen to Hahn?"

It wasn't clear, Morgan said. Hahn has been cooperative. He admitted to killing the drug store clerk in 1945, which District of Columbia authorities were reviewing to determine whether they needed to prosecute.

He detailed his failed mission to assassinate Roosevelt and resurrect the Nazi cause and his decision to assimilate into society. The Justice Department was determining whether hc was liable for war crimes. Now with the execution order the German government would want to talk to him about his role in the students' deaths.

Grey considered what Morgan told him. "It's interesting you showed up. I was planning to visit Hahn this morning."

"I'd like to accompany you, if you don't mind."

"Be glad to have you, but first I have to make a call."

Grey reached Marta at her hotel, catching her as she was about to leave for a meeting at the human rights symposium. He asked her to come to the hospital immediately, but when she asked if he could wait until afternoon, he said, "It's about your aunt."

"What about her?"

"I can't say anymore right now, just get down here; and bring the photo of her."

Marta arrived twenty minutes later to find Grey in a wheelchair waiting with a short man in a gray suit and red tie. Grey introduced her to Morgan and explained briefly why he needed to have her aunt's photograph. Marta gasped when he finished.

"My God, is it true?"

"I don't know, sweetie, it's just a hunch, but you have to do me a favor, ok?"

Marta nodded. "Yes?"

"Let me do the talking."

She smiled knowingly at him and they went to Hahn's room.

They found Hahn sitting up, watching television, when they entered the room. It was the first time he and Grey had seen one another since the fateful day.

"Gut morgen," Marta said sardonically as she pushed Grey in his wheelchair. He leaned his head back and glared at her for disobeying his request. She said nothing more.

Hahn acknowledged Marta with a perplexed look, but greeted Grey and Morgan warmly; he came to trust these men. He found them straight-forward, understanding. He and Grey briefly exchanged funny nurse stories before Grey told him about Gerhard.

Hahn appeared unsurprised.

"Why is Gerhard trying to kill you?"

Hahn sighed. He told the story of his work infiltrating the student movement, of helping point out the students to the Gestapo – of chasing down the one student leader who was the first under the guillotine's blade.

"Do you remember what she looked like?" Grey asked him.

Hahn shrugged. Grey asked Marta for the photograph. Her hand trembled as she handed it to him. He showed it to Hahn who studied it carefully before slowly nodding his head. Marta cried and Hahn noticed Marta's resemblance to the young woman in the picture.

Hahn looked questioningly at Grey who answered, "She was her aunt."

Hahn's body sagged as if unseen weight was set on it. Remorsefully, he said to Marta, "I am very sorry." She felt cold hatred toward him.

Morgan handed Grey the yellowed envelope and he showed Hahn the documents. "These were found in your home, how did you get them?"

Through his friendship with the students, in particular Marta's aunt, Hahn came to doubt they were a threat to the state as Gerhard claimed. Their beheadings horrified him and afterward the general's attempt to seduce him sexually complicated his feeling. He turned resentful.

Shame and remorse came when a clerk he befriended at Munich's Gestapo headquarters – while never knowing Hahn's role in the executions – expressed his view to him in confidence: *Why not just imprison them, Martin? Was it necessary to kill them?*

Hahn wanted to harm Gerhard some how and he thought about the clerk, who was often stationed at the file room. He visited there late one afternoon and stood making small talk while trying to figure out how to ask for access to the files when the clerk asked him a favor.

Could you watch the desk for a few minutes? I need to run something upstairs.

When Hahn finished, Grey asked, "Does Gerhard know you stole the orders?"

Hahn shook his head. "I'm sure he doesn't."

"Then why's he trying to kill you?"

"I'm probably the only witness left to his crime."

Morgan, who stood quietly listening while holding his accordion file against his chest, asked Hahn gently, "Why risk stealing orders, if you never used them as evidence?"

Hahn reflected for a moment. "I did it for Marta."

Grey looked at Marta who stared at Hahn – first in disbelief and then understanding. She turned and smiled at her lover teary eyed and in an emotion-choked voice said, "I'm named after my aunt." She turned back to Hahn, "If you loved her, why?"

Grey was confused. "Help me here, I don't understand?"

Morgan said, "Marta's aunt and Hahn were apparently lovers."

"We were lovers only briefly," Hahn said, his eyes watering. "I was too torn between my loyalty to the state and my loyalty to another human being to realize how much I loved her."

He recalled his relationship with Marta's aunt, a vivacious, strong-minded young woman who studied to become a doctor, but soon became involved in a burgeoning anti-Nazi movement with the underground campus intelligentsia.

She spoke at the first meeting Hahn attended undercover for Gerhard. She moved him in her profession of love for the Fatherland, but he became uneasy when she raised a fist and shook it in the air as she decried Hitler's war and blamed the Fuehrer for destroying Germany.

He found her exciting, like forbidden fruit. She had noticed him at the meeting and again at the café where the group regularly met afterward for ersatz coffee.

They came together and talked for hours. His quiet, reflective demeanor attracted her. He found much of what she said enlightening but conflicting. Passion and intimacy followed, but he worried he had gone too far. Regrettably, he pulled away from her.

Gerhard sensed Hahn's sympathies and reminded him of his parents' deaths and warned him of the penalty for fraternizing with enemies of the state. He told him war was about making difficult choices. So Hahn made his, though with painful reluctance.

He stood there among the ruins of Munich, watching as they kicked her before dragging her away. Anger had welled up in him – anger that she had to be such a radical against the state; anger at her for having put him in the position to make such a choice – his life or hers.

"She could have had me killed, but she never said a word about our relationship," Hahn said. He looked at Marta with watery eyes. "She was braver than I."

Pity pierced some of the hatred Marta felt toward Hahn.

He turned to Grey to apologize for the pain his son had inflicted, but the trooper waved a dismissive all-in-a-day's work hand.

Hahn shook his head and cast his eyes to the Bible on his nightstand. "It's true; the sins of the father are visited upon the son."

Chapter 15

Dover, Delaware

On a crisp autumn morning a few weeks later, Jack Davis looked across his desk at Sam Grey and considered his trooper's request.

"You have vacation time coming," the lieutenant said. "You are to take it, understand?"

Grey nodded. "I plan to, afterward."

"Where're you going?"

"Europe, to finish the vacation I started there."

Davis shook his head in wonderment. "Why don't you let someone else handle it?"

Grey became agitated. "I always finish my cases and I want to finish this one."

Davis nodded. He understood. Until a week ago, he considered Hoest's murder a cold case, but Grey persisted, even though he had been reassigned.

"First, tell me what this old Nazi general is to you?"

Grey's mind raced back to the day after his meeting with Hahn, when Marta arrived for a visit. She had brought dozens of photographs from Africa depicting children who were forced to become soldiers and laborers.

One picture in particular struck Grey. It was of a young boy, no more than six years old, his teddy bear strapped to his back, cradling a semiautomatic weapon in his arms, squatting on the ground with other boys around his age.

"Taken from his family and put into an army," Marta said, softly. "He was killed last year in a border skirmish, part of a genocidal war the two sides have been waging, and which Gerhard gets paid handsomely for providing weapons and children soldiers."

While she had been unable to convince Grey with stories about Gerhard's exploitation of children, Marta found pictures that made an impression. He had stared a long time at the photo of the boy with the teddy bear.

Africa was a thorny thicket, he thought. Maybe he could rid it of one less prick.

Grey said to Davis, "I did a lot of thinking while in the hospital – "

"And?"

"I spent my life ignoring racism. Whenever it confronted me, I let it be the other person's problem, but it's not just someone else's problem, it's also mine."

Davis leaned back and sipped his coffee, letting what he just heard sink in before making his decision.

"This going to become a crusade, Sam? Now you want to start saving the world."

Grey shook his head. "Not at all; I just want to finish my case. I always finish my cases."

"Ok, but this time you will engage fully the German and Swiss authorities. You will have a U.S. Marshal accompany you, and I don't want another mess like we had in Philadelphia."

The following afternoon Grey's plane landed in Geneva, a Peugeot sedan waited for him at the rental car office, and he headed to Adelboden.

He had reached an unhappy conclusion after hearing Hahn's story and seeing Marta's photos, and it bothered him greatly, but he knew there could be no other answer. Upon return from the hospital, he sought help from Wolfram and his colleague, Heinz Manfred.

Grey promised Marta he would spend vacation with her in the Swiss city of Luzerne, but first he had an errand. Grey expected it to take no more than two days. They arranged to meet at an Old City café with a panoramic view of the Alps.

At Adelboden, he found Wolfram and Manfred waiting for him in the lobby of the Hotel Baren. They gathered in Grey's room.

"Some news about Gerhard, *Herr Grey*," Manfred said. "He was diagnosed with prostrate cancer about a month ago."

Grey was skeptical and spoke harshly. "Where did you hear this?"

"My sources in the intelligence community," Manfred said, taken aback by Grey's tone.

"Do you trust the person who's telling you this?"

Manfred nodded.

"Does this mean he's in the hospital?"

"No, he has returned home."

"Good."

Wolfram noticed a troubling change in his friend. Grey spoke to him perfunctorily. "Did you get the weapon?"

Wolfram took a newly made Luger from his suitcase and handed it over. Grey mumbled "thanks," as he examined the weapon to make sure it was loaded. He had not wanted to take his state police-issued Beretta through airport security.

"Sam, do you want to tell us what you're planning to do?" Wolfram asked.

"No. I want you to tell me how to get to Gerhard's villa."

When Manfred finished providing the directions, Wolfram became nervous over Grey's secretive demeanor. "I thought we had a friendship."

Grey looked coldly at Wolfram and aimed the Luger at him. "So did I."

Manfred whimpered, *"Mein Gott."* Wolfram felt his legs shake and slowly sat on the bed, speechless for a moment. "You know?"

Grey nodded.

"How?"

"A lot of little things – took me awhile to add them up, but mostly you made my search for Hahn too easy; you made Heinz too accessible and he made Gerhard so readily accessible it made me wonder. I dismissed it as luck, but later realized it was too lucky."

Wolfram smiled wanly. "Your hunches were always pretty good, Sam."

Grey shook his head and sighed. "Yeah, well, I didn't want to believe this hunch. But just to make sure I was wrong, I obtained a copy of your prints the German Bundsewehr keeps on file from your army days."

Reluctantly, Grey said, he had the lab tech compare Wolfram's prints with the fingerprint found on Hoest's door knob. "The tech said he was one-hundred percent certain about the prints; they were identical."

The room fell silent for a moment.

"What are you going to do with us?" Manfred demanded.

Grey sat in one of the room's two chairs and motioned for Manfred to do the same as he set the gun down on the table next to his chair. "Don't worry. I've got to make a phone call in a few minutes." He looked at his friend and asked, "Why did you kill Hoest?"

Wolfram, wearing a mixed expression of defeat and relief, shook his head. "Sam, it was an accident. All of this was a stupid accident."

"Tell me about it."

Heinz, who had known Gerhard professionally and socially for years, had approached Wolfram one day with a lucrative proposition. The old general had read the wire service story about Hoest and wanted to know what Hoest knew about Hahn.

Heinz told Wolfram: "Just ask him if he knows anything and report back to us quickly."

It appeared to be easy money for a college professor whose lifestyle of late – gambling at the casinos in Wiesbaden and Stuttgart – left him deep in debt. When Heinz told him the general also would pay all of his travel expenses, he agreed.

Wolfram now eagerly looked forward to his task, but his enthusiasm waned when Heinz handed him a Walther P-38 pistol belonging to Gerhard. The Americans, as they had done with most German officers at war's end, let him keep it when he surrendered to them in 1945. Heinz assured him it was only a precaution – for his protection.

He let that rational appeal to him because he wanted the money.

He flew first class to Philadelphia, spent a few days at Heinz's urging at one of the city's most expensive hotels, dined at exclusive restaurants while he toured the city. When he indulged enough, he rented a car and drove to Lewes.

Hoest, just back from Longwood Gardens and starting dinner, heard the knock. The man on his porch read the news story about him and as a young German visiting Delaware he wanted to meet one of Germany's war heroes. Hoest modestly scoffed, but was flattered.

He invited Wolfram to sit on one of the porch's wicker chairs and asked whether he had served in the military. Wolfram explained his compulsory duty in the army and told Hoest how much the wartime U-boat service fascinated him.

Hoest relaxed amid the friendly conversation and spoke a little, though generally, about his experiences. Wolfram asked about Hahn, and Hoest became suspicious.

"How do you know about him? The mission is still a secret."

Hoest knew something. Wolfram saw it in his face and eyes. When Wolfram answered in silence, the old commander became uncomfortable and asked him to leave immediately.

He returned to Philadelphia that evening. After another splendid meal Wolfram reported to Heinz who told him to wait for a call. It came the following morning. The incessant, pulsating ring of the telephone woke him and he answered groggily.

"The general wants to you to go back and ask him again."

"He's not going to talk to me."

"The general said you have so far spent $3,764 in travel and hotel expenses that *you* will have to pay and no fee will be paid unless he gets an answer."

Wolfram flew into a rage, cursing Heinz for setting him up. He didn't have enough in his savings to return home. Heinz sympathized, explaining it was the general's doing, not his. "I will try and help you pay, if you can't succeed," he told Wolfram.

"No!" Wolfram decided to get Hoest to answer. He desperately needed the money. "I will handle this."

Wolfram returned to Hoest's house in the evening. When the old commander opened the door he demanded he leave, threatening to call the police. To Wolfram's surprise the Walther P-38 came out and he motioned Hoest inside. They went into the study.

Wolfram, nervous and tense, stuffed his free hand into his pant pocket and pulled out the newspaper clipping about Hoest. He shook it at him. "You know where Hahn is, tell me!"

Hoest shook his head as he stared at the pistol. He worried about Erica, who was still in the bathroom. The sudden sound of an old, squeaky faucet turning and water running distracted Wolfram momentarily. His eyes searched the room looking for the source of the sound.

The old U-boat commander, wanting to protect his new-found daughter, made a move toward the bathroom, panicking a nerve-wracked Wolfram.

Wolfram pressed the trigger twice.

His ears rang from the deafening gunfire as he stood in shock, staring at Hoest's body on the floor. *What had he done?* The bathroom door opened. He threw a glance at the doorway and got a brief glimpse of a person standing there before turning and fleeing.

"Gerhard paid all of my expenses. He wanted me in Germany immediately, away from a murder he was connected to. Then, what are the chances? I don't know, but you contact me and it's about the murder *I* committed. What are the odds of such a chance? It's too fantastic."

Wolfram stared at the floor as he spoke. "At first, I thought you knew, but you quickly assured me otherwise when you had me check Hoest's old crew and translate the ship's log. I had to play along; then Gerhard decided to use you to find Hahn."

"Did you know he was planning to kill Hahn?"

Wolfram, his eyes still cast to the floor, nodded. "I was too involved, what else could I do?" He looked at Grey. "I told him, though, I didn't want you hurt."

Grey found his friend's remark painful.

"Do you know where Gunter is?"

Wolfram looked genuinely uninformed. "Who?"

"Gerhard's fair-haired hit man – the guy who followed me."

Wolfram shook his head. Grey started to get angry with him when Manfred interceded to explain the general always protects himself on espionage assignments by using intermediaries to hire agents. One intermediary hires one agent and their information is limited to the assignment.

"We were used for one task; whoever followed you was used for that task, but none of us knows who the other is," Manfred said. "The general has more control this way."

Grey addressed his next question to Manfred. "Why did Gerhard want Hahn killed?"

Manfred sat silently, casting worried glances at the Luger and Grey.

"Nothing's going to happen here," Grey assured him. "There's a group of German, Swiss and American police waiting for you guys downstairs, but before you get to meet them I want an answer to my question."

"Tell him," Wolfram demanded.

Manfred prefaced with, "The general is a powerful man in western espionage circles."

"Yeah, so I've heard," Grey said, tiredly, as he prodded the professor.

Manfred recalled the day Gerhard contacted him, worried about a wire service article he just read in a Swiss newspaper.

Since the end of the Cold War, the old general had increasingly become insecure about his station. He feared that the Americans would turn on him – if given the chance – in order to put yet another Nazi away for war crimes.

Last year's petition to the American government by the students' families concerned him, despite his CIA sponsors' assurance nothing would come of it. Gerhard was somewhat confident knowing the execution documents were destroyed at war's end, and the last witnesses had died a few years ago.

But Hahn's whereabouts had remained a mystery since 1945, and the old general worried now. If the U-boat captain who he thought was dead was still around, maybe Hahn was, too.

"We need to find out what this naval commander knows," Gerhard told Heinz.

Wolfram hadn't entirely botched the job – a contingency the general had planned for by having him use an untraceable pistol and ammunition. Wolfram's report on Hoest's reactions to his inquiries convinced Gerhard that Hahn was indeed alive.

Manfred shrugged. "It became an urgent matter to have Hahn disposed of."

Grey shook his head in disbelief. "A doddering old general thinks a man unheard from in fifty years needs to be executed and everyone hops to attention without question – I thought you guys gave up that kind of crap in '45?"

"I told you, *Herr Grey*, he is a powerful man."

"Yeah, I keep hearing that, but I don't buy it."

Grey picked up the phone and pressed the button to call the front desk. "Okay," he said into the receiver. Moments later a handful of men and women, some in uniform; others in plain clothes, entered the room.

A U.S. Marshal handcuffed Wolfram and read him his rights. A plane waited to fly him to Dover Air Force Base where Lewes Chief John Christopher and another officer were waiting to transport him to the Suffolk County jail.

A German polizei detective did the same with Manfred. The German prosecutors wanted to interrogate him about Gerhard before he faced murder conspiracy charges.

Disappointment etched across Grey's face as he took one last look at Wolfram. When he concluded two weeks ago who his likely suspects were, a part of him had hoped he was wrong.

Wolfram sensed his unhappiness. "I'm sorry, Sam."

Grey nodded sadly.

Night fell as Grey finished the last of the extradition paperwork and conferred by phone with Davis and Christopher. They complimented him on his hunch paying off, but he wasn't in the mood to celebrate.

He ordered dinner in his room, but had little appetite. He retired early, but was unable to sleep as he plotted the next morning's actions. Tom Morgan, with Davis' consent, arranged with Swiss and German authorities to allow Grey to serve the arrest warrant on Gerhard.

Arresting the general became important to Grey as he recalled memories of his mother's death by the habitual, remorseless drunk who not only killed her, but the child she carried. Until the accident, the driver had managed to escape the law.

Grey heard his anguished father shouting at the prosecutor – "If someone had done their job my wife and child wouldn't be dead!" And watched the prosecutor do what he routinely did, nod sympathetically and give a pathetic shrug.

His mouth became dry as his thoughts returned to what he intended to do in the morning. He went to the bathroom for a glass of water and spent a night in fitful sleep.

He checked out the next morning and left the village behind, driving several miles before turning off the paved roadway to follow a windy dirt road a quarter mile into a forest of towering pines. He slowed, passing between twin plaster-cracked pillars holding open a wrought-iron gate.

The car rolled up the crushed-stone driveway of a quiet, weathered villa secluded in the forest. Grey stopped the car and stepped out. As he did, Paul, Gerhard's guard, emerged from a side door and stared at him.

The cold air snapped at Grey and he zipped his jacket. He felt the Luger in his pocket as he walked toward the villa, his footsteps crunching stone. After what happened in Philadelphia, he wasn't taking chances.

"Is he in there?"

Paul nodded. "He wants to see you."

"Then let's go."

Grey figured Gerhard knew he was coming. Just as he knew the train he took to Berlin so he could have Gunter and Bill Smith onboard; just as he knew the flight he took home.

He followed Paul through a large living room elegantly furnished with an onyx-colored grand piano. It was quiet, almost monastic. Grey reached in his jacket pocket and removed the Luger. Paul, who walked ahead of him, said, "You don't need that here."

"We'll see."

They went up a wide staircase and down the hall to the open door of a small bedroom, kept dark by closed blinds. A light on a table illuminated a bedridden Gerhard, emaciated from radiation treatments. Paul stepped aside for Grey to enter.

The old general recognized the figure before him. He always knew it would end badly for him, but to him fate had decided to be even crueler, sending him a member of what he viewed as an inferior race to kill him. How laughingly absurd, he thought.

Gerhard smiled weakly at Grey. "You remind me, corporal, of the boy soldiers I train in Africa; eager to fight though they have no idea why, only some vague notion. They hurry off to do their killing – "

"You mean *your* killing."

The old general stared at the trooper, studying for a moment the sweat beading across his forehead. "They reminded me of the little chocolate figures a Berlin candy maker sold before the war." He stifled a cough as he laughed. "They were my little chocolate assassins."

Grey dismissed the rambling. "I know about Wolfram and Heinz."

Gerhard looked impressed. "You know about Heinz, too?"

"It took me awhile, but I figured him out – loyal to the past, not the present."

"Yes, Heinz, all caught up writing history, as you are, I understand – "

Grey became impatient. "I'm not here about Heinz."

Gerhard smiled and made a faint, sardonic laugh.

"What are you here for then, my *chocolate* assassin?"

Grey looked at the Luger, realizing he had been holding it on the general, and shoved it into his jacket pocket.

"No, though killing you has crossed my mind. It would be easier, easier for everyone all around, but I'm not a murderous thug … like you."

The old general scowled.

"Why are you here?"

Grey removed the arrest warrant and dropped it on the bed. "I just wanted the satisfaction of arresting you. In a few minutes the German and Swiss authorities are arriving to take you back to Germany for a war crimes trial."

"Such a thing will never happen."

"Oh? Hahn, if you don't already know, survived your assault and has agreed to testify."

Gerhard chuckled and raised a fist. "You'll be disappointed."

"Oh, I don't think so."

Gerhard brought his fist to his mouth and before Grey could react dropped something in and bit down. His face folded in pain; death was upon him instantly. Grey leaned over the body to whiff the odor of almonds emanating from the mouth.

Gerhard had taken a cyanide capsule.

Grey stared at the general's corpse and suddenly felt nothing. It's probably just as well, he thought, and went outside to wait for the polizei.

A chilly, bright mid-afternoon greeted Grey's arrival in Luzerne.

Marta waited for him at a table at an outdoor café. She wore a black turtleneck sweater, her blond hair cascaded over her shoulders. Her warm smile lifted his spirits. They embraced – he held her close, whispering into her ear how much he missed her.

The drive from Adelboden had been long and tiring. Grey had not yet informed her about what had happened. He planned to do so later, but at the moment he wanted to enjoy a stiff drink, the snow-capped mountain vista, and Marta.

Strewn on the table were newspapers and magazines she bought while she waited. The *International Herald Tribune* had a front page story about Lieberman and other congressional leaders questioning the government's use of Nazi war criminals.

Marta handed Grey a German magazine. A picture of the general in his uniform, taken during the war years, splashed on the cover.

"The German government is getting pressure to prosecute him."

Grey nodded and leaned back in a relaxing pose, taking in the mountain-view. "I don't think anyone has to worry about Gerhard anymore."

She gave him a strange look. "Why do you say that?"

Grey closed his eyes. "Just a hunch."

Author's Note

Though this novel weaves historical facts and figures to tell the story, it is nonetheless a work of fiction, and as such, the personalities of Hitler, Himmler and Hoover were placed within that context. German Professor Hellmuth Walter did indeed design a U-boat as described in the novel, but I took some license with its design and capabilities. A German student movement against the war – *die Weiße Rose* or the White Rose – did exist in Munich, but I have mostly fictionalized those characters and the events. My research resources – periodicals, books, websites such as U-boat.net, academicians, researchers, etc. – are too numerous to mention, but some of the more pertinent include "Hitler's U-Boat War" by Clay Blair, "The Battle of Hamburg: The Firestorm Raid" by Martin Middlebrook, and the Naval History & Heritage Command and the Franciscan Monastery of the Holy Land in America, both in Washington D.C.